MAGE OF MONROVIA

THE MAGIC OF INHERIAN, BOOK 2

TERRY SPEAR

~

Heart of the Wolf Series: Heart of the Wolf, Destiny of the Wolf, To Tempt the Wolf, Legend of the White Wolf, Seduced by the Wolf, Wolf Fever, Heart of the Highland Wolf, Dreaming of the Wolf, A SEAL in Wolf's Clothing, A Howl for a Highlander, A Highland Werewolf Wedding, A SEAL Wolf Christmas, Silence of the Wolf, Hero of a Highland Wolf, A Highland Wolf Christmas, A SEAL Wolf Hunting; A Silver Wolf Christmas, A SEAL Wolf in Too Deep, Alpha Wolf Need Not Apply, Billionaire in Wolf's Clothing, Between a Rock and a Hard Place, SEAL Wolf Undercover, Dreaming of a White Wolf Christmas, Flight of the White Wolf, All's Fair in Love and Wolf, A Billionaire Wolf for Christmas, SEAL Wolf Surrender (2019), Silver Town Wolf: Home for the Holidays (2019), Wolff Brothers: You Had Me at Wolf, Night of the Billionaire Wolf, Joy to the Wolves, Wolf Wore Plaid

SEAL Wolves: To Tempt the Wolf, A SEAL in Wolf's Clothing, A SEAL Wolf Christmas, A SEAL Wolf Hunting, A SEAL Wolf in Too Deep, SEAL Wolf Undercover, SEAL Wolf Surrender (2019)

Silver Bros Wolves: Destiny of the Wolf, Wolf Fever, Dreaming of the Wolf, Silence of the Wolf, A Silver Wolf Christmas, Alpha Wolf Need Not Apply, Between a Rock and a Hard Place, All's Fair in Love and Wolf, Silver Town Wolf: Home for the Holidays (2019)

Wolff Brothers of Silver Town

Billionaire Wolves: Billionaire in Wolf's Clothing, A Billionaire Wolf for Christmas, Night of the Billionaire Wolf

Highland Wolves: Heart of the Highland Wolf, A Howl for a Highlander, A Highland Werewolf Wedding, Hero of a Highland Wolf, A Highland Wolf Christmas, Wolf Wore Plaid

Red Wolf Series: Seduced by the Wolf, Joy to the Wolves

~

Heart of the Jaguar Series: Savage Hunger, Jaguar Fever, Jaguar Hunt, Jaguar Pride, A Very Jaguar Christmas, You Had Me at Jaguar (2019)

Novella: The Witch and the Jaguar (2018)

∼

Romantic Suspense: Deadly Fortunes, In the Dead of the Night, Relative Danger, Bound by Danger

∼

Vampire romances: Killing the Bloodlust, Deadly Liaisons, Huntress for Hire, Forbidden Love

Vampire Novellas: Vampiric Calling, The Siren's Lure, Seducing the Huntress

∼

Other Romance: Exchanging Grooms, Marriage, Las Vegas Style

∼

Science Fiction Romance: Galaxy Warrior

Teen/Young Adult/Fantasy Books

The World of Fae:

The Dark Fae, Book 1

The Deadly Fae, Book 2

The Winged Fae, Book 3

The Ancient Fae, Book 4

Dragon Fae, Book 5

Hawk Fae, Book 6

Phantom Fae, Book 7

Golden Fae, Book 8

Falcon Fae, Book 9

Woodland Fae, Book 10

The World of Elf:

The Shadow Elf

Darkland Elf

Blood Moon Series:

Kiss of the Vampire

The Vampire...In My Dreams

Demon Guardian Series:

The Trouble with Demons

Demon Trouble, Too

Demon Hunter

Non-Series for Now:

Ghostly Liaisons

The Beast Within

Courtly Masquerade

Deidre's Secret

The Magic of Inherian:

The Scepter of Salvation

The Mage of Monrovia

Emerald Isle of Mists (TBA)

PUBLISHED BY:
Terry Spear

Mage of Monrovia
Copyright © 2010 by Terry Spear
Cover by Vibrant Designs

Print ISBN: 978-1-63311-059-5
Ebook ISBN: 978-1-63311-061-8

Discover more about Terry Spear at:
http://www.terryspear.com
ISBN Print: 978-1-63311-059-5

SYNOPSIS FOR MAGE OF MONROVIA

An apprentice of the mage they had destroyed earlier, now threatens Inherian once again. But when Mexia arrives at Langdon to become school trained, she learns the school will not permit a woman to attend. Mexia has already done much more than most school-trained mages when she and her companions had gone in search of the scepter of salvation. But now one of the apprentices of the evil wizard they had destroyed, has stolen his spell book and plans to take up where he had left off, and she has to try and stop him.

Mexia believes the only way for her to defeat the mage is to become school trained like he was with the eventual goal of becoming a high wizard—the first of her kind in Inherian. But the current headmaster denies her entrance because she's a woman. Though if she can get the former headmaster's recommendation, she may attend.

And that's the beginning of the trouble.

First, there's the wizard

Then, the immovable headmaster.

And then, the circle of misfortunes.

It all goes downhill from there…

CHAPTER 1

The humid air hung heavy with the odor of freshly caught fish as Lady Mexia and her companions, crossed the main square of the port city of Langdon. Just a brief walk away stood Mexia's destination, Langdon Castle, the wizard's school of higher learning, and the surprise that awaited them that even her companion, Princess Talamaya, with her ability of second sight, had not foreseen. Or so Mexia thought.

The princess and Lady Kersta of the Kingdom of Damar, and their dwarf friend, Gallant of the village of Kern, strode with her, just as determined to see her attend the school as Mexia was. Dread bunched into knots in Mexia's stomach as the twelve white towers surrounding the castle, came into view.

On top of several of the spires, owls of various kinds, slender bodies with long close-set ear tufts; rounder, larger shaped bodies with large farther set ear tufts; heavily fringed facial disk owls with no visible ear tufts...and more, posed as if waiting to have their portrait painted on the spot.

Mexia studied the birds, most watching the party with intrigue, and she wondered if they were the mage apprentices' familiars, out for a breath of fresh air or exercise. None of her wizard family had ever had familiars before, and she wondered then, would they help or hinder a mage's work?

Kersta's pixie face illuminated with a sunshiny smile. Though many from Damar had brown hair and eyes, of the three ladies, her hair was the darkest. Her curls, nearly black, dangled free from her braids secured against her head from the sea breeze's constant tugging. She patted Mexia's shoulder. "I can see the apprehension in your thoughts. But your father gave you all the knowledge he had of wizard ways, and I'm sure you'll do fine."

Princess Talamaya patted the golden rod secured at her waist. "And the spells and trials you overcame with us as you helped us to claim the Scepter of Lanai should give you an edge." Her heart-shaped face tilted upward slightly with triumph as her lips curved up with reassurance.

Gallant grunted, yanking at his partially braided brown beard that reached all the way to his belt. "Schools of learning like this are for those who never truly venture into the world and experience it for themselves. Ye are better off without them."

Mexia observed the rainbow of lights swirling before closed iron gates. "I wish to be a High Wizard, someday." She stretched her hand toward the portal. "I have not learned how to close or open a portal for one. Not even my father knows how to do such a thing." She turned to the princess. "And though we destroyed the blood-thirsty wizard, Grimoria, the mage apprentice who stole his book of spells is certain to strike out against us one of these days, once he feels he's powerful enough. With the training I receive here, hopefully I will be better prepared to defeat him, too."

"Of course," the princess said. "I worry you have such high hopes for the school, but may be disappointed."

Mexia frowned at her. "You have seen a vision about this, my lady?"

"I am sorry, Mexia, that I have said nothing about this before, but yes. I see the four of us trekking through a forest filled with dangers." She waved her hand at the town. "There are no dangers here, no woods inside the city of Langdon. So why do I see this if you are busily studying in these hallowed halls?"

She took a deep breath, exasperated that the princess would withhold the information from her. Did the princess think Mexia would falter to attain her quest over such a vision? "I am determined to do this."

The princess smiled. "And we are just as bound to see you succeed. Our home of Damar will benefit from everything you're able to learn here. Shall we enter?"

Mexia nodded. "I sense the gates are locked. If we step into the portal at the same time, we should be transported into the castle, I suspect."

"Or the woods where the beasts lay in wait for us?" Gallant grumbled.

"You can wait for us here," Kersta responded.

"Aye, and where will ye be if ye need my protection?"

Kersta chuckled. Mexia shook her head, amused. The two of them would never quit squabbling.

The four stepped into the portal. Instantly, they were transported into a massive hall where youthful mages, their faces sporting a trickle of whiskers, or none at all, stared at the party briefly as they hurried on their way. Marble floors inlaid with wizardry symbols met her eye. The room seemed larger for the twenty-foot ceiling that rose above them painted in images of wizards mastering various skills: levitation, casting lightning spells, taming dragons.

Then three of the students, who appeared older than most already having reached the height of men, and each wearing the start of a beard, watched the newcomers with interest. There was some discussion between them as the princess whispered, "I see no sorceresses."

Kersta nodded. "The notion has crossed the mage apprentices' minds…why are three women and a dwarf standing in their school with magically-enhanced weapons at their beck and call?"

"I have no magic," Gallant argued patting his war hammer secured in his belt at his waist.

"They are eyeing the Scepter of Lanai. Do they know about it?" the princess asked.

Mexia nodded. "Yes, my lady. They would be able to sense every item we carry that has some magical powers."

"One of the men is approaching," Kersta whispered.

Out of the three, he was the shortest and least appealing. Mexia turned her attention to the other two, the one who was speaking, and the other who remained silent but studied her with intrigue.

Kersta whispered, "The one you find most appealing, Mexia, is the most dangerous. Use caution."

Mexia turned to her. "I am not interested in any here. I am only concerned with further schooling."

She focused on the mage who drew close to her. His hair, beard, and beady eyes were colored a monotonous coal black as he stood before her. His attention darted nervously from one of the companions to the other, then back to her.

"What do you wish here?" he asked, directing his question to her, his words meant to intimidate, but his voice slightly high-pitched making him appear more anxious than anything.

"I wish to see the High Wizard. I came here to take the test of admission."

He snorted and folded his arms. "Women do not attend Langdon Castle. Learn your witchery skills at home, little girl."

Mexia's blood boiled, but she curbed her anger, and smiled sweetly instead. "Perhaps you are mistaken."

"I told ye, woman," Gallant said, "ye are too good for the likes of this place. This young upstart paid his way to get in here and has not half the wizardry skills of ye, I tell ye."

The mage quickly shifted his gaze toward the dwarf and glared at him.

The princess motioned her hand at Gallant to silence their companion. He grunted in response.

Kersta tapped her staff on the marble floor. "You wonder about the Scepter of Lanai."

The mage eyed her suspiciously.

"Lady Mexia," she said pointing at her, "turned the wizard, Grimoria, to stone to help the princess retrieve it."

The mage shook his head. "You lie. There is no way a female mage ever did something like that. Furthermore, women will never train here!" Without another word, he vanished.

Ignoring his vile comments, Mexia sighed. "That's what I want to learn to do. Vanish like that."

The second mage apprentice approached her, his hair and beard a lighter brown color like the princess's, and his eyes a hazel tone, but there was no smile on this one's stern lips either. "You were told to leave this place, were you not?"

"I wish to speak to the High Wizard about attending school."

"And were you not told witches do not go here?"

"I'm a mage apprentice, taught by my own father, a wizard in his own right."

The mage's thick brown brows rose slightly in amazement. "He was schooled here?"

"No, he learned on his own."

"A country wizard?" He laughed.

Mexia gripped her staff, annoyed beyond reason to be treated in such a manner by a fellow mage, then noticed both her lady companions did the same with their own. She loosened her hold on her staff. Fighting with a mage apprentice would not help her to enter the school, she suspected. Keeping one's temper, was the basis for all wizardry training, after all.

"I have every intention of attending school to further my training."

He clicked his fingers, and the other mage joined him. "Tell the witch, she is not welcome here."

"She wishes?"

"To see the High Wizard so she may be enrolled in classes here."

The man stroked his blond beard as his blue eyes remained fixed on Mexia. His disarming gaze spellbound her as she considered his sturdy jaw, softened by the beard, while his wavy hair flowed past his shoulders in strands of sun-drenched golden strands. "Then she shall see him."

"What? If you bring her before the High Wizard, he will have a fit!" the other mage exclaimed.

"Your name?" he asked Mexia, ignoring his friend.

"Lady Mexia of Damar."

His eyes widened, their rich blue color darkening to stormy midnight. "You helped..." He paused as he turned to consider her companions. "Princess Talamaya." He bowed. "Lady Kersta, and the dwarf, Gallant. You defeated Grimoria." He looked at the scepter. "I thought that was the Scepter of Lanai."

Mexia folded her arms. "Yes, but one of Grimoria's mage apprentices has stolen his book of spells, and now threatens to take his place."

"See what happens when a witch does a job more suited for a mage?" the other apprentice said.

"There are none in Inherian but my father and me to fight this rogue wizard. I must further my training to ensure the safety of our realm."

"She has a noble cause, do you not think, Ros?"

"It will matter not to the High Wizard. No women are allowed, no matter what the reason, Derek."

"Your friends will have to wait for you here," Derek said to

Mexia. "And you will be required to leave your staff behind. No weapons are allowed in the High Mage's chambers."

She handed her staff to Kersta.

"Good luck," the princess said and gave her a warm embrace. Kersta followed suit.

Gallant grumbled something inaudible.

Derek said, "Do you need help to get to his office?"

Despite hating to admit she could not go there on her own without needing his aid, she said, "Yes."

He smiled the most heart-warming smile. Kersta scowled at him. Mexia knew Kersta was reading his mind and his actions didn't reflect what he had on his mind. At least that's what she assumed.

He reached out his hand to Mexia. She hesitated. He raised his brows. "Are you coming?"

She placed her hand in his, and he drew her close. Despite his touch warming her entire body with intrigue, she heeded Kersta's words. The mage apprentice was a danger to her, and she had to keep her distance.

Instantly, they arrived at an office where shelves filled with books lined three of the walls. A massive oak desk filled a quarter of the floor space in the room.

"Master Harazod?"

The wizard appeared. His white silky beard reached down to the toes of his shoes that curled up to the strands. He narrowed his eyes at Derek, ignoring Mexia completely, annoying her at once. "The news of our uninvited guests has filled the halls. I cannot believe you, of all of my star pupils, had the audacity to bring one up here to see me."

"This one is Lady Mexia, my lord, of Damar."

The wizard stared at Mexia for a moment, then tugged at his beard. "Grimoria," he said under his breath.

"Yes, my lord. She is the one who turned him to stone...well and drowned him." Derek's voice was laced with enthusiasm.

Harazod waved for Derek's silence.

"What do you want here?" Harazod asked Mexia.

"To attend school, my lord." Despite wanting to stick her chin up in the air and fold her arms in defiance, she curbed her feelings. Attending the school was more important than giving in to malicious slights. "I wish to learn all that I can so that I may one day serve as the High Wizard of Damar. But before this, I must prepare to meet Grimoria's mage apprentice, who is as evil as his master. He stole his spell book and threatens revenge against my kingdom."

"Women do not attend school here."

"But I've studied for the entrance exams required to attend here. And your school policy states that a mage may attend who has used his magic to save others' lives, without even taking the exams. I have saved many lives through the use of my spells on several separate occasions."

"His magic, not hers." The wizard furrowed his brow, then his face brightened. "Obtain a letter of recommendation from the mage of Monrovia, the High Wizard Parenkin. If he gives his recommendation, you may attend as the only woman ever to do so."

Mexia smiled. "Thank you, my lord, for giving me this chance to attend your grand school." She caught Derek's eye. She couldn't tell what he was thinking from the scowl on his face. Was he angry that Harazod would even consider allowing her to enter the school? Or was there something else brewing underneath that wrinkled brow?

"I will return you to your companions. Wait there while I have a word with Derek. Then he will join you and send you on your way."

Before she could open her mouth to utter a word, he nodded

his head at her. In the next instant, she stood beside her friends as soon as she blinked her eyes.

"What did he say?" the princess asked.

Kersta handed Mexia's staff back to her. "She has to get a recommendation from the High Wizard Parenkin."

"Do not tell me," Gallant said, "he is in the Darkland Forest that we must now trudge through."

"He resides on the highest peak of Mount Monrovia," Derek said, startling them as he appeared next to Mexia. His arm brushed hers while his breath touched her cheek as he spoke. "You will need a map." His close proximity heated her whole being once again and a flush of heat rose to her cheeks.

He handed her a piece of leather parchment where rivers and towns, mountains and forests, were drawn in a crude manner. "Truthfully, it grieves me to see the first sorceress I have ever met who has already done so much for the cause of magic by ridding us of the rogue wizard, Grimoria, is made to do such a quest. Personally, I would have welcomed you to the school for all you have already accomplished. But unfortunately, I am only a fourth-year student, soon to get my wizardry status, mind you. I still must follow the rules."

"And?"

"All I can do is warn you. The path you take to Monrovia is fraught with danger. You'd best give up this quest and return to Damar before you or any of your companions can get hurt."

Kersta said, "And?"

He shrugged. "That's all I can say."

Mexia could see the intense look on Kersta's face as she studied Derek closely with narrowed eyes, meaning only one thing, she attempted to find out the truth to the matter by reading his mind further.

He held his tongue.

Kersta smiled. "We will speak of this further, Mexia, once we leave here."

Mexia ran her finger over the map, then looked up at Derek. "Which way is the best for us to go?"

"None. The continent of Albion is an inhospitable place, except for the city of Langdon, and two cities you may pass on the way, should you be lucky enough to reach them. Dark elves inhabit the forests. The mountain cheetaur and white devil wolves guard the pass of Monrovia. Trolls have become a plague along the river of Nenda. Trekking across the bridges often leads to a much shortened life span."

"And those who can aid us?" the princess asked.

"None can aid you."

"Why?" Mexia asked.

"I do not know what the people are like on the continent of Inherian. But here, you will not find any who will help you. Everyone goes about their own business. No one cares about anyone else's."

"Thank you, Derek." Mexia tucked the map into her cloak pocket. "We will see you upon our return, I suspect."

She stepped into the portal along with her companions and before they were whisked away, caught his eye one more time. What was there about the man that sent every bit of her body into a tingling mass of nerves? Was it the same as the princess felt about her betrothed?

When they reached the outside of the castle gates, Mexia stood in a daze still, not being able to get her mind off the mage apprentice.

Kersta broke into her thoughts. "Are you sure you want to do this, Mexia? I feel he was hiding something from me. I believe he sensed I could read his mind and didn't wish to reveal anything he ought not to."

"Like?"

"I'm not certain, Mexia. I believe he feels you cannot make it to the mountains of Monrovia, first off. But, there is something more. Something that he was thinking that I couldn't quite reach."

"What?"

"I sensed he is torn between the admiration he feels for you, well and something more, and wanting to keep the status quo. They're attempting to keep you out of the school, and if you're trying to get in gets you killed, it proves their case. You didn't belong."

"I do not wish for any of you to come with me," Mexia said, "if the way is as dangerous as he says. But I must go to Monrovia. If the rogue mage apprentice attacks us at home, and I am not prepared, all of us are as much at danger."

"I agree," the princess said. "I have every intention of helping you, dear Mexia. I am ready to go to Monrovia."

"Aye," Gallant said. "I wish to see my wife in the city of Barston. I've heard tell it is located in the valley outside of the Darkland Forest. I am game."

"And me," Kersta said. "I would not let you go alone." She turned to Gallant. "I thought your wife left you for another man."

"Aye. I wish to see her is all, woman."

She smiled. "And yet you say you do not love her."

"How can I love a woman like that? I just want to see her is all."

"Then we head to Barston first?" Mexia asked, interrupting the conversation before it got out of hand.

"I say we get an early morning start," the princess said. "What with our trip across the sea, it is already late afternoon. We should eat, sleep, and first thing in the morning, be on our way."

Mexia studied the map of Langdon City. "There is a tavern located on the other side of the castle. I wonder if they will let women stay there."

"We will have to check it out, eh?" Kersta said as she headed

11

in the direction of the tavern.

Twenty minutes later, they reached the two-story stone building, the sign freshly painted, swung slightly in the breeze.

"This is it," Kersta said. "The Dragon's Keep."

Mexia pushed the door open, and instantly, the room filled with boisterous conversation died to a perceptible hush. A barmaid sashayed over to the party of four. Her red curls partly squashed on top of her head, the rest dangling down to her shoulders, looked to have been given nary a thought. Her faded blue gown revealed her breasts in ample proportion. She patted Gallant on the head as his eyes remained focused on the low cut of her gown. She waved at an empty round table. "Ye wish meal and some ale?"

"A meal, yes," the princess said. "We bring our own drink with us."

Mexia touched her flask at her waist. The gift from the soothsayer, Modi, a healing tea that replenished itself in their flasks was all that they drank on their travels.

The woman eyed them with suspicion, then nodded. "Very well. Have a seat and I'll bring out your meal."

She hurried off as the ladies and Gallant sat down on the wooden chairs. Gallant grunted as he peered at the women, nose level to the table. "Ye think they'd be a bit more considerate and make taller chairs for dwarfs."

Kersta smiled. "Maybe they have a pillow for you to sit on."

He shoved his bedroll underneath him. Now he sat higher and smiled back at her. "Sometimes, ye have clever ideas. Sometimes."

Mexia looked around the room at the men gathered at several of the tables, all bearded, mostly unbathed, appearing to be rogues...all of them. "Seems the place is lacking in women here, too."

"Aye, they be pirates over there," Gallant said, motioning to a table in the far corner of the room. "We should stay clear of the likes of them. No one would be interested in a dwarf, but if they knew Princess Talamaya was King Lazarion's betrothed, or that the two of ye ladies come from the noble families of Damar... well, ransoms for your safe return would be on their minds."

"Then we must not mention this to anyone," Kersta said, casting a dirty look at Gallant. "Anywhere."

"Aye, but all they have to do is see the way ye are dressed. It doesn't take a High Wizard to be able to sense ye ladies are of nobility, and your kin would have means."

"How do you know they are pirates and not just seamen?" Mexia asked. "It is a seaport after all and to me, they look just like the sailors on the ship we were transported here on. Same knee-high boots, knee-length breeches, blousy shirts with the full sleeves ruffled at the wrists and beaded, braided, dirty matted hair."

"It is the beady eyes that give them away."

Mexia smiled as she considered Gallant's tiny black eyes. "Were you once a pirate, too?"

He growled at her. "Woman, are ye trying to be as dense as that one?" He pointed to Kersta. "Look at the scabbards they carry."

The women cast casual glances at the four men, chugging their ale, deep in conversation some of the time, staring at the women most of the time.

"Scabbards," the princess said.

"Aye. The Black Hawk ship I heard tell frequents this port. The captain is Prince Eric, the Mad, they say. He leaves the town well enough alone. The wizards wouldn't permit his pirating here. That's why the place is safe for travelers."

"But?" Kersta asked.

"If we leave the town, and they should wish to pursue us, well, ye ladies rather, the wizards would have no say in it."

"They would not wish to travel through the Darkland Forest, would they?" Mexia asked.

"They are cutthroats themselves. A few dark elves would not discourage them, I assume, if they figured the three of ye would be worth the trouble."

Mexia sipped from her flask, then turned to Kersta. "Can you read their minds?"

"Too much distraction in here with so many people. But they definitely are interested in us. They're just wondering how strong the dwarf is."

Talamaya ran her hand over her staff. "They will find trouble if they think the three of us women incapable of a good fight."

Mexia nodded. Glancing over to the other corner of the poorly lighted tavern, she noticed a cloaked figure sitting in the shadows, his hood pulled over his head, hiding his face. Did he watch them, too? Every male in the room, from the pirates at the one table to the men who looked like some kind of soldiers of fortune at another, observed them.

"What do you think about the men sitting at those three tables?" Mexia asked Kersta.

"The soldiers?" Kersta said.

"Yes."

Kersta considered them for a moment. "Not sure. They seem to be lower-ranking foot soldiers wearing the poorer padded leather armor rather than chain-mail. None have helms. I don't see any with broadswords. All carry short swords."

"And no leader?" Mexia asked.

"Doesn't appear to be any."

Mexia took a deep breath. "Deserters, do you think?"

"They might be."

"What about the man in the corner of the room? The one hidden beneath a hooded cloak?"

Kersta concentrated. "He's angry. But I cannot tell what

14

about. He feels the whole world owes him, and he'll rip it apart until he gets what belongs to him."

"Something was stolen from him?" Mexia asked.

"I don't know. Like the pirates, he wonders who we are and how much we are worth."

"Maybe this was not such a good place to come."

The barmaid balanced two trays as she hurried across the floor, then slammed them down on the tables.

Gallant scowled at her. "The lady said we did not wish to drink anything."

"The gentleman in the corner of the room over there," the maid said pointing with her elbow to the cloaked man, "wished to buy you each a drink."

The princess nodded. "You may tell him we thank him for his generosity."

When the maid left them alone, Kersta said, "But we will not drink this ale, will we, princess?"

"We drink Modi's tea. Nothing else."

Gallant dug into his wild boar steak with enthusiasm as the ladies buttered the hot pieces of bread they tore off the loaf in front of them. The door to the tavern opened, and a breeze of warm air filtered in.

They turned to see Derek and his two mage friends enter the room, their velvet cloaks, brocade gowns and neat appearances giving them away as mage apprentices from the wizardry school.

The maid hurried to see to their needs. They motioned to an empty table, two tables away from Mexia's.

Kersta cut up a slice of boar. "Kind of unusual, I would think."

"What's that, Kersta?" the princess asked.

"I would have thought they would have to eat at the school."

"Derek said he was a fourth-year student. Maybe he and his friends have more freedom."

Kersta nodded. "And yet, there are no others here."

"What do you see, Kersta?" Mexia asked.

"They are purposefully blocking my reading of their minds. Which makes me think they do not usually come here."

Mexia studied Derek. His angular jaw was softened by his curly blond beard and his blond hair was neatly tied back in a knot behind his head now. But it was his eyes that drew her in.

Kersta touched her hand. "He is dangerous, Mexia. He's more powerful than you. I fear he's casting some kind of spell over you."

"Aye, my wife did the same thing to me." Gallant ripped off a piece of bread.

The princess studied Derek and frowned. "He is the one I saw in my vision, wearing regal blue velvet robes. He appears to have some kind of royal lineage by the way he dresses. And as Kersta says, he has some kind of power over you, Mexia."

Mexia shook her head as her gaze remained focused on Derek's eyes. Her lips turned up slightly, making *him* smile back.

Gallant cleared his throat. "Maybe ye have it wrong. She seems to have all the power over him."

Kersta grabbed her staff as one of the soldiers stood and sauntered over to the mage apprentices' table. "There's going to be trouble now."

"What's wrong?" Mexia grabbed her staff and scooted her chair away from the table.

Kersta shook her head as she considered the confrontation between the men. "The soldier doesn't like mages, and he intends to throw them out of the tavern."

Mexia laughed, setting her staff back down. "Oh, that's all. I thought something awful was going to happen. The mages can handle one drunken soldier."

Kersta raised her brows. "Then the soldiers intend to bed *us* for the night."

CHAPTER 2

Immediately, chairs scooted back as several of the soldiers joined their comrade as he poked his finger at Derek. The mage apprentice spoke to the man. The soldier shook his head and pointed at the solid oak door.

Derek looked over at Mexia briefly, and she wondered if he was embarrassed by the soldier's action, or concerned about fighting him in front of her.

The mage, called Ros, stood up and waved his fingers in the air. Then six of the soldiers hurled their chairs at the wizards.

The chairs shifted their course and dropped on the pirates' table, knocking over their tankards of ale. Enraged, the pirates jumped into the fray, their fists punching the soldiers' faces.

During all of the ruckus, the cloaked man slipped away, and the remaining six soldiers headed for the ladies' table.

"Now," Mexia said as they all hopped from their seats and readied their staffs while Gallant continued to tackle his meat.

Mexia glimpsed Derek look her way as two of the men headed for her. Did he wish to rescue her? He was still dealing with a soldier himself. She turned her attention to the men whose leering eyes and ale-wreaking breaths told her just what they had in mind.

Swinging her staff, she struck one in the chest. He collapsed to his knees and fell to his face on the floor as the other grabbed her arm. Another fell against her when Kersta hit him. To her horror, Mexia lost her hold on her staff.

Before she could retrieve it off the floor, the other dragged her toward the stairs of the tavern. Frantically, she attempted to conjure up a spell, fear and anxiety muddling her thoughts.

Then suddenly, the man rose in the air, letting loose of her arm as his eyes widened with terror. Mexia looked across the tavern to see Derek motion at the man with his fingers. She dashed back to claim her staff, and Derek dropped the man to the floor.

"Debt of gratitude?" the princess said to Gallant as the soldiers and pirates lay still on the tavern floor. "Did you not accompany us to protect us?"

"Ye I owe a debt of gratitude to, woman. But I knew ye could handle it. Didn't want my food to get cold. Besides, this way the pirates know ye are not an easy target." He licked his fingers.

Two of the mage apprentices walked by the ladies' table, their noses held high in the air as they narrowed their eyes at them and continued on past. Derek brushed off his velvet cloak, then crossed the floor and paused in front of Mexia. "You see, even here, it is dangerous for you and your companions."

"It wasn't dangerous until you arrived."

"If we hadn't been here, you would have been upstairs with the lot of them. With us here, we cut down more than half the number you had to fight...to keep your virtue." He bowed his head slightly to her, then hurried after his friends.

Mexia's whole body heated to new levels with a mixture of anger and desire. What made him cause her heart to beat at twice its normal rate every time he drew close? Did he cast some kind of a spell over her as Kersta suggested?

"He is not to be trusted," Kersta said.

They retook their seats.

The barmaid wandered over to their table. "Supposing you want a room for the night."

"Aye. Two rooms."

"One for Gallant," Mexia said, "and one for the three of us ladies."

Gallant waggled his brows as he smiled at Kersta.

The barmaid grabbed Gallant's empty plate. "If you had started this brawl, I would have sent you from here, but it was the wizards that shouldn't have been here."

"Do they come here often?" Mexia buttered another piece of bread.

"No, their headmaster don't allow it."

"So, why would they come here today?"

The barmaid smiled. "You have to ask, missy? We don't get women in this place ever. But one of the soldiers said three women and a dwarf entered Langdon Castle. So now I never heard of a dwarf being a wizard. And I know the school don't allow women, but still there would be no other reason for you to enter it. So which one is it? Or are all three of you wizards?"

None of the ladies answered. The barmaid cackled. "Yeah, well, I would not tell any either, if I were you. No more fighting in here, or I'll boot you out."

"Will you tell the men when they come to, that we sleep in the rooms upstairs?"

"I'll tend to a few of them myself. If they find out where you stay, it won't have been my saying so." She hurried back to the kitchen.

Mexia looked over to the corner where the cloaked man had sat. "In the midst of the trouble, he sneaked out of here."

"Do you blame him?" Kersta asked. "He has his own demons to fight, and no interest in getting involved with a tavern brawl."

19

Mexia rubbed her chin. "I've got to learn how to concentrate in the thick of battle better. When I lost my staff and that barbarian grabbed my arm, my thoughts became as scrambled as the way I like griffon eggs for breakfast."

"Practice makes perfect," the princess said. "Just like sparring with our staffs. Modi's enhancing the oak with magic wouldn't do us any good if we didn't already know how to fight with them. When you have practiced enough, you will be able to think of your spells without trying to remember how to conjure them up."

"I was busy with the last of the brutes, Mexia. If you had lost your staff, how did you overcome the soldier?" Kersta asked.

Mexia didn't have to answer.

Kersta groaned. "Derek aided you. I still say he is dangerous, Mexia."

"Do not worry, Kersta. I feel as you do about him."

"That is what I fret about. You definitely have a fondness for him. And he will break your heart."

They looked over at the princess. She nodded. "I fear he is up to no good."

"Have you seen any visions in this regard?" Mexia poked at her meat, hoping the princess had not had any such vision.

"I cannot say, Mexia, exactly. In a mist somewhere that we visit, I think I see his distinctive cloak. Have you seen how the edge is embroidered with golden threads interwoven with both silver and copper? It's very unusual, and the sign of nobility."

"And there is a golden emblem in the shape of a leaf on his lapel." Mexia looked at her companions to see them all staring at her. "Did you not see it?"

They shook their heads.

"Well, maybe it was because I was closer to him than you were."

After they finished eating, they headed upstairs to the two rooms assigned them. Gallant paused at his door. "Are ye sure ye don't want me to stay with ye women in case someone gets the notion to join ye tonight?"

"If you hear hollering from our room in the night, you may join us," the princess said. "Debt of gratitude, of course."

"Aye." He opened his door and walked inside.

The ladies entered their room and closed the door, then Mexia latched it. Against one wall, a worn wooden chest sat and over this, a brass mirror hung crooked on the wall. Mexia walked over and straightened it. Two blond curls hung down from her braids, and she wrinkled her nose at her disheveled appearance. Derek must have thought her a sight.

A lantern sitting squarely on a bedside table washed the room in a soft yellow glow. And a thick, pieced quilt of an assortment of colors and fabrics from blue wool to green brocade, covered the enormous bed that took up more than half of the floor space.

Mexia pulled off her cloak and laid it on a wooden chair near the window. "You would think Gallant would quit saying he owed you a debt of gratitude as much as he has saved your life in return, my lady."

Princess Talamaya smiled as she yanked her boots off her small feet. "I believe he has grown attached to us, for whatever reason. Kersta, he likes to mix words with. Maybe she reminds him of his wife."

Kersta groaned as she shook her head. "Poor woman." She patted the quilt and a layer of dust lifted into the air.

Mexia unbraided her hair. The thick blond curls unfolded into wavy strands reaching past the worn leather belt at her waist. She pulled a brush from her pouch and ran the bristles through her hair as she studied the silky strands. "Gallant feels he must protect you, princess, but as for me, I am just part of the forest." She wiped away a smudge of dirt on her cheek and groaned. Her ivory skin was now covered in a fine layer of dust, graying the color somewhat.

"He is quite awed by your wizardry skills, Mexia, as we all are. And you rarely argue with him, so he hasn't much to say to you. But he likes you just the same."

Kersta pulled off her skirt-like trousers that each of the women wore, lending to the ladies' modesty, but making it easier to ride, fight, and travel when away from their castle.

Mexia slipped out of her gown, leaving her silk underdress on to sleep in. She turned to see the princess studying the map. "What do you think?" Mexia asked, joining her.

"I think the trek to Barston is not too far. Our difficulty will be in getting through the woods and across the river. That's what will slow us down."

"Had you planned on getting horses? I know you talked of not having to, since we were going to stay in the city of Landgon, but now that we are traveling—"

"The distance through Darkland Forest is not long. And the dark elves we encountered in the woods back home fought us on foot so it was easier for us to fight them that way. We will have the same difficulty when we come to the river. It will be easier to fight the trolls on foot. Perhaps when we get to Barston, we will find riding the best way to go. But for now—"

"We walk," Kersta said as she and Mexia pulled the quilt from the bed then shoved it out the window and banged it against the stone wall. "Perhaps we can solve another quest for a dragon, and he can carry us a bit further."

Mexia smiled as they carried the quilt back to the bed. "Now that is a pleasant thought. We could soar high above the forest, river, whatever dangers there are, and go straight to the mountains."

"Now what you talk of is pure fantasy." Kersta washed up in a basin, then dried her face. When she climbed under the covers of the bed, the ropes holding the mattress in place creaked slightly.

The princess separated her light brown hair wound in braids.

"Who knows? Perhaps dragons do live somewhere along the way we must travel." She washed, then slipped into bed.

Mexia said an incantation as she wiggled her fingers at the door, "May the pain of light protect us tonight."

Kersta said, "What did you do?"

"Cast a protection spell on the door." She cleaned her face and arms as best she could in the rose-scented water, dried herself, then joined the other ladies in the bed. "It should last most of the night, if wizards do not use offensive spells against our door to get in. But against pirates or soldiers, it should remain in place until morning."

A couple of hours later after the ladies fell asleep, the sound like a hundred horses stomping on wooden planks disturbed Mexia's sleep. Voices grumbled as men walked past the door.

The doorknob jiggled briefly, but curses followed as a spark of light illuminated the dark. Mexia smiled. Her door protection spell still protected them.

"Come, boys," the barmaid said. "I'll keep the lot of you satisfied. The ladies and their dwarf companion are long gone from here. No. Come this way."

When the doors squeaked closed, Mexia stared up at the ceiling, not even visible in the dark room. Then a light knock on the door made her turn her head that way.

"Lady Mexia?" a voice whispered.

Derek? He couldn't be seeing her at this late hour. What was he up to now?

She climbed out of bed and grabbed her cloak. Pulling it over her shoulders, she padded barefoot maneuvering to the door, trying to avoid tripping over anything in the dark.

When she reached the door, she laid her hand upon it. "Derek?"

"Yes, yes, I must see you."

Kersta's words of warning plagued her as her heart beat out of control. Despite Kersta's counsel, Mexia longed more than anything to know what he wanted of her. Did he wish to offer them some kind of aid? She hoped that Kersta was wrong about Derek's intentions.

Mexia unlatched the door and peeked out.

Derek held a candle, the flame highlighting his fair features. But his liquid blue eyes quickly shifted from her face to the sight of her curls cascading to her hips in waves of thick hair. She pulled her cloak tighter wondering why she'd ever opened the door for a stranger, dressed in only her skimpy silk underdress, hidden beneath her cloak.

"I need to speak to you in private. Can you leave the room for a moment?"

She glanced back at the ladies, still sound asleep. He reached out and touched her hair to her surprise. Startled, she stepped back.

"Please, a word?"

Her fingers clutched the cloak at her throat with a death grip as she shook her head. "I must return to bed. I should not have opened the door in the first place."

He offered his hand to her. "Please?"

His word was spoken so urgently, so coaxingly, she assumed he'd ask on bended knee if he could get her to comply. She rested her hand in his and he pulled her close. The heat from his body touched her, but in the next instant, they stood in the dining area of the tavern on the first floor.

Astounded, she blurted, "What are we...how did I...you shouldn't have—"

"Shh, I must speak with you. You must return home. The High Wizard doesn't intend for you to attend the school ever."

"Even if I get the letter of recommendation?"

"All I know is he doesn't intend for you to get to Monrovia in the first place."

"Why?"

"I have already told you. The way is too difficult. You and your friends will never make it."

"You need not worry about us. We'll make it just fine."

He furrowed his brow at her, then set the candle on a table. Turning again, he faced her. "You must return to Damar for your own safety. I cannot stress my concern for you any more than that."

She folded her arms. "It doesn't matter to me that you do not want me to attend the school. And I only even wish to go there because I can learn nothing further from my father as he never had enough schooling to become a High Wizard. But neither you, nor anyone or anything else, will stop me from achieving my goal."

He stepped closer to her. She moved back. "Are you afraid of me?"

She tilted her chin up. "No. Why ever do you ask that?" She couldn't help the venom that seeped into her words. There was no way she was afraid of this mage apprentice, though goose bumps dotted her arms as he drew near.

"Because it is warm in here, yet you tremble." He smiled. When she didn't respond, he rested his hand on her shoulder. She shrugged it off.

"I am not dressed properly, and an unmarried lady does not visit with a gentleman unless she's well chaperoned."

"And if you attended the school? Then what? You would be the only lady there."

He touched her hair again. She stepped back, only this time her heels ran into the wall. His lips inched up as his eyes sparkled with amusement.

"I do not want to hurt you," she said under her breath, her blood rushing to her head as she considered what she could do to him that would not be too harmful.

"You can only do something to me if I am evil. I sense this in you."

"I wish to return to my room. I have nothing further to say to you, and you will permit me to leave, now."

He placed his hands on her shoulders and leaned over to kiss her. She should have turned him to stone, though his body pressing against hers already felt as hard as rock. But his lips pressured hers to respond, and she gave in to the moment, the warmth, the tenderness, the desire to be loved.

She touched his waist, intending to push him away, but instead, she gripped his body and kissed him back, encouraging him further. Then to her astonishment, his hands slipped beneath her cloak. He touched her breasts, the filmy silk sliding over them as he attempted to feel the tips tightened in anticipation. She gasped as she grabbed his wrists to stop his touch.

"You want me, like I want you," he whispered in her ear, his breath warm against her cheek.

She mouthed an incantation, "Memory lapses, everything collapses, with the blink of an eye."

He stilled his hands. Then he chuckled. "You have gotten the spell wrong if you are attempting to make me forget what I am doing."

She raised her knee to his groin, but he jumped back before she connected. Then she dashed up the stairs in the dark as he laughed out loud.

Tears flooded down her cheeks. Kersta was right. The mage apprentice could do nothing but hurt her. Mexia ducked into the room, shut the door, and locked it.

"Mexia?" Kersta called out.

"Yes, it is just me."

"Are you all right?"

Mexia wiped the tears from her eyes as she dropped her cloak onto the chair. "Yes, I am just fine." But she wasn't. She wouldn't let Derek get under her skin again.

~

*E*arly the next morning while Mexia braided her hair, she glanced over at Kersta to see her studying her. "What, Kersta?"

The princess stopped dressing and looked over at the two of them. "Have I missed something?"

"Do you want to tell the princess who you were seeing last night? Or shall I?"

"What happened?" The princess straightened her back.

"Derek came to see me last night." Mexia looked back at the mirror. Her ivory cheeks instantly colored red with the recollection. Wrapping her hair in coils against her head, she bound the braids close with golden clips. "He warned us not to continue on the journey any further."

Kersta frowned at her. "Anything else?"

"No." Mexia fought the tears collecting in her eyes as their green color turned even darker. She couldn't let her friends know how foolish she'd been to leave the room in the first place. And then to have tried to cast a spell on the man to stop him in his actions, only to foul it up. She had to learn to concentrate, no matter what the distraction. Her stomach sickened as she recalled his laughter, echoing in the recesses of her mind still.

When she finished securing her hair, she looked over to see Kersta and the princess still waiting for further conversation on the subject.

"That was all," Mexia said. "Are we ready to breakfast?"

The princess finished rolling her light brown hair into curls on her head. And Kersta finished securing her hair, the darkest brown of the lot, nearly black except when the sun shown on it revealing the distinctive brown coloring. Many Damarians had the same color of hair, truth be known.

She could see why Princess Talamaya had been so intrigued with the Mesa elves and their fair coloring, and King Lazarion with his blond hair and blue eyes. Was that what attracted her to Derek, too? His difference?

Derek was a mage like her also. That appealed. He understood some of how she thought, being a wizard, too, and they had similar abilities. Well, except he could vanish, or take her to places when he held her hand. Her stomach tightened.

That's what she wanted to do. Just wave her hand in front of her face, and poof, she would be transported somewhere else. Somewhere she truly wanted to be. Like at the castle of the High Wizard of Monrovia.

She pulled her cloak on, then grabbed up her staff. Turning, she realized the ladies all waited for her.

She avoided their looks of concern and headed for the door. "I am starving. Are you, ladies, not also?"

When they knocked on Gallant's door, there was no answer. Kersta twisted her mouth in annoyance. "Maybe he has already begun eating."

They walked down to the dining hall and saw him sitting at a table, already ripping off a portion of bread. He waved to them.

"No manners, whatsoever," Kersta grumbled under her breath.

Six soldiers ate their breakfast at two of the nearby tables. As soon as the ladies stepped into the room, one of the men spoke and the whole lot of them looked in their direction. But there was no sign of the pirates, or of the cloaked man.

When the ladies took their seats, the frazzled barmaid joined them. Her red hair looked even more unkempt this morning. She cocked a brow. "I take it you want breakfast, nothing to drink?"

"Yes, please," the princess said.

"I'd be careful on your journey this morning. Some of the

soldiers were put off they didn't get to share your company last night."

"Are they not worried we might be sorceresses?" Mexia asked.

The woman smiled a lopsided smile. "They do not like the male mages. A roll in the hay with a female might prove to be fun, eh? Besides I'm sure they figure if you haven't been to the school, you cannot be that powerful."

"Their folly," Gallant replied. "Where is the food, woman?"

The barmaid smiled. "We don't have dwarves in here very often. You're kind of cute." She flipped around and headed back to the kitchen.

"Sleep well?" Gallant asked.

The ladies looked at Mexia.

She cleared her throat as Gallant shifted his gaze to her. "Well enough. The brigands made enough racket last night to disturb my sleep when they finally removed themselves from the tavern floor."

"Aye, well, I slept like the dead." He pointed his knife at the princess. "There is an adventurers' guild in Barston I wish to stop in at."

The princess took a deep breath. "You wish to be paid for a quest?"

"Aye. I have not earned money in a while."

"We must not delay in getting the letter of recommendation for Mexia."

"Aye."

"If you find a quest you must complete and it takes you out of our way—"

"I will find one that is along the way, woman. How can I protect ye, if ye are not with me? I only want a quest that is in the same direction as we travel."

The ladies smiled.

He grunted.

The barmaid returned to the room and laid a tray on the table. Fishcakes, scrambled griffon eggs, and boar bacon filled the pewter plates to the edges.

Gallant dug into his eggs with enthusiasm. "It's about time, woman."

The barmaid chuckled under her breath, then hurried off to the kitchen again.

As the ladies poked their forks into their food, a shadow descended over the table. They turned to see one of the soldiers smiling at them.

"I am Lentoris. The barmaid said you be traveling our way."

"What way is that?" the princess asked.

"Through Darkland Forest. We go that way, too. Seeing as you are three women without escort..."

Gallant poked his knife in the soldier's direction. "They have protection."

"As I said, seeings as we go the same way, we could offer you our protection."

"We thank you for your kind offer, sir," the princess said, "but we will be fine."

He nodded, then looked the three women over once more. "You'll be fine with the mage apprentices' help. But you won't be when you enter Hell Forest."

"Darkland Forest?"

"One and the same." He shook his head. "You should have taken us up on our offer. We shall try to avoid stepping on your bones left strewn on our path in the meantime." He bowed slightly, then turned and motioned to the men. One of the soldiers dashed up the stairs.

Within a few minutes, the twelve soldiers gathered on the first floor. Lentoris stopped at the ladies' table on his way out. "One last chance."

"Nay, the lady has declined your offer once, man. How many times does she have to say it before ye get it through your thick skull?" Gallant grumbled.

The man stared at him, hard. "Good day to you, ladies. Safe journey then."

He waved to his men, several of whom cast glances back at the women as they headed out.

Kersta sighed. "They are planning on ambushing us in Darkland Forest. Only, if the dark elves get to them first, they will be the ones whose bones will lie scattered about in the woods."

Mexia nodded. "Perhaps I can call on the wild boars to aid us against the dark elves."

Gallant frowned. "As long as ye do not have them attacking the wrong foe."

They finished their meals, then paid the barmaid. "When you return, will you stop here for the night again?" she asked.

"We plan to. The food and lodging were most agreeable," the princess said.

They walked through the door and crossed the square as the sun peeked its head out of the sea. Darkland Forest filled with a mixture of pine and oak stood before them, waiting for new visitors to enter.

"The quickest way," Mexia said referring back to the map, "is to go straight."

The princess tucked a loose curl behind her ear. "But that's where the soldiers will lie in wait."

"Still, should we not go through the shortest part?" Kersta asked. "Traveling farther into the forest would not be a safe venture."

"I vote we go the shortest path," Gallant said.

Mexia and Kersta nodded.

The princess pointed with her staff. "The shortest path. Let us hope it is not the deadliest."

CHAPTER 3

The party of four strode into the pine tree dominated woods, each listening for any signs of danger. The fragrance of the pine wafted on the slight breeze. Mexia whispered, "The birds still sing their heartwarming tunes."

"Yes," Kersta said, "that means the dark elves are not about."

"At least not close at hand," the princess added.

"Can you cast a protection spell over us, Mexia?" Kersta asked.

Mexia mouthed the words for the spell. "Provide an impenetrable wall to protect my companions, all." Irritated with her inability to not always be able to control her powers, she shook her head. "Not for a while. The one I used on the bedchamber door to keep the soldiers from bothering us has taken most of my defensive spell energy. I will try again later."

Gallant touched his helm. "I guess this won't help me none against the dark elves."

"Certainly, it will," Mexia said. "Of course it is designed to protect you against the most powerful wizard mind spells, but it'll save you from a weapon, too."

Kersta wrinkled her nose at him. "His head is hard enough. He doesn't need to have a helm to protect it."

"Didn't I say ye liked me, woman?"

"Shhh," the princess said. "I thought I heard footfalls deeper in the woods."

They stopped walking. The sounds of birds still filled the air, lilting, sweet, cloaking the danger that lurked in the forest.

"Not the dark elves." Mexia readied her staff for trouble as she carried it across her body diagonally.

"The soldiers?"

"Might be." The princess began to walk again, this time quickening her pace. "The path is well worn and you can see where woodsmen have trimmed the lower branches of the trees to keep it open for travelers."

Mexia recognized the princess's ploy of attempting to change the subject to calm the fear rising deep inside them. Always calm in a crisis, she made for a great companion in times like these.

A yell from men deeper in the woods, Mexia assumed the soldiers' voices, made the companions continue on their way without hesitation.

"Dark elves!" one of the men shouted.

Then the woods grew quiet all around the party.

"Dark elves," the princess whispered, holding the Scepter of Lanai tightly in her grip.

They stopped and waited, forming a circle, facing outward, weapons readied.

All at once the elves appeared from the woods. Their ebony hair hung loosely about their shoulders, their lithe bodies cloaked in green shirts as dark as the oak's green leaves and their trousers as brown as the bark of the trunks. They studied the women and dwarf with oval black eyes glinted with red as if they were coals burning with a slow flame. Their short swords caught the rays of the sun streaming through the branches of the oaks surrounding them as they held them ready to do battle.

"Are they waiting for a Dark Elf lord?" Mexia asked, trying to settle the nervousness filtering through every fiber of her body.

"Aye, just as they did in Wildwood Forest. Nothing changes in their actions from continent to continent," Gallant said.

The clomping of horse's hooves on the spongy woodland floor made the party glance over at the new arrival. Only it wasn't a Dark Elf lord as they expected to give the order to kill the companions.

"Derek?" Mexia said, her voice confused and surprised at the same time.

"I killed him," Derek said with triumph. He jumped down from the horse. "The Dark Elf lord's dead. Return now to Langdon and take the ship home to Damar, I tell you."

The elves exchanged glances. Leaderless, they seemed at a loss as to what to do momentarily. Derek took the opportunity and spoke an incantation. "Disband the elves who encircle the Albion party." He parted the elf party with the spell briefly and joined Mexia.

Without a word to the others, he grabbed her hand and instantly they were transported to the edge of the woods rimming Langdon City.

"Troll's dung, Derek!" Mexia screamed at him as she realized he'd ferreted her away from her friends using his transportation spell as she now stood on the outskirts of Langdon. Nothing could have infuriated her more as her head nearly exploded with frustration.

He stared at her for a second, his mouth dropped open, undoubtedly to hear her swear, and then he smiled. His face turned dour at once as he pointed to the shipyard. "Go! Return home. I will not save you again."

34

"I didn't ask for you to and now you've put my friends in great peril!"

She dashed back through the forest, running as fast as she could to join them. Her heart pounded with anxiety. If in her absence her friends were hurt or killed because of their fewer numbers...

"Mexia!" Derek shouted as he ran after her. "Mexia! Quit being such a fool!"

He soon caught up to her with his longer stride, but when he grabbed her arm, arrows zinged through the woods, catching their attention. He reached for her hand, but she darted off again toward her friends whose weapons clashed with elves' short swords some distance away. A flash of light from the princess's scepter appeared like a lightning bolt, then vanished.

Again, Derek tried to grab Mexia's hand. Only he cried out in pain when his fingers touched hers. She turned to see an arrow wedged in Derek's arm, the blood already soaking the sleeve of his shirt.

"Derek!" she screamed. Her anger instantly transformed into fear for him. She grabbed his good arm as he collapsed.

"Come with me," he pleaded.

She pulled out a healing kit from the pocket of her cloak.

He shook his head. "The arrow tip is poisoned. Take my hand."

"I can heal you of the effects."

"No! Give me your hand!"

She ignored him and wrapped the healing patch around the arrow and his arm, her head throbbing with worry, her breath still short from running. But when two elves ran onto the path with their swords drawn, Derek moved his hand before his face and vanished.

Mexia jumped to her feet and struck the first elf with her staff. He collapsed to his knees, the magical effects of her weapon instantly killing him with its touch. Turning, she managed to strike the second elf's sword as he thrust it at her. The sword shattered and the jolt through his arm made him cry out in pain. She quickly slammed her staff against his chest, and he buckled to the ground.

At a full sprint, she ran in the direction of her friends, but to her horror, she saw no sign of them when she reached their last location. All that remained were dead elves strewn all about. Her heart gladdened to see none of her friends' bodies lying amongst the evil-hearted elves', but her blood quickly turned to ice as she worried her companions had left her behind for good.

The screech of an owl made her glance up to see one swooping into the dense forest.

Without further hesitation, she ran toward the clearing she hoped she would soon find, and with it, her friends resting while they waited for her there.

But when she reached the meadow that stretched for a couple of miles before the river cut it in two, all that filled her vision was tall, gold-tasseled grasses swaying gently in the breeze. She attempted to catch her rapid breath, and settle the growing fear that threatened to undo her thoughts. Calmly, she had to figure out what to do next, she urged her mind...only with her wits about her, could she survive alone.

Then a golden head bobbed up and down, moving toward her. She stood still waiting, panic filling her stomach. Her friends wouldn't leave her here all alone, would they? Maybe they thought she couldn't return, that Derek had cast some kind of spell on her, that she couldn't break the influence. Had they gone ahead, then, to receive the letter of recommendation on her behalf?

The notion sickened her. She had to find them and quickly. No way could she handle all the dangers she'd have to face on her own. Even returning through the woods alone would surely be the death of her.

As the figure drew closer, she could see it was a young boy now, clutching a wooden sword in his right hand, a tin shield in the other. "You be a warrior?" he asked, enthusiasm spilling from his child's lips. "You looking for your friends?"

"Two women and a dwarf?" she asked running to join him, her only thoughts, finding her friends and reuniting with them.

"This way," he waved his sword. "They be this way!"

"What are you doing on this side of the river?" Mexia asked as the boy ran beside her, the concern evident in her voice.

"To fight the monsters. On the other side of the river is the city. No fighting monsters there."

"Are you alone?" Her mind sifted through the situation. No way could the boy have survived a trek alone across the bridge, could he have?

He laughed. "Nah. Me and me friends, we play here all the time."

"Surely your parents are worried about your being over here. How did you cross the bridge without the trolls hurting you?"

"We fight them." He motioned with his sword. "Ha! Ha!" He nodded. "Me and me friends kills them."

She shook her head, not believing his story entirely. "Have you seen soldiers? Or pirates?"

"Pirates?" He laughed. "Too far from the sea here. Nah, no pirates. Soldiers? A couple."

"Where did they go?" She tried to keep her voice cheerful, not harried like she felt.

"We brought them here."

"Where's here?"

"Our cave. It's like home."

He pointed to a waterfall pouring down a cliff face. "Behind the water."

"Why did my friends come this way?"

"They said they wanted to help me. Well, me and me friends. It's funny because we wanted to help them, too. We are adventurers from the adventurers' guild. The dwarf scoffed. Said we were too young, but we rescued your friends. Is that not what adventurers do? Help others in their time of need?"

"Yes, of course. Which bridge is the best one to take to get to Barston?"

"The one without all the missing boards. We can show you. We killed the trolls there, but they keep coming back."

"How long have you been here?"

"Days, maybe weeks. I'm not sure."

As they drew closer to the waterfall, the roar was nearly deafening. Wet moss covered the rocks surrounding it while the air smelled fresh as when it was cleansed with a spring rain.

He motioned to the cave. "Shall we?"

Already suspicious, she balked. "What did my friends say their names were?"

"Uhm, I'm not sure. I'm not too good with names. You can ask them yourself." He pointed to the cave again. "Come on."

She turned back toward the way she had come, her pace hurried. "Can you show me the bridge first?"

"Me and me friends can show you the bridge. Come, meet them now."

Mexia shook her head, the fear rising in her throat. "I will meet your friends later. I must make it to Barston today." She turned away from him and headed for the river.

She ignored his hurried footsteps as he ran after her.

"Do you not want to meet me friends?"

"I'm sure that I do. Can you tell me your parents' names so that I may let them know where you have been playing?"

He stopped. She turned to face him.

Scratching his head with his play sword, he said, "They will be angry with me."

"Mexia!" Kersta shouted from some distance away.

Mexia flipped around, but saw no sign of her friend.

"Kersta?"

"Mexia! Thank the gods you are safe!"

"Kersta?"

"Oh, oh," Kersta whipped off her invisibility cloak and suddenly appeared a hundred yards away.

The boy laughed. "Me thought she be a ghost."

Kersta was the most beautiful sight in the world to Mexia. She ran to join her.

The women embraced, Mexia never wanting to let go. "I thought I'd lost you for good." A couple of tears drizzled down her cheek.

Kersta gave her another heartfelt squeeze. "I knew you would be safe. Come, we have found the bridge to cross."

"The one with no missing planks?"

"How did you know?"

"The boy." Mexia turned to point at him. All that stood before her were the meadowland grasses rippling gold in the brilliant rays of the sun.

"Come, Mexia. We must join the others and figure how to cross the bridge."

"Did you see the boy?"

"No children would be over here on this side of the river. It's too dangerous."

"That's what I told him."

Kersta grabbed her hand and hurried her toward the grassy knoll where the princess and Gallant waited. "She is safe!" Kersta said, her words proudly spoken. "I told you I read her frazzled mind, and she was safe in the meadows."

"Thank the gods." The princess hugged Mexia, warming her clean through.

Gallant shuffled his feet. "Aye, good to see ye back with us, woman. We could use your spells against those." He motioned to the bridge.

"I see nothing there." Mexia peered at the wooden bridge in the distance, its flimsy wooden railings the only thing keeping a person from falling into the swiftly moving waters where boulders blanketed in moss, poked out of its dark depths.

Gallant pointed at the bridge again. "They hide underneath, just waiting for the likes of travelers like us to make an attempt to cross it. And then they will rip out your heart and eat it for supper."

"Did any of you see the boy in the meadow?" Mexia asked, trying to curb her unsettled stomach as she considered facing the trolls.

The princess shook her head. "No children would be over here. They'd never make it across the bridge from Barston. Nor could they have come from Langdon City through the Darkland Forest with the dark elves about."

"But the boy said he spoke to you. That you were in the cave beneath the falls over there." Mexia pointed in the direction the boy had taken her.

"We saw no one, woman," Gallant said shaking his head. "Just as the ladies have said."

"But he said that you had told him he was too young to be from the adventurer's guild."

"If I had spoken to him, I would have said such a thing, but I have not seen the lad."

Mexia studied the meadows, but there was no sign of the boy. "He would not give me his name. I wanted to tell his parents where he was. He said there were others, and two soldiers also." She couldn't shake the concern she had for the

40

children whose parents must have been frantic over their disappearances.

"We spoke to no one." Kersta rubbed her arms. "But we were worried sick about you, Mexia. When Derek grabbed your hand, I could see he intended to whisk you away to safety. I felt you wouldn't return to the woods, that he wouldn't permit you to. He's more powerful than you, in some regards. But in others, you are more powerful than him. And then the princess had a vision you were in the meadows. I read your mind, too, confirming this."

"In what way am I more powerful than Derek?"

Kersta took a deep breath. "I'm not certain. It is as though you have some kind of innate abilities that he does not. He has learned much in his four years of schooling, but you possess a power that's…well, that's greater than his, to some extent. He senses it, too, and he's drawn to you…because of that, but something more."

Kersta shook her head as she continued. "I don't know what goes on in his mind. For brief seconds, I gleam some meaning, then all of a sudden, he throws up a wall, as though he realizes I am attempting to read his mind. As to your abilities, they exist, but just haven't been trained."

"My father always said I learned faster than he ever could. I think it disturbed him some as he felt a woman should never be able to best a man…in anything."

"Yes, but he changed his mind after you helped me claim the scepter," the princess said, patting her on the shoulder.

"He did. I don't think I've ever seen tears in his eyes as when he saw me off to attend the school here. I will be the first wizard from Damar who ever had formal schooling. And if I ever make it to that level, I will be the only Damarian mage to hold the distinction of High Wizard."

"You will succeed," the princess said, "as your heart is in it."

"What are we going to do about Derek?" Kersta asked.

"He was wounded by a Dark Elf's poisoned arrow. He returned home, but before this, he told me he would not attempt to rescue me any further."

Kersta and the princess exchanged glances.

"What?"

"We do not believe he has finished with us...or with you, Mexia," the princess said.

Gallant pointed at the bridge with his war hammer. "Are ye ready?"

"Mexia, can you cast your protection spell?"

Mexia tried, then shook her head. "Not yet. I'm sorry."

"Kersta, wear your cloak. See if you can cross without their detecting you," the princess said.

"But we need to stick together. To fight together."

"If they appear, we will swoop down on them using the advantage of surprise. If they do not, you can wait for us on the other side of the bridge, and again, attack them from behind, to their surprise."

"All right." Kersta pulled her cloak over her shoulders, then situated the hood over her face and clasped it with its golden fastener. Her actions showed bravado, but her words were said with timidity.

Mexia knew she felt the same sense of despair she experienced when she had to go it alone. She squeezed Kersta's hand. "We will be right behind you, should they attack."

Kersta chuckled. "I will expect it."

For some distance, they heard her light footstep, the invisibility cloak hiding her completely. Then a clunk resounded as she kicked a stone with the toe of her boot.

Mexia cringed. Would the planks of the weathered bridge creak as Kersta crossed it and give her away?

The women waited, their weapons readied, their feet itching

to sprint toward the bridge, if need be. Gallant stood just as tense, his war hammer held in his hands, ready to do battle.

They couldn't tell how close Kersta was to the bridge as they waited, every minute seemingly endless.

"Can we move a little closer?" Mexia asked. "I hate to be such a long distance from her if she needs our help."

"No," the princess cautioned. "If we near the bridge now, they will undoubtedly swarm all over it. Even if they cannot see her, they will run into…"

Mexia gasped. A troll, gray mangy fur covering his entire body, scrambled out from underneath the bridge. He swatted at the air with his long dirty clawed fingers as he stood, close to the women's height, shy a couple of inches of five and a half feet tall. Mexia held her breath.

"He must have heard the boards creak with Kersta's footstep," the princess whispered.

"He must be the guard. Nay doubt others lay in wait beneath the bridge," Gallant said. "But there will be one less if we kill this one. Are ye game?"

The troll sauntered to the farthest side of the bridge, then suddenly a staff whipped through the air. The beast cried out and fell between the crooked posts of the scanty railing, and into the turbulent water.

The staff disappeared.

"Kersta," Mexia said under her breath.

"Aye, she is clever." Gallant began to walk toward the bridge, but the princess grabbed his arm to halt him.

"Wait a minute more."

Again, a troll crawled out from underneath the bridge, this one as gray-haired as the other, beady eyes of black, and teeth jagged and yellowed as it wrinkled its nose up to smell the air. "Where be you?" it said, its throaty voice hollered in annoyance, grating on

Mexia's nerves. "Where be you? Me smell the sweet meat of a huuuuuman. But me no sees you."

The staff suddenly appeared and with a strike at the beast, the troll screamed in pain and dropped into the raging river. Two trolls scampered onto the upper side of the bridge and stood next.

"It is time," the princess said, then ran like the wind toward the bridge.

Mexia joined her as Gallant tried to keep up, his short legs running twice as fast.

"Huuuuumans!"

"And a dwarffffff!" the other shouted.

Five more trolls appeared on the bridge, but one quickly fell to the river with a groan as Kersta's staff struck him.

The adrenaline surged through Mexia's body like a forest on fire as she thrust her staff at one of the trolls. Her staff hit his chest and instantly, he collapsed to his knees.

Gallant struck another with his war hammer as the princess used her scepter on one. A flash of light followed, making one of the trolls scream out at the sight. Farther along the bridge, panic filled the trolls as the unseen force wielded a staff from behind, striking at them again and again.

As soon as the last two trolls scampered for safety underneath the bridge, the companions hurried to cross to the other side.

Mexia pointed to the village in the distance. "Barston. And no more obstacles."

"Aye. We see my wife now. And then we visit the adventurers' guild."

"You did great, Kersta," Mexia said as Kersta unclasped her cloak and became visible again.

"Aye, woman. Being as feisty as ye are, ye clobbered them good."

"Yes, Kersta, you certainly spooked them," the princess said. "Which way, Gallant?" She motioned to the town as it stretched across a verdant valley, surrounded by crops of wheat and corn bending in the breeze.

Gallant pulled out a city map. "Millicent is supposed to be living on the east side of the town. Third house down from the butcher's shop."

"And the adventurer's guild?"

"The building before the butcher's shop."

"Perhaps we should go to the adventurer's guild first?"

Gallant tugged at his braided beard. "Aye. It is first on the way. My wife can wait."

"Will the man she ran off with not like it that you wish to see her?" Kersta asked.

"He will not mind."

"I don't understand," Mexia said, thoroughly confused about Gallant's strange relationship with his wife. "I would think you would want to wring his neck, or hers."

"Or both," Kersta added.

"She did not want me adventuring, woman. Haven't I told ye this before? Can ye blame her? Worried that I might never return home to her? Constantly, off slaying beasts, rescuing damsels who need my aid," he said pausing to wiggle his brows at Kersta, "and being gone long days without word."

"I see your point. So then why did you choose to join the adventurer's guild?"

"My brother, who owned the tavern in Kern, did not want me to help him. And my brother, who owned the dwarf mine, was a disagreeable sort. So I chose to strike it out on my own. Though dwarves do not normally join the adventurers' guild."

"You are like us then," Mexia mused. "Women were not mages in Damar, nor were they allowed to cross the continent on quests. So we all are doing something that does not come naturally to us."

"Aye."

When they spied the sign displayed across the guild in bold letters, Gallant stood straighter. "I will be but a moment."

"Gallant! Gallant! Is that ye?"

The ladies turned to see a bearded female dwarf running toward them, her skirts shifting at her ankles as she hurried to greet Gallant.

"Blasted, woman. I have business to take care of, can't ye see?" He pointed to the guild with his war hammer as he narrowed his eyes at the dwarf who ran across the street to join him.

Mexia and the other ladies smiled. "Your wife, Gallant?"

"Aye."

The woman grabbed his hand and yanked at him to follow her. "Come, come, ye have come all this way to see me. I will take ye to my home."

"And my friends?"

She glanced back at them. "Ye have taken up with a bunch of female humans?"

"The one saved my life."

"Aye, debt of gratitude."

"Well?"

"We have no room for them. They will have to seek lodging at the tavern on the other side of town."

He yanked his hand away from his wife. "Wait for me here. I must see to the guild first."

"If ye go in there, ye are not welcome in my home."

Gallant hesitated.

Mexia tried to smooth things over between them. "Perhaps the guild can wait until later, Gallant. We will eat at the tavern and meet you here in a couple of hours. That'll give you time to visit with your wife and plan things from there."

"Aye, two hours it be then. Meet me here." His wife dragged him away.

Kersta chuckled. "You can see who wears the breeches in that family."

"I heard ye!" Gallant shouted as he scowled at Kersta.

"Come, ladies, let us find the tavern and rest a while. I would welcome a place to sit for some time. My feet are much wearied." The princess began to walk toward the other side of town while the ladies hurried to keep up.

"Maybe we can get some horses here," Kersta said, her voice sounding hopeful.

"No horses here," a man said as he strolled behind them.

"No horses at all?" Mexia asked, as they turned to face him.

The gray-haired man, his face wrinkled with years of working in the sun, nodded. "They have all run off."

Mexia frowned. "Why?"

"You would have to ask the soothsayer that. But none of us are welcome in her cave."

"Why not?"

"The last of those who believed in her died off some years back."

"You do not believe in her, either?"

He shook his head. "Not when there is so much evil in the world. The people feel she has let them down."

"Where is the soothsayer's cave?"

He motioned toward the river. "Back across the river. Underneath the waterfalls that pour over the cliff face to the west. That's where she lives."

"Where the boy was leading me," Mexia said, under her breath. A chill twisted down her spine. "It had to have been."

"A boy? No, no children would ever venture across the bridge. They'd be killed for certain by the trolls."

Mexia frowned. "What if some children did make it across the bridge, but could never return here because of the powerful trolls that still protect it? Would the soothsayer provide them a safe haven?"

He shrugged. "How would I know this? I have never ventured across the bridge since the trolls moved in. Foolhardy at best. Only the soldiers of fortune who pass through this way from time to time, attempt it."

"Are there any children reported to be missing?" the princess asked.

The man motioned toward the adventurer's guild. "You will have to see the guild master to ask your questions of him. He would know if a family posted a reward for the return of their missing children."

The women looked back at the guild hall. Mexia said, "Should we check and see? If the boy was correct and there were more of them, we need to bring them home."

She turned to speak to the man, but he had vanished.

"Where'd he go?" Kersta asked.

Chill bumps trailed up Mexia's arms. "Let us go to the adventurers' guild at once."

CHAPTER 4

Kersta opened the door to the adventurer's guild and the ladies frowned to see five of the soldiers from the Dragon's Keep Tavern in Langdon there.

A man who was speaking with these turned his attention to the women. "You seem to be lost, ladies. May I direct you somewhere?"

"We wish to know if you have a list of missing children posted by some of the townspeople who wish their return," the princess asked.

"We do, but what would you wish of this information?" His gaze trailed from the top of her head to the tip of her boots and back up again.

"We intend to bring the children home, if this is even possible."

The soldiers laughed.

"I have spoken to one of the boys," Mexia said. "Beyond the river. A blond-haired lad of nor more than eleven."

The man's eyes grew big. Then he shook his head. "They could never have fought the trolls and survived. And had they,

they would never have lived this long in the wilderness. If they were dead and you spoke to them, you are dead, too."

"So you do not wish them returned, if any of them do live?" Kersta asked.

He shuffled his feet as he looked over at the soldiers. "These men will find them."

"And if they do not?"

"I would not send women out, well, in truth if you are not members of the guild, you cannot go on a guild quest at all."

Mexia smiled. "How do we become members of the guild?"

Again the men chortled.

Mexia tightened her grip on her staff.

The princess pointed back to the river. "We have already solved many quests in Inherian."

"The continent of Inherian is an island paradise, not like here. There are no dangers there."

The women exchanged glances as Kersta rolled her eyes.

"Ah, but we journeyed through the woods here and fought the dark elves…and survived," Mexia said.

"And we fought the trolls on the bridge and lived to tell of the tale," the princess added.

"And," Kersta said pointing at the soldiers of fortune, "we bested these very same men in a barroom brawl in Langdon."

"The ladies are a bit…daft," one of the soldiers said. "Can you believe a word of it? We cleared the way for them through Darkland Forest. After we finished off the trolls, they had no trouble crossing the bridge. As for the tavern in Langdon… wizard apprentices used their magic. Who can fight something like that?"

Mexia whispered to the ladies, "We do not need to be certified by the adventurers' guild. Come, let us see the soothsayer and bring the children home."

The princess waited for Kersta's concurrence, then nodded.

"Thank you, guild master. We apologize for inconveniencing you so. We will be on our way."

The ladies headed out of the building, but before they had made it very far down the road, one of the soldiers called out to them. "If you women insist on traveling the same way we do, we might as well go together."

"If we are able to bring the children home, these men will try to take credit for our actions," Mexia cautioned the ladies under her breath.

"More than that, I don't trust their intentions," Kersta added.

"I was going to let Gallant visit with his wife a bit longer, ladies," the princess said, "but I believe we will fetch him. I'm sure he would grouch the rest of our journey if he knew we did not take him with us on our quest." She turned to the men. "We are not leaving town, just yet. So best of luck to you on your quest."

The men hesitated.

"What? Did you think we'd clear the way for you, again?" Kersta asked.

"You think the three of you are very clever. But we will catch up to you, soon enough."

The soldiers hurried through the meadow toward the bridge.

"Come, ladies, let us see how things are going with Gallant."

It didn't take more than a few minutes to find the one-story, pink stone house where Gallant stayed. Blue and pink flowers filled window boxes to the brim, cheering the green glass of the window panes arching above them. A sweet fragrance drifted from the flowers and another of...well, Mexia couldn't be sure. Some kind of sweet confection she assumed baked inside.

When they knocked at the door, Millicent answered it, but the look of disdain on her face showed how displeased she was to see them again.

"He is busy." She tried to shut the door in the princess's face, but Talamaya shoved her foot in the room to block the door from closing.

"Gallant!" the princess hollered into the hallway.

"Aye? What do you want, woman?" He hurried to the door.

"We need to do a quest, but we cannot speak to the guild master about it as we are not certified members of the guild," the princess said.

"Aye. That was why I was to go there to speak to him. Why did ye go there instead?"

"We need to rescue the children on the other side of the bridge, if we can. But we need to know who they were and how many there are."

He scratched his head. "But we didn't see any."

"A man told us there was a cave where a soothsayer resides. It is located underneath a waterfall, sounding very much like the one described to Mexia by the golden-haired lad."

"Aye."

"We need to speak to the soothsayer. No one has been permitted to see her in years. If this is so, no one will be able to free the children from her safe haven. That is, if she will allow us a visit."

"Why would she not see ye?"

"We think she will. The townsfolk don't believe in her. But we believe in soothsayers, so I think we will have no difficulty."

"Aye." He rubbed his whiskers. "But she will not see me for the same reason."

"You can remain outside the cave like you have done in the past when we have visited the soothsayers of Inherian."

Millicent gave him the look of the devil.

The princess tried to soothe things over with Gallant's wife. "If you could get the list of names for us, Gallant, you could return to visit with your wife longer. There is no need for you to stay with us. It shouldn't take us very long."

"Nay, I would not have ye go on a quest on my behalf. If I get the names, I am obligated to fulfill the quest or die trying."

Millicent folded her arms.

"I will be back, wife."

"If ye leave, Gallant, ye need not come back."

He smiled. "Ye say that but ye still love me." He patted his war hammer. "Let us be off then. I wish to be tucked into bed by the time it is dark."

The party of four walked back to the guild as Millicent slammed the door behind them, the angry noise reverberating off the cobblestone road.

When they arrived at the guild, the ladies stayed outside this time.

In a few minutes, Gallant returned to them with the paper in hand. "Ready, women? Just takes an adventurer to speak the words right."

"How many are there, Gallant?"

He handed the princess the list. "How would I know? I cannot count."

"Ten...all under the age of eleven. The youngest two were eight."

"All boys?" Kersta asked.

"One girl."

They crossed the fields before the bridge, then when they came in sight of the wooden structure, they paused. "Shall we do as before?"

Kersta clasped her cloak shut. "Worked well the last time."

After several minutes, she pulled down her hood as she stood on the other side of the bridge and waved her staff.

"Is it a troll trick, do you not think?" Mexia asked.

"They are not that clever," Gallant said. "I think they're afraid."

"Or perhaps the soldiers killed the last couple when they passed over this bridge a while ago," the princess said.

They readied their weapons and ran across the bridge. Other than the creaking of boards and their boots banging along the wood, there was no other sound.

When they reached the other side, they continued through the meadow following Mexia's direction this time.

"Hello?" she called out twice.

"Do you think the soldiers are around?" the princess asked.

"Who knows what those idiots would be doing? They may have gone in the opposite direction. No telling," Kersta said.

When the waterfall came into view, Mexia took a deep breath and pointed at the fall. "There is where he said he and his friends waited for us."

"Why would he have told such a lie?" Kersta asked.

"I think he wanted me to come rescue them or see the sooth-sayer so badly, he would have said anything for me to enter the cave. He kept wanting me to meet his friends."

"Are you ready, ladies?" the princess asked.

"I will wait out here for ye, ladies."

Leaving Gallant behind, Mexia led the way behind the water-fall, clinging to the rock facing in an attempt to keep her footing. She slipped on the wet moss coating the rocks. Her heart raced, fearing a dunk in the swiftly flowing river.

As they stepped into the cave, the princess handed the fairy's wand to Kersta. The golden glow illuminated the dark. Mexia touched the velvety soft moss cloaking the walls in damp green blankets.

Water trickled down them like a stream bubbled over rounded rocks on a never-ending journey. The sound of dripping water deeper in the cave drew them in.

"It is not like Modi's cave," Kersta said.

"Nor like Nania's cave," the princess agreed. "I wonder who the soothsayer is who lives here?"

"You have visited Modi?" a woman's voice called out from deep in the bowels of the cave. "And Nania?"

"Yes, we have visited both," Mexia answered. Her heart couldn't beat any faster from the concern she felt for the children. "Do you protect the children? We wish to take them home if we could."

"Ah, the children. Come and visit with me. Share some goat milk with us."

They walked farther into the cavern, then found two tunnels. "Which one?" Mexia asked.

"Take the one that the children use."

Mexia looked back at her companions. Kersta shined the light from the wand into the one, then walked over to the other. Pointing with it, she said, "There. A sword lies on the floor there, and down the passageway, a shield."

Mexia led the party down the tunnel, then stopped as it opened into an enormous cave. Light streamed in from up above, illuminating pictures drawn on the walls four feet high, then all the way to the floor. Drawings of trolls, the river and the bridges, miniature warriors with wooden swords and tin shields fighting the evil, fairies and unicorns in a hodgepodge of colors filled the walls. In the middle of the room, a crystal blue in-ground swimming pool took center stage.

Seated on a natural step at one end of the pool, a woman watched them, her long black hair curling to her waist, her blue eyes sparkling with the reflection of the water off them. She smiled. "Welcome, I am Marinda."

"Marinda." The ladies all curtsied.

"I am so pleased to see you. Who are you, where are you from, and what do you seek?"

The princess spoke up. "I am Princess Talamaya, daughter of

the late King Sal of Damar. These are my companions, Lady Kersta, and Mexia, both of Damar. Waiting outside for us, is Gallant, a dwarf adventurer from the village of Kern. Lady Mexia wishes to attend the school of wizards, only she has been told she cannot, unless she receives a letter of recommendation from the mage of Monrovia."

"Such is the way of the world."

"But we wish to help the children return home," Mexia said. "Where are they?"

"Playing."

"We also were told you would know the reason why the horses left the village of Barston," Kersta said.

"The unicorns."

The princess sighed. "I have read of these great beasts. Horses of purest white with spiraled horns. I've heard the horns change colors at whim."

"Sprinkled with silver," Marinda said, nodding.

Mexia ran her hands over the paintings on the wall.

"What have they to do with the horses?"

"Magical, are they not?"

Mexia looked over at the soothsayer. "The unicorns?"

"The paintings." Marinda pointed at the murals.

Mexia studied them closer. "The unicorns feel warm to the touch. And the fairies, too."

"You have magic in you then. I knew one of you did. I could sense you carried magically empowered items with you, too."

"But where are the children?" Mexia asked.

"Sleeping."

"But you just said they were playing."

Marinda laughed. "So I did. Some are playing, some sleeping. You know how children are. Did you find the trail of toys they left in the passageway? Messy children. No matter how much I tell them to clean up after themselves, they don't."

"You don't want them to leave, do you?" Mexia said softly.

Marinda didn't respond to the question, just slipped into the pool and swam across its length. "I have enjoyed the children's company. I never thought anyone would come here to visit me again. Their parents don't deserve them, truly they don't."

"Because they don't believe in you?" Mexia asked.

"The children believe in me. That's all that matters. You understand, they wished to see me, when their parents wouldn't allow it. What parents would allow their children to venture into a dangerous world without protecting them, denying that I even exist? The children knew differently. They knew and wished to visit with me. It has been a year since the last leader of Barston sought my council, after all."

The princess knelt down beside the pool. "But we believe in you, too."

"Yes, that presents a problem."

Mexia crouched next to the princess. "If we do something for you? Will you release the children to us?"

The soothsayer stepped out of the pool, the water curling down her blue silk gown, then with a wave of her hand, her skin, clothes and hair were dry. "Drink with me."

She motioned to white fur cushions sitting in a corner of the room. "The children made those. They said my home needed something to soften it."

"The boy I spoke of said two soldiers came here also."

Marinda smiled. "Ruston? He makes up stories all of the time. Anything else?"

"He wished me to come here because he said my friends were waiting for me in the cave. But they were near one of the bridges instead."

"Ah." Marinda sat down on one of the cushions, then poured tin cups of milk for the ladies as they took their seats around her. "Yes, well I told him to do so."

"So you made up that tale?"

"I wished to meet the one who had magic. You will be able to approach the unicorns and the centaur who protects them. They will trust you."

"To do what?"

"Help them." Marinda took a deep breath. "It is a circle of misfortune." She paused. "Drink your milk, young ladies. It is good for you."

"What is a circle of misfortune?" Mexia prompted.

"A mage lost his ring in Pala Lake. Before this, he protected the area from the trolls and the like. He coaxed the townspeople into retrieving his ring for him, but five drowned in the attempt. Then the trolls moved in. Unable to rid the area of the trolls, the mage was banished.

"The centaur, that protected the unicorns in the meadow between Darkland Forest and the river, moved them east to Spring Valley where the flowers perpetually bloom to keep them safe from the trolls and dark elves. The unicorns fearing for their four-legged distant cousins, the horses of Barston, called to them to join them. The townspeople fearing the trolls underneath the bridges, couldn't stop their horses from running away. The children wanted to make everything all right again, sought my counsel."

"And now?" Mexia asked.

"You must begin at the beginning."

"First, we must locate the mage's ring?"

"Yes."

"If we're able to locate it, then what?"

"You must give it to the mage."

"Where is he living?"

"No one knows exactly. Perhaps in your journeys you will discover his whereabouts."

"Who is he?"

"Dragonmage, they call him, because he is the dragon's friend."

"You will not release the children until we have done this for you?"

"Solve the circle of misfortunes. Then the leaders of Barston will again seek my counsel and all will be well."

Mexia pulled the map from her cloak and studied it. "Pala Lake is east of here."

"Yes."

Mexia ran her finger across the map a short distance. "The valley of the unicorns is not far from there."

"No."

"But where is the wizard located? Have you a clue for us?"

"I have already given you one. Besides, you must first retrieve the ring. It is not an easy task."

Mexia ran her hand over her skirt, contemplating anything else she could ask the soothsayer before they attempted to find the ring. "How did the mage lose it there in the first place?"

Marinda smiled. "He was showing off to some mage friends. They all believed they could retrieve it first. All of them tried, but alas they failed. Maybe you can do what they cannot."

Mexia nodded. "We can only try."

"I must warn you though. You will find no trouble getting there. The trek is pleasant and unencumbered. The lake is warm and as inviting as much as my own pool is. But the water twists and distorts the magic of the ring. None who have tried to retrieve it can find it. They extend their fingers and though it seems within their grasp, they never manage to touch it."

"We will try." Mexia rose from her pillow.

"Yes, I knew you would. You have helped others in need…the three of you and your dwarf companion. You will help many more on your journey. The children will be waiting for your quick return. They are eager to go home to their parents, despite the scolding and the chores they will return to."

The ladies waited for Marinda to clap her hands and send them to the opening of the cave as the soothsayers of Inherian had done. Instead, she waved at the passageway. "Run along and be quick about it. We all await your return."

The princess led them down the passageway, none of them speaking until they were nearly to the waterfall. Then Kersta said, "Do you think she will release the children to us?"

Laughter echoed from deep within the cavern, children's laughter and a woman's, too.

"We will do whatever we can for these people. It is essential that the leaders believe in the importance of their soothsayer," the princess said.

"I wonder if Gallant can swim," Mexia said as they exited the cave.

"Swim?" Gallant said. "Are ye daft? Geese swim. Fish swim. Mermaids swim. Dwarves keep their feet on the ground, woman." He glanced behind Kersta. "Where are the children?"

"I'm afraid we have to go swimming first," Mexia said, as she began walking across the meadow in the direction of Pala Lake.

"Ye make nay sense, woman," Gallant muttered, trying to keep up as the ladies caught up to Mexia.

"It will be getting dark in a few hours," the princess reminded them.

"The soothsayer said the land was safe. If we have to, we could make camp at the lake." Mexia dug her staff into the ground using it as a walking stick.

"It is a good thing my wife already fed me."

"Good," Kersta said. "Then I do not have to share my bread with you."

He eyed her backpack with interest. "On the other hand, to keep up my fighting strength, a little supper would be welcome."

He smiled at Kersta. "So what would ye be needing to swim for?"

"A magical ring in the lake."

"Aye. And what does the ring do?"

"When a mage wears it, it protects the area from trolls."

"We could have used this ring before this," Gallant said, and Mexia wondered if all of a sudden he might even be willing to swim.

For an hour the party walked, stopping briefly to rest while Gallant dumped a rock out of his boot. Then they continued on again.

When they came in view of the lake, six soldiers drinking from the water dashed their high spirits.

"Marinda never considered the soldiers would be here and might give us trouble," Mexia whispered. "What do we do now, Princess Talamaya?"

"Because they're not innately evil, our staffs will only knock them off their feet for a while. If we have to, we will fight them. We cannot wait for them to leave the area."

Mexia readied her staff. "Let us find the ring, then."

The party headed for the lake when one of the men noticed their approach. He spoke quickly to the rest.

"What have we here?" the leader of the rabble asked.

"Have you located the children yet?" the princess asked.

"They are around here, somewhere. What are you doing here?"

"We wished to see the lake. The children are at a cave in the west, in case you still wish to take them home for the reward money."

Gallant grumbled under his breath, "Ye will be the death of me, woman."

"You try to throw us off their trail," the leader said.

"Whatever you say." The princess motioned to her party, and

they walked around the perimeter of the lake with a cautious step, watching for any sign of the ring. "Do you sense anything, Mexia? Anything magical at all?"

"Not yet, my lady."

Kersta glanced back at the soldiers. "They are watching us."

"We will swim one at a time once we find the location of the ring. When one gets tired, another will try. The rest will be ready to fight the soldiers if need be," the princess said.

"Here!" Mexia called out, her excitement at making the discovery evident in her voice.

"Shall I go first as I am the best swimmer?" Kersta asked.

"Yes," the princess answered. "Do."

Kersta pulled off her pouch and laid it on the grass. "Now they are really watching."

"They're curious as to how much you will take off," Gallant said as he watched her.

"As are you. Turn around. At least they are far enough away it will not matter." Kersta pulled off her cape. "Just tell me if they decide to come closer."

"They are coming closer," the princess said.

"Great. I do not wish to drown in my gown."

"You are swimming naked?" Gallant asked turning back around to take another look.

"Of course not." Kersta motioned for him to face away from her. When he did, she pulled off her skirt and blouse. Dressed only in her underdress, she waded into the water. "Pleasantly warm."

"We will keep the soldiers away," the princess assured her.

Kersta dove under.

When she came up for air, Mexia said, "I believe it's more to the right."

Kersta nodded and slipped underneath the water again.

"Leave us in peace," the princess said to the soldiers as they drew close. She and Gallant faced them, ready to do combat. Mexia's attention was divided between the men and aiding Kersta's search, but her staff was ready, and she'd only have to take a quick sprint to reach her companions to help them with the men.

"We are curious if we may be of some assistance," the leader of the men said.

"We do not need your help. Move away from here."

Kersta resurfaced. She whispered to Mexia whose boots remained at the edge of the water, "It is within my grasp, but I cannot quite get it."

"Perhaps I can reach it then. Come out of the water, and I'll try."

Kersta frowned. "The men must look away."

"I doubt they'll honor your request."

Mexia retrieved Kersta's cloak then handed it to her, making Kersta smile.

Once Kersta became invisible, they could hear footsteps move across the pebble beach. Her wet shift dropped to the grass, then her skirt floated in the air, then vanished. Her shirt did the same. "All right," she said, "you go next, Mexia."

Then to everyone's surprise Kersta's staff floated toward one of the soldiers. She said, "Turn around, or you will be dropped to the ground."

The men hesitated as Mexia pulled off her cloak, then removed her boots.

Kersta struck the sword of one of the men and when it shattered, he yelled out. Finally with much grumbling, the men turned their backs to the women.

"You think you can rush the three of us as there are twice our number," Kersta said, "but I can read your minds and know all you have planned before you can take action. So it would be in your best interest to behave."

Mexia smiled as she hurriedly pulled off her blouse and skirt, hoping no one would chance a peek. The sight of an owl soaring high above caught her eye. Was she mistaken, or was it the same with the orange feathers that brightened its cheeks, while white feathers arched high over his yellow eyes, making him appear more distinguished? His tufted ears perked up as he landed in a nearby tree, then twisted his head to watch her.

She waded into the water. As warm as heated bathwater, she enjoyed the feel against her skin as she dipped beneath the surface.

The gold ring glistened in the sunlight. The metal called to her, begged her to free it from its watery grave. And she longed to make it hers. But when she reached for it, the ripples in the water made it bend, distorting it, making it appear to move with every effort she made to retrieve it.

Her fingers touched it, just the tip, she was certain, but when she tried to grasp it, the ring faded from her touch.

CHAPTER 5

Mexia bounced on her toes in the water and rose to the surface.

"How are you doing?" the princess called back to her.

"I cannot reach it. It is there, but it slips away from my grasp every time."

"Do you wish for me to try?"

Exasperated, but determined, Mexia wasn't about to give up her efforts now. "No, my lady. If only I could see a clearer image of it."

"Modi's tea," the princess said, hurrying to get Mexia's flask. "It helped me see through the blizzard in Elan Pass."

"Yes, it clears the mind," Mexia agreed.

The princess handed Mexia the flask. After Mexia drank of the tea, she returned the flask to the princess, then dove under the water.

This time the ring didn't move from her touch as before. As if it sat on a dry beach, the ring appeared as clear as any of the stones at the water's edge. Her heart soared with excitement to nearly have it in her grasp. She grabbed it, slipped it on her finger so as not to lose it, and then attempted to shoot to the surface of the lake. Her heart beat with enthusiasm to finally reach the elusive ring.

Immediately, the sun that drenched the water's surface disappeared, and the water, too, just vanished. The air turned colder, but dampness still hung about her. Material like wool, woven into a carpet, rested beneath her fingertips to her surprise.

Her whole being filled with dread. She whispered, "Princess Talamaya? Kersta? Gallant?"

But no one responded.

Wearing only her underdress and still dripping wet, she crawled forward, too unsure of herself to attempt to stand and walk around in the darkness.

Voices in the distance seemed to echo off walls, then grew silent, furthering her sense of disquiet.

"Where is she then?" she finally heard a male voice say, his words said in exasperation. His muffled footsteps passed her by, as if a wall existed between them.

Had she been transported to some place when she placed the ring on her finger? Yes, just like when the princess wore the witch's ring in Inherian.

Mexia wished she could vanish into thin air like the mages of the school could do. She attempted to pull the ring off her finger, but it wouldn't budge. "Troll's dung," she said, forgetting to use caution.

A man chuckled.

She stilled her actions, her blood chilled with concern. Had he heard her? She had no weapon to protect her. And though she had her spells, they weren't always totally effective.

"She's nearby. Search the rooms."

This time goose bumps collected on top of the goose bumps already raised on her arms.

A door opened. Light from the hallway spilled into the room. Mexia cringed on the floor. She wished she could vanish like

Derek easily did. Again, she grabbed at the ring and attempted to yank it off.

A redheaded man wearing robes of crimson stepped into the entryway. "She's here!"

Lanterns filled the chambers with light as three men stepped into the room. Each wore a conical hat, indicating they were mages of some distinction and undoubtedly graduates of the school at Langston. All wore short beards, showing they were still youthful. And they all smiled at her as she grabbed a blanket from the bed resting at her fingertips, covering herself instantly.

"You have found the ring," the redhead said as he stepped closer, his green eyes sparkling in the lamplight with delight.

"You are Dragonmage?"

He chuckled. "Only Marinda, the soothsayer, calls me that. Who are you?"

"Lady Mexia. But I must return to Pala Lake where my friends are."

He glanced down at her hands clutching the blanket around her shoulders. "You have my ring."

"And I'd give it back, but it won't come off."

He nodded at the other mages. "This is Fessenwig and Mer. They helped me to lose my ring in the first place."

"Why?"

"We wished to see who could use their powers to elevate the ring from the lake first. Only we didn't realize we have no power over water. And none of us could even swim. So unfortunately, the game ended rather abruptly."

"People died over your foolishness."

He raised his brows at her. "Are you not afraid I will turn you into a frog?"

"Are you not afraid I will turn you to stone?"

He smiled as his friends chuckled. "You are not a mage. We have no sorceresses in Albion."

"I'm not from Albion."

His eyes widened. "Where are you from then?"

"Inherian."

He stroked his curly beard, the color nearly a golden red. "Inherian. I have heard the strangest things said about that continent of late."

Fessenwig cleared his throat. She turned her attention to him and studied his dark brown hair and eyes. He had very much the same coloring as one of her own people. "They say a female mage destroyed Grimoria."

"Lies," Mer said, folding his arms, his black brows furrowed in a frown. "Everyone knows no one could destroy Grimoria and get away with it. No way would a sorceress best the cagey old devil."

"A rogue wizard, who will never return to plague the continent of Inherian, gentlemen," Mexia said, her feathers a bit ruffled. Typical male mage. Uppity with no respect for sorceresses' abilities. Still, she hadn't any urge to make them mad at her, since she still had to somehow return to the lake. "But I must be on my way. My companions will worry about me."

"They have returned to the soothsayer. She will tell them where you have gone."

"But I have other business I must take care of."

"Dressed like that?" Dragonmage said. His lips curved up. "I've never met a sorceress before. I didn't realize how bedraggled and beautiful one could be all at the same time."

She frowned at him. "If you'll return me to the lake, I will retrieve my clothes."

"Your companions have taken your things with them. If I returned you to the lake, you would find yourself in a worse quandary than before."

"Then return me to the soothsayer's cave."

"I cannot. I could only return you to the place you put the ring on." He motioned to the hallway. "Have you eaten?"

She hesitated.

"Are you afraid of me?"

"She ought to be," Mer said. "In truth, Dragonmage has been scouring the countryside for a wife for several weeks. I haven't seen him so…intrigued with a woman, ever."

"I must attend the wizardry school at Langdon so that I may defeat the mage apprentice who escaped with Grimoria's spell book. I have no time for this nonsense."

"You have time to eat." Dragonmage motioned for his friends to move out of the doorway.

Frustrated, but not seeing any way out of her dilemma, Mexia walked toward the hallway with a quickened pace. When she stood in the hall, she waited for direction.

Dragonmage joined her and pointed to the right. "We were just sitting down to supper when you dropped in."

"How did you know I was here?"

"My ring called to me, and I knew it was nearby." He walked beside her, his friends following close behind. "But before this, we watched you through a sphere. We didn't figure any of you ladies would manage to retrieve the ring. But it was fascinating sport to watch you. Then the meal was ready, and we gave up, assuming that you would still be at it well after we had eaten. Then my ring called to me. Of course, I wasn't certain which of you ladies had actually retrieved the ring at that point."

He considered the blanket around her shoulders. "Perhaps we should take a detour." He opened a door to a room and motioned for her to enter. Inside, a bed sat against one wall, bookshelves against another, and a window overlooking the valley from high in the mountains, filled the third wall.

"Where am I?" Mexia crossed the floor and stared out the

window at the jagged mountains where Dragonmage's home was situated.

"Tarrant Mountains."

He walked over to a wardrobe and pulled out a brilliant purple gown. "My favorite, though it might be a little long for you. But I think it would do."

He waited.

She tapped her foot on the floor. "Could I have some privacy, gentlemen?"

The smiles on the mages' faces couldn't have been any bigger.

"Yes, I do believe you've found the one you've been seeking, Dragonmage." Mer pulled the door closed behind him.

"Hmpf," Mexia said under her breath as she dropped the quilt on the floor, then hurried to pull the velvet gown over her under-dress. The silky wet material against her skin still gave her the chills. She slipped her arms out of the full-sleeved mage's gown, then hurried out of her underdress. Pulling the sleeves of the purple garment back up her arms, she shivered.

"Are you coming, Mexia?" Dragonmage called out.

She looked down at the floor. The gown extended six inches past her feet in all directions. The sleeves were at least four inches longer than her fingertips where they should have come to her wrist, though a typical mage's gown's sleeve extended a foot on the part underneath, tapering in a long flowing dramatic point. The neckline dipped down in a v, and she imagined if she leaned over to reach anything on the table, everyone could see clear inside the gown.

Knocking on the door followed. "Mexia?"

"Do you have a belt?"

Laughter echoed through the hall. Her face grew hot. The door opened a crack.

"I have several. Can I come in?"

She folded her arms. "Are you sure you do not have something...smaller?"

"I normally do not keep garments here for stray sorceresses who take a dip in the lake."

"A belt then?"

Dragonmage considered the gown as she held it tightly against her waist. His smile made her cheeks warm again.

"Slightly oversized." He crossed the room to a chest and pulled a drawer open. Holding up a gold cord with tassels dangling at the ends, he asked, "How about this?"

"It'll probably do."

He rejoined her, then handed the belt to her. Before she could take hold of it, he wrapped it around her waist and cinched it tightly, to her annoyance. "How's that?"

"Better, but I could have done it without your help."

She picked her wet gown up off the floor. "Where can I hang this to dry?"

He took it from her, studied the filmy partially transparent fabric, and then tsked. "To think I missed seeing you in it." With a click of his fingers, the garment vanished.

"What did you do to my gown?" Mexia couldn't control the irritation rising in her words or her blood.

"I sent it to my maid. She will surely be astonished to find it in my laundry, however." He took Mexia's arm and led her to the door. "I venture to say, as soon as she can make an excuse to visit my dining room to see who might have worn the garment, she will join us."

Mer walked away from the entrance to the bedchambers as Dragonmage and Mexia walked toward them.

"Looks much better on the lady, than it ever did on you," Fessenwig said.

"If you are trying to make points with the lady," Mer said, "forget it. Dragonmage is already too far gone."

"I have other concerns than finding a suitor," Mexia replied, her tone haughty, meant to discourage their interest.

"This one will be difficult to please," Mer said.

"Have there been many?" Mexia asked.

Dragonmage pointed to the dining hall. "My lady." He led her into the room.

"There have been no other ladies at all," Fessenwig said. "In fact, we've never seen him so interested in a woman."

"You had other concerns after supper, did you not?" Dragonmage asked his friends as he pulled a chair out for Mexia.

Mer chuckled. "I believe he is suspending our Wednesday night wizardry game, Fessenwig."

"Sounds that way. But what if the lady decides to pop right out of here? Then where will you be?" Fessenwig asked Dragonmage. "You will have dismissed your friends, and alas we will be gone for the night."

Dragonmage scooted his chair closer to Mexia. Afterward, he poured a glass of wine for her. "She asked me to return her to the lake. She cannot leave here without my help."

"Not true," Mexia said. "I only asked so as not to tax my own powers."

"What level are you?"

"What level?"

"Yes."

"I don't know what you mean."

Mer laughed. "She is not a mage. I didn't think so."

Fessenwig buttered a slice of bread. "No matter. He still wants her."

Mexia curbed her growing frustration. She had to eat, then somehow find a way down the mountain, back to the lake, and then on to the soothsayer's cave. But how could she travel without even a good pair of boots?

To her surprise, Dragonmage reached over and took her hand in his. "She already even wears my ring."

The others laughed.

"Have you not heard a word I've said?" Mexia asked. "I am going to the wizard's school—"

"They would never allow a woman to go there." Mer sliced up his fish.

"If you are from Inherian, but wish to go to the school, what were you doing at Pala Lake?" Dragonmage asked.

"Swimming," Fessenwig answered for her.

"I have to see the mage of Monrovia. I must get a recommendation from him so that the High Wizard at Langdon Castle will admit me."

Dragonage leaned back in his chair as he studied Mexia. "Parenkin was the old master. He retired after too many years of teaching and dealing with new apprentices. He is now a hermit in the mountains of Monrovia. Why on earth would Harazod send you to him to get a recommendation? It doesn't make sense."

"Perhaps he feels if the wise old gentleman agrees to my attending the school, the matter will be out of his hands. Then he won't have made any enemies over the situation."

Mer snorted.

Mexia looked over at him, but he poked at his fish and didn't say a word.

"What do you feel about this, Mer?"

He glanced over at Dragonmage, then changed the subject. "If she wears the ring, will the protection spell scatter the trolls?"

Dragonmage touched the ring on Mexia's hand, but she pulled it away from him. "As long as it is in my possession, it will," Dragonmage said.

"But it is in the young lady's possession," Mer reminded him.

"And she is in Dragonmage's possession," Fessenwig added.

A bell rang startling Mexia, and she jumped in her seat slightly.

Instantly, a maid entered the room. Her eyes grew big as she saw Mexia. "Who…who is she?"

"A guest, and from the ringing of the bell, I would say we have some other unexpected company. Who might it be, Mistress Darnella?"

"Prince Derek, my lord."

Mexia dropped her spoon into her soup, splattering droplets of the golden broth on the white tablecloth.

Dragonmage glanced back at her, then faced the maid again. "I thought he and Ros were tied up with studies and couldn't make it to the wizardry games tonight."

"He asked if there were three ladies and a dwarf here, my lord."

Dragonmage turned to Mexia. His widened eyes revealed his astonishment. "You know Derek?"

"We have met. He took me to see Harazod."

"Your cheeks are cherry. Has he interest in you?" His words were rough, spoken with concern.

"Only to keep me from attending the school."

Dragonmage tapped his fingers on the table. "Tell Derek our game is cancelled as Mer and Fessenwig have other pressing business this evening."

The mages laughed.

Mer said, "I had heard that when a mage becomes interested in a lady companion, his friends would come second. I just never believed it." He saluted Mexia with his goblet, then sipped his wine.

"Sorry, I'm so late," Derek said popping into the room, his blond hair secured neatly in a loop at the back of his head. His attention turned immediately from Dragonmage to Mexia.

"Where are your clothes?" he nearly shouted at her, his blue eyes on fire.

The maid quickly vacated the room.

Fessenwig shook his head. "Now this I have never seen. Two wizards interested in the same woman, who just happens to be a sorceress."

Mer speared a slice of fish. "Should be interesting to see who wins this contest."

Derek sat opposite Mexia and filled his pewter plate with fish and corn. "What are you doing here?" he asked her, his lips an angry line.

Dragonmage took Mexia's hand, but again she yanked it free from him. "She fished my ring out of Pala Lake. For a year, no one has been able to. Anyway, she is wearing it for me now."

Derek's cheeks reddened. "You couldn't have agreed to marry Creighton."

"Who?" Mexia asked, not sure whether to laugh or to scream at the whole lot of wizards.

"She calls me Dragonmage, affectionately."

"Marinda called you that. And you've given me no other name," Mexia corrected him.

Dragonmage smiled at her.

"You cannot still be trying to make it to the mountains of Monrovia. And whatever made you retrieve Creighton's ring for him?" Derek asked.

"Marinda said I had to if she was ever to release the children to their families in Barston."

Derek ripped off a piece of bread with his hands.

Dragonmage pointed to the bread knife.

Ignoring him and after buttering his bread, Derek considered Mexia's robe again. "I asked you why you were not wearing your own gowns."

Mexia folded her arms. No way was she going to let Derek bully her.

"And I told you," Dragonmage said, "she retrieved my ring. The skimpy slip she wore was soaking wet. She'd have caught her death in this cold, drafty castle."

"You saw her in near to nothing?"

"Unfortunately, no. She had the misfortune to arrive in my guest chambers, and promptly covered herself with a quilt from the bed."

Though the look of concern mixed with anger still clouded Derek's face, his jerky actions with the food he chopped in haste, quieted. "You are not marrying her," Derek said finally.

Mexia laughed. "You know it's kind of refreshing to find anyone interested in me. Back home in Damar, most men were intimidated by the notion I am a sorceress. But, gentlemen, I must respectfully say my goodbyes now, as I have pressing business to conduct elsewhere."

When Mexia stood, Derek said, "She cannot leave here without your say so, can she, Creighton?"

"No." He tugged at Mexia's sleeve. "You have hardly eaten. Sit and finish your meal."

She pulled away from him, then walked toward the entrance to the dining room. But when she tried to step outside the room, her toes bumped into an invisible wall. She moaned in defeat.

"Come, Mexia. Sit with us and finish your supper."

Mexia spoke an incantation next as she wiggled her fingers. "Dissipate the unseen wall blocking my entrance into the hall."

Utter silence pervaded the room. She imagined four pairs of eyes studied her every move. When she reached out with her fingers, she touched the glass wall.

Turning, she faced the men. Dragonmage smiled first. Then he said to Derek, "She doesn't understand about mage levels. What level is she? Neophyte?"

"Her father was a country wizard."

"Ah." Dragonmage and his friends laughed, making her seethe with rage.

If one more mage made fun of her peoples' country schooling...

Dragonmage patted the seat next to him. "Come, Mexia. Sit and eat. Perhaps we can play some wizardry games afterward."

"Why?" she asked as she stormed back to her seat, not seeing any way out of her predicament for the moment. "Because you think you can beat me?"

He smiled back at her, but Derek remained somber. Finally Derek said, "You cannot marry her."

"What is stopping me?"

"She must wish it."

"Who says she doesn't?"

Derek tapped his fork on the table. "She doesn't wish to marry you anymore than I do."

Dragonmage filled his goblet with more wine. "She wishes to marry you instead, Derek?"

"No!" Mexia said. "I have never been around so many egotistical males in my life."

Mer laughed. "These weekly wizardry games were getting a bit dull, Dragonmage. I believe the lady has added quite a lot of spark to tonight's activities."

"I will not play these games of yours." Mexia spooned up some of her soup.

"We will be gentle with you," Dragonmage said. "After all, I must win your heart or Derek will have a fit. He seeks it, too, but for whatever reason, he has failed to interest you."

She looked up to see Derek studying her. If she agreed to end her quest to see the mage of Monrovia, would Derek help her to leave Dragonmage's castle? She assumed he would if he was able. But he wasn't a graduate of the school yet. Would he be as powerful as Dragonmage?

"Why do you wear his ring?" Derek asked, his voice softened and deeper now.

"I rescued it from the lake as I have already said. Only when I placed it on my finger so as not to lose it when I swam to the surface, it brought me here. And when I attempted to remove it, I found it stuck."

"You could have lied," Dragonmage said, wiggling his red brows. "It was much more dramatic when Derek thought you wore my ring on purpose."

The muscles in Derek's neck relaxed, and Fessenwig slapped him on the back. "I almost could hear your sigh of relief, Derek. I believe you are as wrapped up in the lady's skirts as Dragonmage is."

"If we are all done with our supper, shall we let the games begin?" Dragonmage asked, a sly smile stretching across his face. "I can see the night's activities will be most entertaining."

Before Mexia could respond to Dragonmage's question, he waved his hand in front of his face, and vanished. She looked over at Derek who kept his eye on her. Did he think she'd suddenly disappear, too? If she could, she would.

Fessenwig guzzled down the last of his wine. "Good, we are playing hide and seek." After he placed his glass on the table, he winked at Mexia. "Being the guest of honor, you're it."

He disappeared.

CHAPTER 6

Mer smiled. "Dragonmage will want to be the first you find, Mexia, so he will not make it too difficult." He waved his hand and was gone.

Derek frowned at her. "Must I always get you out of these predicaments?"

Mexia jumped up from her seat, irritated beyond reason with Derek and his mage friends. Lifting the long robe she wore as she avoiding tripping on it, she hurried toward the entrance. Glancing back at Derek, she said, "Go hide yourself so that I might not find you, Derek."

Laughter resounded and she realized then, the mages watched her, though she couldn't see them, furthering her annoyance. She walked into the passageway. With her heart pounding in her ears, she rushed down the hall to where it turned right. Footsteps followed her. She whipped around to find Derek behind her. "You are not playing the game."

"Nor are you."

She folded her arms. "Won't your friends be mad at you?"

"This one will amuse them as well. In fact, I venture to say, the game you and I play will entertain them more." He bowed slightly to her.

She wheeled around, grabbed the robe, and stormed down the corridor. Stopping at a door to her left, she pulled it open. Inside, the maid stirred a blue liquid in a black cauldron, but nearly dropped the ladle when Mexia stepped into the room.

"You frightened me, miss," the woman said, her hand clutching at her breast.

"Where is my gown?"

The woman pointed to a line hung high above a fire. "Should be dry by now."

"Good." Mexia studied the rope, then frowned. "How do I get my dress?"

The maid pulled a cord and the line moved away from the fire.

"Thank you." Mexia stepped on a stool and pulled her gown off the line.

"You cannot be thinking of wearing that," Derek said, pointing at her underdress. "Anyone can see clearly through that flimsy fabric."

"Are you still here? I thought you were supposed to hide from me." She tucked the gown into her corded belt. Turning to the maid, she said, "Where is the portal chamber?"

The maid shook her head as she returned to her work. "If Lord Creighton wishes you to leave, he will send you to where you wish to be."

Mexia headed for the doorway. She could see if she was to leave, she'd have to do it on her own.

"You will never find a way out of here. Take my hand, Mexia. Come with me," Derek said.

She faced him, her cheeks burning with anger. "If I take your hand, then what? You will return me to Inherian? The city of Langdon? Where? And then how would I get back to my friends?

I would have to face the dark elves with…with, my underdress to slay them."

He smiled. "You're beautiful when you're angry. Actually, you are beautiful every time I see you. Come to think of it, most of the time when I see you…you are angry with me."

"And why do you think this is so?"

She hurried off. His footsteps pursued her as her head continued to pound with annoyance. Certain she'd find a portal room somewhere in the castle, she searched through room after room. From bedchambers to broom closets, she explored the level she was stuck on while Derek stalked her movements with interest.

"There are no stairs in this place," she finally said as she stared out the window of Dragonmage's bedchambers. "And yet as tall as this castle is, there must be other floors."

"None of us have to use stairs to get to the other levels," Derek said.

"What about the maid? She has no wizardry skills. How does she get around?"

"She doesn't need to go anyplace else."

Mexia leaned out the window and looked beneath her. Ten feet below, a window loomed. And directly above, another. Along the wall, wrought iron grillwork provided a ladder for climbing flowering vines. Mexia smiled. Shall I go up, or down first?

Taking a deep breath, she reached out to the railing.

"What are you contemplating?"

"Nothing that would interest you." Mexia grabbed the iron and pulled. It appeared to be secure enough to hold her weight. She glanced down at the two-hundred-foot drop to the valley below, then with trepidation, she climbed out onto the ledge.

"You cannot do this," he said as he rushed forth to stop her.

She grabbed the wrought iron and pulled herself from the window, trying to avoid his stopping her. Her panicky actions nearly caused her to fall. Immediately, she experienced difficulty. The gown encumbered her feet and no matter how much she tried to slip her toes into the trellis, the fabric got in the way.

Her arms stretched to the limit, the muscles strained and wearied as she feared letting go. And yet as she attempted to get a toe grip through the material, she was unable.

"Reach out and grab my hand, Mexia!" Derek shouted, worry evident in his stressed voice.

"No! I will not be taken to Langdon by you...you deceiver."

"You're slipping! You're not going to make it, Mexia. Grab my hand!"

"No!"

She tried to move down a rung, but holding on with only one hand, she nearly lost her grip. The panic surfaced, pebbling her skin with perspiration as her heart rate speeded up. She knew she'd never make it to the other window now. The strength dwindled from her arms, the muscles taut, tense and aching, stretched beyond their limits.

Grasping the iron in her clenched fists, she attempted a spell, any spell that could save her from the fall that now awaited her.

"Where do you want to go? I will take you there, just take my hand!"

"Shut up, Derek! I have to concentrate."

He climbed onto the windowsill and reached out to her.

And then the notion came to her. Marinda called Creighton Dragonmage because the dragons liked him. Would Mexia's ability to call beasts to aid her, work on a magical dragon? Were the dragons even living in the area? She had to chance it.

She closed her eyes and willed a dragon, any dragon, to come to her aid.

Derek grabbed for her hand. The ring slipped off her finger, and she looked up to see him holding it in his hand. He cast it into the room and reached for her again.

Closing her eyes, she concentrated on the dragon again. But to her horror, she lost her hold on the railing, her sweaty fingers no longer able to grip it further.

Could she stop screaming long enough for her whole life to flash before her eyes? Looking up, she realized Derek cried out to her, above her own screams of terror. Then the air filled with turbulence and darkened as several winged creatures flew out of a nearby cave.

Dragons or griffon? Griffon would make a meal of her, Dragonmage's robe and all.

Dragons! A blue-scaled one amongst the green dragons, dipped beneath her and with an oof, she fell on top of his wide back. Grabbing hold, she said, "Thank you, dragon, for coming to my rescue."

"You and your friends brought us back our dragon artifact."

"You're the one from the cave from Inherian? The one who wished the magical mirror back?"

"Yes. Where do you wish to go?"

Glancing back at the castle, she saw it grew smaller. Her heart still pounded out of control as she tried to breathe in normally. She could no longer tell if Derek still watched her from the window. Torn between wanting to see him further, and wanting to laugh at the mages for her ability to win at their dim-witted games, she longed to know what Derek was thinking.

She sighed deeply. "To the soothsayer, Marinda's, cave.

"As you wish. I have told the other dragons of the aid you and your companions provided to us. Should you need them, they will help you, too."

"Is Creighton the dragon's friend?"

"He is."

She hmpfed. Spying her companions near the waterfall, she shouted with glee, "There, there!"

Kersta and the princess waved their arms frantically at her as they bounced on their toes. Gallant stood quietly nearby with his war hammer in hand.

"Dragon," the princess said in greeting as he alighted on the grass.

"Princess."

"Thank you for bringing her back to us," Kersta said, running her hand over his leg in a gentle caress.

"I must head back to Inherian before my mate leaves me for abandoning her with the dragonlings again."

"Why have you left her?" the princess asked.

"I am a member of the chain of dragon counsels. I understand that a wizard apprentice named Rosenthal has taken Grimoria's place. He is not powerful enough yet to do battle with the dragons. But he has the spell book, and from what we understand, he's quite brilliant. Since the four of you defeated Grimoria, I have relayed this information to the dragons residing in Albion. They will help you, if need be, to defeat Rosenthal."

"But we understood he is still in Inherian," Mexia said, her eyes wide with disbelief.

"Word has it, he's here. This is his birthplace. He will learn the spells, then return to defeat us all. Be wary, he can be hiding just about anywhere."

Mexia looked south. "Can the dragons take us to the mountains of Monrovia?"

"Rosenthal isn't located there."

"But you said he could be hiding anywhere. And I need further skills training. I need the spells to be able to defeat Rosenthal."

"The dragons can only be called upon to aid you in fighting Rosenthal. Not only that, but he would not be in the mountains of Monrovia. It is too dangerous for the likes of him. Not with Parenkin living there." The dragon looked back toward the seacoast of Langdon. "I must leave now."

"Too dangerous?"

"Yes, speak to the centaur of Spring Valley. He has been near there. He can tell you something of the journey."

"Thank you, dragon, for saving my life."

He nodded. "Until we meet again."

With a flap of his powerful wings, the dragon lifted off the ground, and headed north over Darkland Forest.

Instantly, Mexia was bombarded with hugs and even Gallant managed a wink at her and a smile. Her heart warmed to be returned to her friends.

"Marinda told us you were a guest of Dragonmage, and we had to wait here until you returned to us," Kersta said.

"I have returned his ring. We must go to Spring Valley to see the unicorns now."

"No," the princess said, as she wrapped her arm around Mexia's waist. "Marinda said we will stay here the night. In the morning, we will make the trek."

"And the children? Have you seen them?"

"She fears the children will be torn to return home to their parents if they see us."

"Dragonmage said that once the ring was returned to him, the trolls would vacate the bridges."

"This maybe so, but the trolls still hide beneath the bridges, according to the soothsayer."

"Then what has gone wrong?" Mexia considered how Derek had thrown the ring into the castle. Had Dragonmage not found it yet? She groaned. No way could she return to that place to help him find the ring.

~

*L*ater that night, the ladies and Gallant lay down to sleep in a cave on mattresses stuffed with down. But after the candles were extinguished, Kersta poked Mexia. "I have tried to read your mind several times about what happened, but you won't think about it."

"I explained to you what happened. I placed the ring on my finger, and it transported me to Dragonmage's castle. Then I returned here."

"But you have not explained why the dragon had to rescue you. Marinda assured us you were safe."

"I was safe, until I tried to escape from the castle, Kersta. That is all."

The princess rolled over onto her side. "You did not explain this."

"Derek?" Kersta said rubbing her forehead. "What was he doing there?"

"How did Derek get into this business?" the princess asked.

"Dragonmage wanted to play wizardry games of some sort. Well, a game of hide and seek. Only I cannot vanish like they can."

"And Derek?" Kersta prompted.

"Friends with Dragonmage. He wanted to take me from the castle. But Dragonmage wanted to keep me there."

"For what purpose?" the princess asked.

"To marry you?" Kersta said with such incredulity, Mexia frowned at her.

Like the princess, Mexia still wasn't used to Kersta's reading their minds at will. "Yes, if you must know. He and Derek fought over me, kind of."

Gallant grumbled, "Can ye keep it down over there? I am trying to sleep."

Mexia lay on her back and stared up at the stalactites clinging to the ceiling. "Derek wouldn't play the game and wished to take me from the castle. But I didn't trust him to bring me here."

Kersta snorted. "I should say not! Not after he took you to the perimeter of Darkland Forest, and you had to fight your way through it all alone to join us on the other side. You should have turned him to stone."

"I feared a trick. If I accepted his help, would he return me to Langdon? I assumed since he did it the first time, he'd have no regret in doing it again."

"I thought the dragon brought you to us at Dragonmage's request," the princess said.

"No. I tried to climb outside of the castle walls to find another level. I just knew somewhere inside the castle, I could find a portal room. Only there were no stairs that I could find on the floor I was searching. So I tried to climb the trellis attached to the outer walls of the castle. However, the gown I wore was too long, and I finally lost my grip on the iron. All I could think of doing was calling for a dragon's help."

Kersta squeezed her hand. "I did not mean to offend you by seeming so surprised that anyone would be interested in you, Mexia. It is just that, well, this is such a new...occurrence is all."

Mexia patted her hand and smiled. "I told the mages how the men back home were not interested in me because I was a sorceress."

"But a mage isn't afraid of you," the princess said. "Someday, you might find one who is suitable."

"Not Dragonmage," Mexia said. "He asked if I did not worry that he might turn me into a frog! The nerve of the guy. Talk about egotistic. Of course, I countered that with offering to turn him into stone."

The ladies laughed.

Gallant shuffled around in the dark. "Ye will never let me get any sleep at this rate." Then his footsteps faded as he stomped out of the cave.

A renewed round of laughing resulted.

"What about Derek?" Kersta asked.

"What about him? When I fell, he yelled out, but I guess he had no spell to stop my fall. Then the dragon came, and he brought me here."

"Derek's going to continually be a problem." The princess sighed deeply.

Mexia closed her eyes. Why couldn't he have helped her instead of hindering her so? He seemed to care for her, and yet, he held back on helping her to reach her goal. What was the reason?

"Maybe the wizard in charge of the school has something to do with it," Kersta said, then yawned. "It's possible he's threatened Derek if he attempts to aid you."

"Or he just doesn't like the idea of a woman going to his school. Maybe it would lower the prestige? Or something idiotic like that."

~

*I*n the middle of the night, Talamaya rolled over on the mattress and found Mexia missing. She bolted upright. "Mexia?" she called out.

"Shh," the word echoed off the cave walls. "Mexia is fine."

"Where is she, Marinda?"

"She is visiting with a mage. Do not concern yourself. No harm shall come to her."

Kersta rubbed her eyes and sat up in their bedding. "Where's Mexia, Princess Talamaya?"

"Sleep, ladies. You have much to do. Sleep. She will return to you soon."

"Where is she?" Kersta asked Talamaya.

"With a mage, Marinda says." Talamaya lay back down, her mind disquieted.

"You had a vision?"

"Yes. That's what woke me. Mexia was gone and her life was in great peril."

Kersta rubbed her forehead. "Where?"

"Somewhere on the path we must take. Smoke, fire, mists fill the air. She cries out, but we cannot reach her."

"And right now?"

"She is with a mage."

"But who? Dragonmage? Derek? Someone else?"

Marinda laughed. "Sleep, ladies. She will return when she is ready."

~

*M*exia walked along the meadow beside Derek as his amulet lighted the way in a soft blue glow. The grasses slapped at their long gowns but when he reached over and touched her arm, she froze in place.

"I told you before not to touch me, Derek, or I'll return to the cave at once."

He nodded. "I had to…to see that you were all right, Mexia."

"Why? You sometimes act as though you care for me a great deal, then do the most despicable deeds."

"I cannot help myself."

She shook her head. "Cannot, or will not?"

"I am drawn to you. I cannot explain. I have to keep you safe. It's like a dragon who returns to the nest year after year. A natural instinct, so to speak. I've never felt this way about anyone before. When you fell from the castle wall, I nearly died. Not any of the spells I knew could have saved your life."

She smiled. "Then I am more powerful than you."

He grabbed her arm with a light touch and pulled her to a stop. "How did you do it?"

"I can call some beasts to my aid. I didn't know if I could call a dragon though."

He nudged her elbow to walk again. When she didn't object to his tender touch, he kept his hand in place. "I worried you had some affection for Creighton."

"I cannot think of finding a husband. I have already told you this before. Rosenthal, Grimoria's apprentice, must be destroyed. But before I can do this, I must have more training."

"You do not love Creighton then."

Mexia paused in her footsteps. "Derek, you never listen to me." Her gaze was drawn to his lapel. She touched the glowing leaf on the right, then the one on the left.

His eyes widened. "You see...what do you see?"

"Gold leafs. I have to ask you, why do you not want me to go to Monrovia? Is it that you do not wish me to attend the school?"

He rubbed his bearded chin, apparently deep in thought as he considered his answer.

"Derek?"

"What?"

"You're impossible." She turned around and stormed back toward the cave.

"No," he said as he stepped in front of her. "We walk a bit further." He turned her around and moved his hand to the small of her back, gently guiding her to walk with him.

"What did Dragonmage and his friends say about my escape?"

"They were much impressed. Though like me, they attempted to think of spells to save you. Of course, after you were taken away by the dragon, Creighton became pretty incensed. He couldn't understand where the blue dragon came from."

"Inherian. He helped us on our quest there."

"You are friends of the dragons?"

"Yes."

He stopped her. "If this is so, Creighton says you are meant to be with him. It's a sign."

She shook her head. "I do not care for him." Derek seemed slightly relieved as the look of worry in his wrinkled forehead smoothed out. "So as to my question, do you think the school's curriculum will suffer if a woman is allowed to attend?"

"No."

"Then you do not object to my attending the school?"

"You cannot attend there."

"Because...of the headmaster?"

Derek nodded.

"You admire me for what I have accomplished in Inherian, do you not?"

"Of course. You and your companions have done a great service to all of Inherian."

"The other mages scoff at me."

Derek remained silent.

"Even you ridicule my father for being only a country mage."

"I didn't mean to. When Creighton asked what level of mage you are, all I could say was that your father was a country wizard. I didn't mean it in a derogatory fashion, only that mage levels are not important in your realm."

He reached for her hand, but she hid it in the folds of her gown. "I will not take you away from here, as much as I'd like to, Mexia. Please trust me."

She hesitated. More than anything she wished to hold his hand as they strolled through the meadows, but she still feared his treachery.

"If you take me from here, I promise I'll turn you to—"

"I pledge we will continue to walk right here in this very meadow with one another."

She held her hand out to him. He grasped it in his hand, greedily as if in doing so, she'd agreed to be his forever. He seemed to relax all at once.

Derek cleared his throat. "Finding a wife has been the farthest thing from my mind, I wish you to know. My studies have come first and foremost. I mean, I never even gave it a thought until you appeared in the school portal. Though each of your companions are beautiful and share the same fair complexion, and petite statures, you stood out amongst them. At night when I close my eyes, all I can think of is you."

He turned to her, his eyes almost pleading with hers. "And you? Do you not think of me, too?"

She tried to hide the smile on her lips and the blush that rose to her cheeks. She couldn't stop thinking about the kiss they had shared and how much she wished for him to kiss her like that again.

He squeezed her hand lightly. "I know you are the one for me."

"I have never had men interested in me before. How can I know it is not just an infatuation because you show me so much attention?"

"Ask the soothsayer about us." His words were spoken so seriously, she wasn't sure what to think of it. He turned and touched her lips with his free hand. "She will tell you we were meant to be together."

The crunching of boots on soil made them turn in the direction of the sound.

Derek sighed. "Ros, I thought it was someone else."

"Creighton, perhaps? He is pretty incensed the woman got away from him. But do not tell me you've grown interested in her, too." He folded his arms. "The headmaster is looking for you. If you do not return at once, he'll terminate your schooling."

"I'll be there in a minute. I must return Mexia to the cave."

"The soothsayer's cave?"

"Yes."

"I'll return her there. You run along before the old man turns somebody into a toad."

Derek squeezed Mexia's hand and when she blinked, she stood before the cave with him. He leaned over and kissed her lips. "The soothsayer will know the truth."

Before she could respond, he waved his hand in front of his face and vanished.

CHAPTER 7

Concerned with what they had to face in the morning, Mexia rejoined the princess and Kersta on their mattress, ready to finally get the sleep she knew she needed if she was ever to make it to Spring Valley.

"You were seeing Derek?" Kersta whispered.

"Yes," she whispered back.

"What happened?" the princess asked.

The ladies laughed to hear the princess was awake also.

"I'll tell you in the morning. For now, I must sleep, ladies." Mexia closed her eyes, but she couldn't help wondering if Derek was right. Was she meant to be his? What would Marinda say? She rubbed her temple. Sleep was what she needed more than anything. There wasn't any way she could deal with her feelings for Derek if she didn't get enough rest.

Early the next morning, Marinda shared sweet breads with them. After Mexia finished drinking her goat's milk, she said to the soothsayer, "Prince Derek, mage apprentice at the school in Langdon, told me to ask you if he was meant for me."

Gallant grumbled under his breath as the princess and Kersta stared at her in surprise.

Marinda smiled. "He wishes it to be so, yes?"

"He seems to think we were meant to be. He told me to ask you about it."

"Do you see something of his?"

"Pardon?"

"Something he wears on his cloak?"

"Well, yes, of course, if you mean the golden leaves on his lapels."

Marinda raised her brows in surprise. "Two of them you saw?" The soothsayer didn't wait for a response. "Hmmm, earlier than I expected."

"Is he right then? Are we meant for each other?"

"Have you told him what you must do?"

"Yes, Marinda. But he doesn't pay much attention to me."

She smiled. "Well, it is too early to tell."

"If we are meant to be with each other?"

"You must see the centaur." She clapped her hands. "Come, ladies, gentleman, off with you. The children wish to go home. Finish your quest."

Disappointed, Mexia rose from the cushion she sat on. If she saw Derek again, well, when she met up with Derek again as she could see now he wasn't going to stay away from her for long, what would she tell him? Just what Marinda said, she supposed. But would that satisfy him? For her, it didn't. She couched the irritation disturbing her digestion that morning, and headed out of the cave with her friends.

Before long, the companions reached Pala Lake. Mexia turned to her friends and said, "What happened to the soldiers? When you left here to go to the soothsayer's cave, what did they do?"

"No telling. They were sure you'd come out of the lake, and couldn't understand that we'd leave you there alone. But the princess had a vision, and saw that we were to speak with the soothsayer about your disappearance."

"What did you see of me? I thought I had broken free of the water. The next thing that happened, I was crawling around on a carpet in Dragonmage's castle. Did you see me come to the surface?"

"No. The men had begun to get troublesome," the princess said. "Kersta had to quiet them down as she hit one with her staff. Once he collapsed to the grass, the others quit causing difficulties. That's when I noticed you were no longer in the water. Then I had the vision that we needed to see the soothsayer."

They headed next in the direction of Spring Valley. Tall, willowy branching trees covered in pink blossoms and tiny heart-shaped green leaves, dotted the land. The green grass shortened, then finally gave way to drifts of purple flowers. Through this, a well-worn trail appeared. The party walked along it to avoid stepping on the flowers' lacy petals.

"Did he really think you were supposed to be his betrothed? Derek, I mean, Mexia?" Kersta asked.

"That's what he said. What do you think about the soothsayer's response?"

"It is too early to tell. So she says. But you know, they often speak in riddles." Kersta tapped her staff on the ground.

"Aye, most women do," Gallant grumbled.

Mexia turned to him. "Did you get a good sleep last night, Gallant?"

"Hmpf. Aye, I did, when the likes of ye were out of hearing."

The ladies laughed.

When they arrived at the valley, they noticed clusters of horses and unicorns alike, grazing beneath the trees.

"Do you see the centaur?" Mexia asked as she surveyed the valley. "I see no sign of him."

"There." Kersta pointed farther south. "He is shooting something with a bow and arrow."

Her words must have traveled on the breeze as suddenly, all of the horses and unicorns turned their heads in the party's direction. Galloping across the valley, the raven-haired centaur headed straight for them.

"He would not harm us, would he?" Kersta whispered.

"Most are good from what I have read. Healers, like us, hunters, and some are even philosophers. This one who protects the unicorns, must be decent. Even Marinda said it would be safe for us to come here," the princess said.

"You are here finally! I am Chernon." The centaur looped his bow over his quiver of arrows hanging diagonally across his back, then folded his arms. His ebony eyes looked from one of the women to the other, ignoring the dwarf. Then he focused on Mexia. "You are the one who embraces magic."

"Not enough, but I hope to work on that."

"Good, come with me."

"But my friends—"

"They must take the horses back to Barston."

"But the trolls—"

"You have returned the ring to Creighton, have you not?"

"Yes."

"The trolls have been vanquished. Come with me. The horses will follow your friends to Barston. Your companions can wait for you at the soothsayer's cave afterward. This is what has been foretold."

Mexia looked over at the princess, who nodded. Already the horses drifted toward them as several neighed to the unicorns, she assumed, saying their farewells.

The princess and Kersta embraced Mexia. "We will see you soon, Mexia."

Kersta squeezed her hand. "Soon."

Gallant waved his war hammer at her. "Keep out of trouble, woman. I do not wish to have to rescue ye on an empty stomach."

"You just ate, Gallant," Kersta corrected him.

"Nay, ye do not call sweet cakes enough sustenance for an adventurer, do ye?"

Mexia waved to her friends as they walked back with the horses along the trail they used, each following the one ahead of them like goslings pursued their mother to the water. She couldn't help but worry about her companions as they left her behind. Were the trolls truly banished? Or would her friends find them still hiding beneath the bridges, lying in wait?

"Come, they will be fine. We have work to do." Chernon motioned for her to join him.

"The dragon from Inherian said you could tell us what awaits us on our journey to the mountains of Monrovia."

"Many perils. The swamps between Barston and Cramer take the lives of many travelers every year. The word has spread that a wizard has unleashed the undead in a cemetery in the center of the swamps. You must past through it to reach the village of Cramer. The people of Barston normally trade with those of Cramer, and all trade with the seaport of Langston. Now they are effectively cut off from one another by the dark elves of Darkland Forest and the Malayn swamps."

"Is there not a trail across the swamps?"

"Yes," the centaur said, then pointed to a small stone house. "Come inside."

When they entered the place, he pulled off his quiver and bow and hung them on a wooden hook on a wall. "Sit."

She sat down while he walked over to a pot bubbling over an open fire, his hooves clicking on the wooden floor, the aroma of sandalwood and beef gravy mixing in the air.

"Some broth?" he asked.

"Thank you. So if there is a path through the swamps, what makes it so difficult to travel through the region?"

"The deceptive mist that cloaks the area in an impenetrable

blanket. And the fire that shoots out of the earth fills the air with flame and smoke. Deadly."

"How can we manage to get through there then? It sounds impassible."

He set the bowl of broth in front of her. "Griffon broth." He folded his arms. "You are magical, like the unicorns. You will know the way."

"But I have not had the training like those who attend the school in Langdon. How can I manage such a place without additional help?"

Smiling, he ladled broth into a bowl for himself. "One of your companions carries the Scepter of Lanai."

"Yes."

"You have been to the Cave of Sorrows."

"We have."

"And have treasures from deep inside."

She touched the worn leather belt at her waist. "The belt protected me, well, more than that, when a mage tried to strike me with an offensive spell. I was able to take the power he cast against me and returned it to him full force."

The centaur joined her at the table. "Yes."

"But it was used against a wizard's spell. It wouldn't work against fire cast from the swamps, would it?"

"The fire is a trigger spell set by the wizard who plagues you."

"Rosenthal." The notion the wizard had already begun to cause trouble for the peoples of Albion, angered her as she clenched her teeth.

Chernon nodded.

"But how can we see through the mists?"

"You found the ring in the lake? No one could find it as it magically shifted out of anyone's grasp. How then, did you manage to grab it?"

"After drinking Modi's tea."

"Yes. So you see, you have helped many in the past, and they still aid you."

Mexia sipped some of the hot broth, the salty, spicy flavor of beef tantalizing her taste buds. "This is very good."

He nodded.

"What about the cemetery?"

"The cemetery will be another story. There you must use your magic."

She groaned. "Lately when I get flustered, I cannot remember my spells. I do not know what the matter is with me."

"It is like my hunting, practice improves my skill. Think, what is the spell you cast that you excel at?"

She scooped another spoonful of broth and paused. "Turning living things to stone."

"And why is it your best spell?"

"I used to turn poisonous frogs to stone, so the children wouldn't fear swimming in the lake."

"So with practice…"

"I improved the skill." She pointed her spoon at him. "But can I turn the undead to stone?"

"No." He shook his head, then returned to the pot and refilled his bowl. "Having magic is much more than just possessing it. You must be able to train your mind when and where to use the right kinds of magic. Sometimes spells, sometimes potions work best. At other times magically-enhanced items will aid you most."

"So what must I do?"

He shrugged. "What does your mind tell you?"

She grunted in annoyance. "You are like Marinda, talking in riddles now."

He smiled. "Being likened to her is not so bad. So what riddles does she tell you?"

"She says it is too early to tell if a mage is the one who is meant to be my betrothed."

"He has already approached you with such a notion?"

Mexia looked up at the centaur as his words grew dark. "Yes. You seem troubled. What is the matter?"

"You must avoid the young man at all costs."

"Derek?"

"The mage will be your undoing."

"He is dark-hearted then?" She shook her head and rested her spoon in her bowl. "I do not believe he is evil. Just overly infatuated with me."

"Stay clear of him, is the only advice I can offer." He set his empty bowl down. "Come, if you are done here, you will join me in a cave where you will learn how to defeat the undead."

"But I'm not sure what to do."

"You will learn to be sure."

Mexia followed the centaur out of the house, then walked half a mile to an opening in the rocks of the cliffs, stretching toward the sky. When she looked up, she saw Dragonmage's gray stone castle nearly blending in with the rocks high above.

"He watches you through his sphere of sight. I have sensed the eye concentrating over the valley. He could not see inside the house, nor will he know what goes on in the cave. But while you are in this region out in the open, he watches you."

"Me or just what goes on in the valley?"

"You. One of the dragons he befriended came to visit me last night. He said Creighton could have breathed his own fire like the dragons do, he was so angry he'd lost his sorceress. Creighton couldn't understand why you were rescued by a dragon cousin from Inherian. Then he assumed it was because you were meant to be his betrothed. He feels it is a sign that you have a way with the dragons like he does." He glanced back at her. "I knew you'd come see me soon, though, and you'd solve the circle of misfortunes."

"The other mages don't believe I'm capable of doing anything."

He smiled at her. "But you'll prove them wrong, no?"

"I don't understand. If Creighton can keep the trolls out of the area, why can't he also get rid of the dark elves in Darkland Forest?"

"The ring works on simpler minded creatures, like the trolls."

"And the undead?"

"They are mindless. It will not work on them."

When they stepped into the dark, he pulled a lantern off the wall and lighted it. "Deep in the cave there are undead souls, roaming aimlessly. Take care of them, and you will successfully navigate the cemetery."

"And beyond the cemetery?"

"The city of Cramer. I have not been past there."

She shivered, her heart picking up its pace as a scream echoed off the stone walls. "What am I to do?"

"Practice. Anything you can think of. Truthfully, I am not like Marinda. I do not know how to kill them, or I would willingly tell you."

"And if they kill me?" she asked, her voice unsteady, her fingers gripping her staff with uncertainty.

"My apologies. The cave is protected by the unicorn's magic. You cannot die in here. But you will have every opportunity to kill the undead. They cannot run away from the cave, and they cannot kill you. So I leave you now to work your magic."

When he left her alone, another soulless spirit cried out, and she nearly dropped her staff. She had to come to grip with her fears or she'd put her companions and herself in dire danger when they arrived at the cemetery.

The notion she couldn't be killed didn't soothe her shaky nerves either as her hands grew sweaty and her teeth chattered. Then she thought of the poisonous frogs she turned to stone. Practice. She was able to turn the Cyclops to stone. She could kill a few undead people.

She carried the lantern into a cavern where tunnels appeared at five different locations in the gray stone peeking out from patches of green moss. Out of one of the passageways a man appeared, dressed in armor, his shirt sleeves tattered, his skin bloodied, his eyes vacant. He moaned as he looked in her direction.

She set the lantern down on a rock ledge in a hurry. With her staff readied, she attempted a mind spell. "Halt your assault."

He ambled toward her. The first spell wouldn't work. Despite the centaur's caution that it wouldn't succeed, she used the stone spell next. "From rotting skin to brittle bone, turn this dead man into stone."

The dead soldier groaned, but continued toward her at his slow pace, his hands outstretched, ready to choke the life from her. Did the centaur know what he was talking about? Would the unicorn's magic keep her from turning into the vile creature who intended to kill her?

Then she considered the fireball spell she'd learned from the belt's absorbing it. She tried casting it on the creature. "With fire from the sun, your will be undone." It went straight through him, slamming into the wall instead, charcoaling the moss gripping the wet surface.

Two more undead, more soldiers of fortune from the looks of their armor, appeared from other tunnels. She stepped back. They couldn't kill her, she reminded herself as she barely breathed.

She thought of the love spell she had learned and quickly wiggled her fingers at the first of the creatures as he drew closer. "Love one another as you once did your mother." No effect. Mind spells wouldn't work. She sadly realized then, they had no mind to control...not any longer.

The first grabbed for her arm. Instinctively, she hit him with her staff. He collapsed, but after some struggle rose to his feet again.

Their magical staffs wouldn't work. She tossed some of Modi's tea on him. Every place the droplets touched, his gray skin turned pink. She stared at it for a second, then ran to the other side of the cave to give her more time to cast her spell. The three turned and headed for her again at their baby-step pace, one foot in front of the other, unsteady and unsure.

Wiggling her fingers in the air, she spoke a healing incantation on the one closest to her. "Heal this man from inside out. Remove his death that gives him clout." His skin renewed to its former healthy state making him appear human once again. Then instantly, he turned into a pile of ashes. She turned to the next and did the same to him. In a puff of dust, he vanished.

She took care of the next more quickly this time. Then she realized she could use the spell she had worked so many times over the years to heal the wounded and sick in Damar, to destroy the undead. Though she was the best at it, both Kersta and the princess were able to heal as well. They'd be able to make it through the cemetery now.

Another scream met her ears and two more undead approached her, one a woman, and another, a soldier. This time she attempted to cast a spell for a group. She'd only done it once before when several children had come down with a sickness all at once. For those less ill, the group spell had worked. For those who were sicker, she had to use more potent magic. But using a spell like that could significantly aid them in clearing the cemetery of the undead more quickly.

She attempted her group healing spell. "Sybillant notious!"

Both of the soulless people looked more human as the spell took effect, then they dissolved.

Grabbing up the lantern, she hurried into the closest tunnel. Determined to finish her task, she wanted to return to the soothsayer's cave, then take the children back to their families in Barston. Afterward, it would be time to continue on their way to the mountains of Monrovia.

When she had finished clearing the undead out of the caverns, she turned to hear someone tsking behind her. "Dragonmage."

He smiled at her as he leaned against a rock ledge. "Want to join me for lunch?"

She brushed past him as she headed toward the exit of the cave. "I have business to conduct."

"I wondered what you were doing down here. Chernon said you were cleaning out the cave." He reached to touch a curl that had slipped out of her braided hair.

She pushed his hand away.

"He shouldn't have had you do such a dangerous thing. He could have asked me."

"I'm sure you'd have had a difficult time breaking away from your wizard games."

Dragonmage smiled at her. "Did you not like our game?" Then his smile turned sour. "You could have been killed to have pulled such an unbelievable stunt as you did. Derek said you were looking for a portal room, and thought it was on one of the other floors of the castle. But to have attempted to climb to the other window…"

Mexia hurried outside of the caves.

He touched her sleeve. "Where is my robe? I think I liked that better on you. Though, this one does help to reveal that lovely shape of yours better."

"Marinda has it. Whenever you wish to get it, you can pick it up from her." She glanced down at the ring on his finger. "I see you found your ring."

He frowned. "Yes, underneath my bed. Derek went after you later last night, didn't he? I told him to forget you. You and I are meant to be together." He studied her as she looked for the centaur. "Why didn't you tell me that you could call the dragons to aid you? I would have known for certain you were the one for me. You see, I can do the same thing."

"I know. That's why they call you Dragonmage."

"Marinda calls me that. And now you. I like the name."

Mexia waved at Chernon. As he galloped toward her, she said to Dragonmage, "Keep the area safe from trolls. Maybe when I return from the mountains of Monrovia, I will have the opportunity to visit with you again."

"Let *me* teach you the skills you need to know. You need not go to Monrovia."

"Show me how to vanish."

He smiled. "If you will join me up there." He pointed to his castle. "I will teach you all I know."

"More than I would wish, I am sure."

Chernon came to a stop in front of them. "You have accomplished your task?"

Mexia smiled. "Yes, Chernon. Thank you for your guidance to me. I will be on my way now to see Marinda."

"May you be successful in your quest, my lady."

She leaned over and kissed his cheek. "Thank you." Glancing over at Dragonmage, she smiled to see the frown return to his face. She hurried off toward the path out of the valley. To her annoyance, he joined her.

"I have a quicker way to get us there."

"For some reason, I don't trust you. If I went with you, I'd worry I'd end up back in your castle with no way to return here."

"You cannot be serious about still going to the mountains of Monrovia."

"I am."

"What has Derek told you?"

"The same as you. We are meant to be together."

"He's wrong. Why would he say something like that, knowing

how wrong he is?" He rubbed his bearded chin. "You did not let on you cared for him, did you?"

"Dragonmage, I have told him, as I have told you, I am on an important quest, and not interested in *any* man."

She could sense him staring at her. Was he trying to determine the truth?

"Did he kiss you?"

"That's really none of your business."

"When did he do this? Last night? Before? I'll have words with him over this."

She smiled. The notion she had two mages fighting over her really tickled her. Even though in her heart she knew nothing could be done about it…not until after she killed Rosenthal. And then? Well, she wasn't sure even then if either man was right for her, though Derek tugged at her heartstrings whenever he drew near. "The soothsayer says it is too early to tell who is right for me."

"She said this?" He shook his head. "She is wrong."

"Do you know of this wizard, Rosenthal?"

"No, I've never heard of him before, though the dragons told me he is the one who has taken Grimoria's place."

"Will you help me to fight him?"

He smiled. "Will you join me? I would do anything for you."

"Take me to the mountains of Monrovia?"

"No. It's too dangerous. And I would not wish you attending the school."

"Why?"

"As my wife, you will not need any more wizardry skills."

"Are you afraid I might be more powerful than you?"

He laughed. "You have a cute sense of humor."

Everything about him rankled her. He definitely wasn't the right one. She quickened her step. The sooner she returned to Marinda's cave and lost him, the better.

When they finally reached the cave, the princess and Kersta hurried to greet her. Both stared at the mage, then frowned at him. "Who is this?" the princess asked.

"Dragonmage."

"Ladies." Dragonmage bowed.

Both Kersta and the princess grabbed Mexia's hands and pulled her into the cave.

To her disappointment, Dragonmage followed close behind them.

"Ah," Marinda said, her arms opened wide. "You have returned. The horses are back in their stables in Barston. I see you wear your ring once again, Dragonmage. The trolls are gone. Now all we need do is return the children home and convince the leaders of the town to come and see me once again."

"We are ready," Mexia said.

"Tell Mexia, she is the one who is meant to marry me, Marinda," Dragonmage said.

Marinda chuckled. "You have made quite an impression, Lady Mexia. But, it is too early to say who the lady shall be betrothed to."

Waving her arms, Marinda said, "Come!" Several children ran into the cavern from adjoining tunnels. "Here are the children. Take them home."

"Thank you, Marinda, for all of your help." Mexia and the ladies grew teary-eyed to see the children, every one of them, smiling at them as if they were going on a great adventurous trek.

Mexia offered her hand to the girl, peeking shyly from behind the blond-haired boy, who had met Mexia in the meadow. The two hurried to grab Mexia's hands.

The party headed toward the entrance to the caves, all but Dragonmage, whose voice echoed off the walls, "What do you mean, it's too early to say? You must tell her I'm the one for her.

You must. And you've got to convince her that this notion of hers to go the mountains…"

His voice faded as they reached the waterfall.

When they walked outside of the cave, one of the boys began a verse. The children all joined in, their young voices filling the meadow with sweet song. Mexia glanced over at Gallant who couldn't have looked any sourer, with his lips turned down to his chin as a boy clung onto each of his shirt sleeves.

"You must be happy to be going home," Mexia said to the children with her, once they'd finished their song.

"Me mother and me father will be angry with me to be sure… with me and me friends," the boy said.

The girl looked up at Mexia and nodded.

"Why did you go with the boys?" Mexia asked her.

"We had to have a leader," the boy answered for the girl. "She is the mayor's daughter. His only child."

She had considered the girl thought herself as an adventurer, too, but now she could see she was not, only one who wished to lead. "I can see you have courage like the others, though you are not a warrior at heart like they are," Mexia said to her.

Dimples appeared in the girl's cheeks as she smiled at her.

Mexia turned to the princess. "Did you have any trouble returning the horses home?"

The princess shook her head. "No, but we worried about you. How did you fare?"

"We must use healing spells on the undead at the cemetery. My belt will help with the fire aimed at us in the swamps, and Modi's tea will help us to see the way more clearly."

She considered the concerned look on the princess's face, her mouth turned down slightly and her brow creased. "What is wrong, Princess Talamaya?"

Kersta took a deep breath. "The princess has seen danger for you in the swamps. We could not reach you."

CHAPTER 8

Mexia quashed the anxiety that threatened to undo the courage she'd summoned from solving the dilemma with the fire trigger traps in the swamp and the undead in the cemetery.

Now what would be the matter?

Before she could concern herself further, bells rang all over the town and people emerged from every building.

"Our welcoming committee," Mexia said.

"They were delighted we returned the horses, but they did not believe the trolls were gone," the princess said. "And further, they did not believe we could return their children."

The adventurer's guild master hurried to greet Gallant. "You have brought the children home. Your reward will be paid at once."

"I told ye what our bargain was, man. If ye do not wish to hold up your end of the deal…"

The guild master looked from Gallant to the ladies, then back to the dwarf. "I have agreed and will make the announcement at once."

The children stayed with the ladies, seemingly not willing to face their parents' wrath, as the townspeople gathered around.

Their parents seemed afraid to take a step forth to reunite with their children who stood with such powerful benefactors.

Clearing his throat, the guild master motioned for silence as everyone spoke in a rush of words. "I declare that Princess Talamaya, Lady Kersta, and Lady Mexia, shall henceforth be members of the adventurers' guild. Every courtesy is to be bestowed upon them whenever they partake in a quest that any adventurers' guild has asked of them. In light of this, any monies owed to them for bringing the children home will be paid in full."

Mexia turned to Gallant who nodded. "Ye are adventurers and are now members of the guild."

Princess Talamaya spoke, "We are honored to be members of the Albion guild and will do our best to do what we can to help others in need. Your children are now returned to you, but I must ask that the mayor and his other council members see Marinda at once. She wishes to speak to you about many things, I am sure."

"At once," the mayor said as he motioned for his wife to get their daughter. "Upon our return, we shall have a feast in your honor."

"But we must go to Cramer," Mexia objected.

The children gripped her hands tightly. "A feast, my lady," the girl said. "We must celebrate."

She smiled. "All right."

Gallant cleared his throat. "Aye, I need a good meal before we trek through the swamps."

"Ye are leaving again?" his wife said as she forced her way through the crowds to reach Gallant. "When ye have only just arrived?"

"Aye, I have work to be done, woman." He glanced over at a male dwarf who watched them with narrowed eyes. "But if ye prepare that sweet cake for me at the feast, I will surely be pleased."

Her lips twitched up. "Aye, I can do that." She patted his

hand. "Ye have done a good thing for the town, Gallant. I cannot begrudge ye your work when ye do so much for others."

"Ye do not mind then?"

"Of course I mind. Come see me on your way back through here, will ye?"

"Aye, for a good hot meal."

She laughed. "Ye only think of your stomach, my love."

He kissed her on the cheek quickly. "I cannot say what else I think of, in front of the children."

~

*L*ater that afternoon, a celebration was in full swing as music filled the air, and food on white linen-cloth tables was served.

Dragonmage showed up, to Mexia's discomfort. Tugging on her sleeve, he said, "I was at Marinda's home when the mayor and his council members arrived. I do not believe I have ever seen the soothsayer more pleased. The circle of misfortunes has been broken. I know you have every desire to continue on to see Parenkin, the mage of Monrovia now. But still, I can teach you a few things that might aid you. Would you delay your trip a few days and stay with me so I could show you these things?"

"No."

He frowned at her. "You are *most* stubborn."

She smiled. "You are most persistent." She grabbed a slice of bread, then buttered it. "Could you show me these things here?"

He shook his head.

"And why not?"

"Imparting magical knowledge must take trust. Since you do not trust me…"

"You are quite right about that."

"Do you trust Derek?"

"You know that I do not. You watched us while you played your game of hide and seek. He offered to take me away from your castle, and yet I would not take him up on his offer. I do not trust him any more than I trust you."

His lips turned up. Was it because he was glad she didn't believe Derek had her best interests in mind either? Certainly, that would work in his favor.

"Do you know anything about Grimoria?" Mexia raised a goblet of goat's milk to her lips.

Dragonmage lifted a bowl of stew off the table. "Grimoria was the High Wizard, formerly the headmaster of Langdon Castle. But he wanted more power for himself. Now you've got to remember, this was five hundred years earlier."

She nodded, then grabbed a slice of sweet pinion melon. "Yes, and Princess Aralias imprisoned him in stone for five hundred years."

"Yes. Then he returned here, convinced nearly the whole senior class of students of Langdon to go with him, and take over Inherian."

"Rosenthal was one of these students?"

"The star pupil, actually."

"Was he in the same class with Derek then?"

"Yes. There are only three left in Derek's class now."

Mexia thought back to when she first arrived at Langdon Castle. Ros, Derek, and the unnamed mage apprentice had stood isolated from the others, speaking to one another. She assumed they were the three seniors then that had remained at the school. "So, why did they not go along with the others?"

"They were considered dangerous to Grimoria's cause. Untrustworthy, dedicated to the school and its noble beginnings, they assumed Derek and his friends wouldn't go along with it.

And in truth, they might have attempted to stop the rogue wizards, had they known. That night, a fire in the records room quickly spread to the sleeping chambers, creating destruction and confusion. Many hours later, the headmaster determined that the senior students had left of their own accord."

"So why wouldn't you nor any of the other mages be angry enough to stop this Rosenthal yourselves? You are a graduate of the school, too, are you not?"

He smiled. "I have my hands full with trying to protect the valley and the people who live here. If I didn't have this to do, I could venture through the countryside, straightening out the messes Rosenthal has created. But my duty is to this region."

"And my duty is to straighten out Rosenthal's messes."

"You are going to get yourself killed, then where will I be?"

"You will find someone else."

"If I could, I'd make you stay here with me."

"It is good you are not that powerful, then."

She finished eating her meal, then as she caught sight of the princess motioning for her to come, Mexia grabbed her staff. "Maybe, I shall see you upon my return. Goodbye, Dragonmage."

Dashing across the crowded square, Mexia didn't wait for Dragonmage to respond, nor did she glance back in his direction, though she sensed his gaze never left her.

"Are we ready?" she asked her companions, the dread already filling her stomach as her meal became unsettled.

"Aye," Gallant said. "We should cross the swamp and the cemetery, then reach the town of Cramer before the sun sets."

"Yes," the princess said, leading the way out of town. "Tonight, I wish to sleep in a tavern. No more damp caves for me."

"Yes, a real bed. I'm sure I have a bruise or two on my back from sleeping on the bedding on that rough rock floor," Kersta added.

"And a separate room so I do not hear your constant chatter," Gallant said.

The ladies laughed.

Each of the members of the party took a drink of Modi's tea as a wall of fog appeared before them on the outskirts of town. "Is there any way to clear the fog, Mexia?" the princess asked.

"If we kill Rosenthal, his spell will be broken, which will stop the fog. Though you never know. We might discover a way to end his hold over the region, which may also dissipate the mist that blankets the area. In the meantime, we can set off his fireball trigger spells to at least rid the area of that danger, my lady."

"We must try to get rid of the fog if it is in our power, so that the people of Cramer and those of Barston can trade again."

"What of the dark elves?" Kersta asked. "They're still a problem."

"Perhaps once Mexia has more training, we can resolve that problem. For now, let us concentrate on the path before us."

In a misty haze, a path emerged. The mossy green trail appeared nearly the same color as the scum-covered swamp that licked at its edges. Though the land was wide enough for two to walk abreast, Mexia led the group single file, ever vigilant in watching for the mage's deadly fireball traps.

She raised her hand for the party to stop as the buckle on her belt glowed. "Wait here." She took a step forward trying to draw up her courage as she moved. Immediately, a fireball shot out of the water. The ladies gasped as Mexia's belt absorbed the blast.

"Are you all right?" the princess and Kersta both shouted, rushing forth, then grabbed her arms to make sure for themselves.

She smiled at them. "Yes, ladies. The belt takes all of the impact." Yet her legs wobbled a bit. She tried to lose the shaki-ness draining of her strength. Practice. She had to continue to clear the way and with more practice, the shock of the fire headed at her with deadly speed would no longer shatter her courage. She hoped.

"We should continue as before."

The ladies dropped back behind her as Mexia took a step forward. Again her belt glowed. She feared at their slow pace, they would arrive at the cemetery at the fall of dark, not at the town they'd hoped to be at, sleeping comfortably in beds in a tavern.

She motioned for everyone to stop again. When they complied, she stepped forward. This time, she knew what to expect. As long as she remained cautious, she could clear the path of the triggers and with each fireball, she gained strength for casting the spell herself.

For an hour, the party continued in much the same way, sometimes making considerable progress, other times, stepping only a few feet, then pausing for another assault.

The problem they soon found was that the path didn't lead directly to the cemetery, but instead twisted and turned like a meandering maze full of dead ends and new beginnings.

Mexia turned back to look at the princess who hastily drew up the newest path choices. She pointed to the right.

They continued on that way, then found this one dead ended like a peninsula jutting into the swamp.

"The way to the left then. We have been straight ahead and it led us back to the place at the juncture."

"It is good that you have been mapping this all along," Mexia said, though frustrated at their slow progress. "I would have no idea that we have passed the same way again and again."

"Of course. I intend to put all of our travels into a book, so that those of Damar who wish to know of the peoples and geography of the regions of Albion, can learn about it."

"From a safe distance," Kersta responded.

Gallant shuffled his feet. "Do ye hear something? Something that approaches from behind?"

"I did not think there was anything that lived in the swamps," the princess said.

"No, the centaur said nothing about us having any other difficulty out here."

"I hear something, woman."

"Yes, but can you see what's making the noise you hear?"

"There! A wild boar sniffing at the ground, headed this way. Undoubtedly lost in the swamps like us." Gallant readied his war hammer as the princess joined him with her staff.

"Mexia?" a muted voice called out to her from the path they needed to take. It sounded very much like Derek's voice. He couldn't have been foolish enough to have followed them, could he have?

The pig squealed as it lunged at the princess and Gallant while Kersta waited behind them to help if need be.

Mexia headed down the path they were to take. "Derek?"

A fireball shot out at her and she turned to absorb the impact with her belt. Once she was done she cried out, "Derek!"

"Here," he said, his voice weak and pleading.

Her heart pounded with worry. How could he have been so foolish as to have followed her here?

She moved more slowly now, clearing the fireball triggers along her way, realizing if she wasn't more careful, her friends would only find her as a pile of ashes on the trail before them.

"Mexia!" a voice cried out to her from farther into the swamps. His voice sounded strong again, confusing her.

She stumbled toward his voice. "Derek?" Then she saw him injured, lying in the middle of an island, his head lifted as he held his hand out to her. His golden hair was undone and lay about his shoulders stirring slightly by a breeze she hadn't noticed before now. His blue eyes clouded over.

"Help me." His words were spoken in pain and with fading strength, sending a chill down her spine.

She sprinted down the path, but couldn't see a way to get to him as he seemed stranded on a single island surrounded entirely by the swamp. "Derek? Can you not cast a spell and get to me? I will heal you."

He rested his head on the ground and closed his eyes.

"Derek!" She paced back and forth across the path, trying to think of what to do, then she remembered moving the stone statue of Grimoria in Inherian. Could she move Derek safely across the swamp the same way?

Her brow furrowed. But she'd dropped the statue a number of times before she got it on the ship. She had to be careful and not drop Derek.

Motioning with her fingers, she began a spell. Slowly, he levitated, but then her concentration slipped as Kersta and the princess hollered for her some distance away.

He fell to the earth with an oof. A slew of curses escaped his lips.

She bit her lower lip. Again, she tried to elevate him. What if she dropped him in the swamp? He'd drown for certain in the injured state he was in. Her heart thundered. Her self-doubt ruined her concentration, and she dropped him again.

This time he growled under his breath.

"I am sorry, Derek. Please be patient with me."

This time she managed to move him halfway across the green water when a hand touched her shoulder. She screamed. Whipping around to see what had grabbed her, a splash behind her followed. But before her, Derek stood. "You and your ladies will never make it, Mexia."

She screamed, then her world turned from a white mist to instant black.

"Mexia...Mexia...dear Mexia," Derek said repeatedly trying to revive her from far away.

"I drowned you," she squeaked as her eyes fluttered open.

"I am very much alive. Come, we must find your companions."

"You were injured. I tried to move you over here from that island." She pointed to the small land mass surrounded by water. She couldn't shake the fright she'd had.

He frowned at her. "Either you are imagining things in this creepy place, or someone is playing tricks with your mind." He lifted her to her feet. "Hurry, we must find your friends."

Shifting her thoughts to Derek's safety for when they reached the cemetery and the problem with the undead, she squeezed his hand. "Can you heal people?"

"Slightly. It's not one of my better subjects."

"Then when we reach the cemetery, you must stay back with Gallant. Protect him if need be. The ladies and I have to use our healing spells to put the undead back to sleep."

"Rosenthal has done this?"

"Chernon, the centaur, has said so. In Inherian, Grimoria tried to pit man against man, now he seems to be dividing up the peoples of Albion. Once he conquers them here, he will come back to Inherian to war with us."

"He will never succeed against the wizards of Albion."

"Because you are school trained?" Her words were spoken with bitterness.

He looked over at her, then took her hand and hurried her along. "No, because there are more of us."

She glanced back at the island now hidden by the mists still expecting to see Derek injured, lying there out of her reach.

Noticing her concern, he cleared his throat. "Do you think it could have been Rosenthal pretending to be me?"

"I have seen a mage do this before...give the illusion he was one of our knights, and injured, so yes, he could have done such a thing, I suppose."

Derek nodded. "Did you see the golden leaves on his lapels?"

"No."

"Can you see them on mine?"

She stared at his cloak, then touched it. "There are four now."

He squeezed her hand tighter. "I knew you were the one for me the moment I saw you. Did you not feel that way about me also…when we first met?"

She had been drawn to him immediately. But she'd only thought it was his handsome features and the way he appeared equally interested in her, that made him appeal so to her. "But Marinda said it was too early to tell."

"She doesn't know what she speaks of. It is said, the woman who sees the golden leaves embroidered on my cloak will join me in matrimony. Between the two of us, we shall run the school of Langford and have a child who will be more powerful than any wizard alive today." He leaned over and kissed her cheek. "You are the one." He smiled as she stared back at him. "You will get used to the idea. And if Rosenthal tries to impersonate me further, remember my cloak. He will not know this about it. Even I cannot see what is on my cloak like you can."

Mexia gripped his hand, making him smile at her. She knew he was the one. Why wouldn't Marinda have known also? Then she considered her words. It was too early to say. Did she mean she could not tell her the truth for the moment? That's what she must have meant. It was true, Derek was meant for her, only Marinda could not say it was so. Mexia's mission came first. Everything else would have to follow.

"I have much to do before we can be together, Derek. You must understand this."

"I will not aid my future wife in this endeavor, Mexia. You will die before we can fulfill what has been prophesied for me."

She tried to pull her hand free.

He held it tight. "You cannot fault me for trying to keep you safe." He took a deep breath. "I will go with you as far as Cramer, but from there, I must return to Langdon. I will graduate in two days' time. Once you can see you will have no way to make it through the mountains of Monrovia, I expect you to return to me at Langdon. There, we will wed. Then we'll return to my home in Malar. When the time is right, we will run the school at Langdon."

"Malar?"

"On the southern coast, beyond the mountains of Monrovia. Beautiful place. You will enjoy it there."

She jerked her hand away from his. "This fairytale may have been prophesied for you, but not for me. I will find a husband who would share my adventures and help me in my endeavors. I am now officially a member of the adventurers' guild. As such, I have many noble quests to fulfill."

He snickered.

She turned to him, anger filling her. "Derek, be gone. This place is too dangerous for you. Go home to the school where you will be safe."

"If this Rosenthal is pretending to be me, he means to kill you. I have every intention of putting an end to his miserable life, rest assured. But I must complete my training. In two days' time, I will graduate. Then, after I wed you, I will track him down and put an end to his shenanigans. But only once you are safely at my villa in Malar."

"Mexia!"

"Princess Talamaya, Kersta!" Mexia ran to join them, then embraced them with exuberance. She smiled at the dwarf. "Gallant."

"Ye should not have run off like ye did," Gallant groused.

They all looked around her at Derek.

Gallant frowned at the mage. "What are ye doing here now?"

Derek folded his arms. "Trying to keep my bride-to-be from getting herself killed."

"Not that again," Kersta said, shaking her head.

"You have cleared the path this way?" the princess asked.

"Yes."

"What made ye run off without us? I killed the boar fast enough."

"Derek, or I should say, Rosenthal called to me from the swamps. I thought it was Derek who was injured."

She led the way again, but when Derek tried to hold her hand, she stopped. "I must clear the area of fireball traps, Derek. If anyone walks with me, they will be incinerated."

"I wished to hold your hand because I cannot see through this damnable fog."

"Oh." She handed him her flask. "Drink of Modi's tea. She is a soothsayer in Inherian. Her tea helps us to see our way clearly."

He drank of the tea, then handed her flask back to her. He smiled. "I thought you were much more powerful than me."

"I am." She took a step forward. He stopped her. Mexia crossed her arms. "What?"

"I can help." He considered the area ahead of them, then pointed his finger at the swamp. A fireball exploded in the water sending the scum flying. Now drenched in the green plants, Mexia shook her head.

She wiped some of the gook off her cheek and shook her hand to get rid of it. "We'll do it my way. Less messy."

Less than twenty feet away, she motioned to her companions to stay back. Though they did as she ordered, as soon as the blazing fire shot out of the water and headed straight for Mexia, Derek took a step in her direction. Both the princess and Gallant grabbed his arms.

Her name died on his lips as her belt absorbed the blast.

"You could have warned me," he grumbled as they released his arms. He hurried to join her and held her tightly. "You could have told me what to expect."

She loved the warmth of his body pressing hard against hers. She ached for his kisses and much more, but when she turned her face up to his, Gallant cleared his throat.

"If ye do this every time she rids the swamp of a fireball trap we will never get to the cemetery before nightfall."

Mexia smiled, but when she attempted to pull away from Derek, he kissed her lips with the same kind of desire he'd shown her before.

"I thought I'd lost you, my love," he whispered in her ear. "I nearly died."

She kissed him back with the same kind of hunger, the fire kindling deep inside. "We must go, Derek. Remember, when we get to the cemetery, you must stay on the path through the swamps while the three of us ladies use our healing spells to put the undead to rest."

He nodded.

Then they were on their way again, twisting turning, choosing the wrong path, and then the right. After several hours, they ended up at the northern edge of a vast cemetery. Headstones appeared to rise out of the ground at close intervals with narrow paths to maneuver between sections. A white stone building lay straight ahead.

"The crypt?" the princess asked.

"Most likely." Mexia pointed to movement to the west. "Five or six of the undead are headed in this direction. Come with me, and I will attempt to use my group healing spell. If it doesn't work on some, then you ladies can kill the others."

"Be careful," Derek whispered.

"I would put them back in the grave with my war hammer if ye would let me," Gallant griped.

"Our weapons will not work on them," Mexia warned. She and the ladies left their staffs with him. Then she motioned for the ladies to follow her.

Here, they had no protection from the undead, no unicorn magic. Here, they were on their own.

CHAPTER 9

Mexia summoned the courage just lying in wait as she and the ladies crossed the cemetery. She intended to keep the undead creatures far away from Gallant, who had no skills in the art of healing, and Derek, who at his own admission, wasn't very good at it.

Five men, their clothes ragged, moaned under their breaths as they caught sight of the women. They turned and headed for them, ambling like toddlers taking their first steps, one foot in front of the other, tilting unsteadily, pausing, and then moving forward again.

"Keep watching for others," Mexia said, the sight of them sending shivers up her spine, "while I use the group spell on these. Keep away from them. They don't move quickly. We should be able to outmaneuver them if they don't surround us."

She hurried to work her group spell as the princess watched their backs, and Kersta aimed hers at one of the men closest to her.

The five men's flesh turned pink all at once, their eyes seemed to have life, and then they dissolved to ashes, to Mexia's relief.

The princess said, with hint of dread to her voice, "Behind us, three more."

Mexia hurried to use her spell for the whole lot of them.

For an hour, they moved cautiously through the cemetery, putting the undead to rest, searching for more signs of them, but when Derek yelled out, the ladies dashed through the headstones to come to his and Gallant's aid.

A cluster of twenty approached the prince and the dwarf. Mexia worried she couldn't handle that large a group, as she gnawed on her lower lip. Though she had to try anything she could to save them.

"Gallant, strike at them with your weapon!" she ordered. "Though it will not kill them, they have a time getting back to their feet."

She quickly cast her spell as Gallant struck at the outstretched hands of a woman intent on choking the life from him.

The ladies each concentrated on a man of their own while Derek gave up his healing spell and disappeared.

Derek. Mexia couldn't squash the irritation rising in her blood that he would leave them to fend for themselves once again. Just when she needed him, he'd vanish like a puff of blue smoke.

To Mexia's relief, fifteen of the undead returned to their former state of health, then disappeared in clouds of dust. She hurried to take care of the last five. She knew she couldn't take credit for having returned all of the undead to their resting state, but she realized her skills at healing were improving with practice.

When the last of these disappeared, the princess said, "Where'd Derek go?"

"Guess he's rather faint of heart," Kersta said.

Mexia took a deep breath, trying to quell the annoyance she felt that he'd up and leave them again in their time of need. "He said his healing spells weren't very good, and he didn't have a weapon with him."

Kersta pointed at their staffs lying on the ground. "He couldn't have used one of our staffs?"

Mexia grabbed up her staff. "Perhaps he's not trained with a weapon. I mean, we are. It doesn't mean everyone is." She hadn't meant to defend him, but she couldn't help herself.

Kersta shook her head and lifted her staff off the ground. "Can you believe she's sticking up for him?"

"Ye have to agree he tried. He cannot do what he cannot do, woman," Gallant argued.

The princess pointed her staff at the crypt. "We have cleared all of the undead from the cemetery. But what about the crypt?"

Mexia motioned to Gallant. "Stay here. We'll make sure it's free of undesirables."

The three women crossed the cemetery to the crypt where a metal door barred their entrance. Mexia reached for the handle and pulled. The door creaked and groaned its displeasure at being disturbed. The noise sent her skin crawling with apprehension.

The air inside smelled of earth and dampness, thick mold and decay, heavy and difficult to breathe in. Kersta sneezed, sending a spark of fright through Mexia's spine.

"Sorry," Kersta whispered, then sniffled.

Another sneeze reverberated off the crypt walls.

"Who goes there?" a deep voice asked, the figure hidden in the shadows in the far corner of the crypt.

Mexia answered for the group, "We are members of the adventurers' guild and seek to put the undead to rest."

A figure strode forth and the ladies stood fast. The man, dressed in golden armor, his tunic covering this, red velvet proudly displaying the golden embroidered image of the sphinx, stopped in front of Mexia. His blond beard and hair extended below his helmed face as his green eyes peered out from the golden metal. "I am Sir Farrington."

His figure wavered slightly and Mexia wondered if something in the air made her see things not as they were.

"This is my crypt," he said. "You do not plan to steal from it, do you?"

"No, we only seek to help those who need our assistance."

"A man named Boras stole my sword. I cannot leave my crypt to tear his heart out for leaving me weaponless, but I will do anything I can to repay you for aiding me in my quest."

"Boras?"

"He lives in Cramer."

"We need to know how to stop the wizard who has cast a spell of mist over the swamps. Can you help us with this?"

"Return my sword and I will see what can be done about the wizard's magic."

"Do you know where this Boras is in Cramer?"

"He is a thief, a sewer rat."

"We will return as soon as we are able." Mexia thought for a moment, then said, "What is distinguishing about this sword, Sir Knight, so that we may know it is the right one when we find it?"

"Shaped in the head of a snake, the handle has emerald eyes and a ruby tongue."

"All right, we shall attempt to find it and bring it back to you."

The ladies turned to leave, but the ghostly knight said, "Wait."

He pointed to a place beside a sarcophagus. "He dropped a key. Perhaps it will unlock something for you that will aid you."

Mexia retrieved the key, then stuffed it into her pouch. With a brief farewell to the knight apparition, the ladies hurried out of the crypt.

Kersta sneezed with her exodus. "Sorry, ladies. I couldn't help myself."

Gallant hurried to join them. "Off to the village of Cramer now?"

"To the sewers it seems," Mexia said.

"But first, a meal and rest," the princess reminded them. "There will be plenty of time to search the sewers for this Boras who stole Sir Farrington's sword."

"Who's he?" Gallant asked as they headed out of the cemetery and into a verdant valley.

"The knight whose crypt we just came from. Boras is a thief." Mexia followed the others, still glancing over her shoulder, wondering if either Derek or the imposter, Rosenthal, followed them. Though she assumed Derek returned safely to Langdon, she still worried that he might not have made it. Then what?

Her thoughts shifted to the conversation they'd had. Could what his people had prophesied be true?

"What?" Kersta asked. "Who prophesied what?"

Mexia shook her head. No way did she want to explain what Derek had said to her about the prophecy.

The princess glanced back at her with one brow quirked. "What is it, Mexia?"

"Nothing, really, my lady." What he'd said wasn't important...not really. She had a job to do. And yet, if what Derek said was true, that she and he would preside over Langdon Castle, what about her desire to be the High Wizard of Damar?

He had to be wrong. He just had to be.

She diverted her gaze from her feet to her companions and noticed they were eyeing her suspiciously. "What?" she said with irritation.

Gallant shrugged. "They seem to think something is wrong."

The princess looked over at Kersta. "Lady Kersta seems to think something is wrong."

Mexia frowned at Kersta. "There is nothing the matter."

Kersta shook her head. "Something always is the matter when

it has to do with Derek." She turned her attention toward the dirt road at their feet, avoiding Mexia's glare.

When they arrived at Cramer, the town was cloaked in shadows. Lighted lanterns illuminated the main road, but areas shrouded in darkness filled the alleyways. And whispered voices hissed in the blackness.

Kersta readied her staff. "I sense trouble."

"What kind?" the princess whispered.

"Thieves. They wonder how much we are worth."

"They will find we are not worth messing with." Gallant readied his war hammer. "Ren will take care of the likes of them."

Mexia looked warily at the dark alleyways on either side of the street, her heart picking up its pace a couple of notches.

Then Gallant pointed to a building to the right. "The adventurers' guild of Cramer."

"But you have already done a quest and earned your money, Gallant," the princess said. "We must continue on our way to Monrovia."

"Ye wish to retrieve the knight's sword, do ye not? That quest takes us in the opposite direction. And when ye were made members of the adventurers' guild, ye not only took half of my quest money for the last mission, but ye promised to take on a quest every time ye arrived within sight of an adventurer's guild, should they need our services."

"Half your money?" Kersta said. "Why, there are four of us."

"He can't count," the princess reminded her.

"Oh." Kersta smiled. "You may have my share of the money, Gallant. I have plenty."

He furrowed his brow at her. "I would not think of taking your money. And as before, I will find a quest that will take us in the direction we are headed, unlike this knight's quest from the crypt." He raised his brows at the princess.

She smiled. "All right. Will the adventurers' guild still be open?"

"They stay open the whole night, woman. Weary adventurers may sleep there if need be, should they have no money for fancier lodging."

A small boy approached them, his feet bare, and face smudged with dirt, while his breeches and shirt appeared two sizes too small for his thin body. "Have you a coin for an orphan, lady?" he asked Kersta.

"No as you would rob me blind if I allowed it. I have a special gift, young man, and can read every thought of yours and your companions'. If you do not wish me to turn you in to the town constable, you will make yourself scarce."

The boy's eyes grew big. He dashed off into the alley without another peep.

"Couldn't we have given him a coin, Kersta?" Mexia asked as they headed toward the adventurers' guild.

"Not to the likes of them. As soon as you had your purse out, it would have been snatched by another. There were at least three others just waiting for one of us to pull our purses from our cloaks."

Mexia glanced back at the shadows and saw the same boy watching them. "He is not convinced you would turn him in, I don't think."

Kersta smiled. "And yet he didn't make an attempt to steal from us. We have set a niggling of worry in his youthful mind."

Gallant pulled open the door to the adventurers' guild, then walked into the building with the ladies following close behind.

A large black-bearded man rose from a wooden chair, his face deeply scarred from what looked to be sword play.

He looked from the dwarf to the ladies and pointed to a ream of paper. "Fill in your concerns there, if any of you can write."

"We are adventurers who seek a quest in the direction we travel," Gallant said.

The big man laughed. "I'm Cirrus, and you are the new court jester, no?"

"I'm Gallant, from the adventurers' guild in my home town of Kern. The ladies are certified by the guild in Albion." He crossed his short arms over his broad chest. "Now do ye have a quest for us, or have ye nay trouble in town?"

The man pointed to several scrolls of posters hanging on the wall. "Take your pick, little one." He eyed the women from one to the other. "I have never heard of women adventurers before. Nor of a dwarf who does such a thing for a living."

Mexia motioned to the ladies. "We are seeking a way to reach the mage of Monrovia. Can you tell us anything about the journey there?"

"Nobody is foolhardy enough to attempt to make their way through the mountain passes. The mountain cheetaurs blending in with the snow would devour you before you made it very far. Snow devil wolves, avalanches, snow spirits, and..." He glanced over at Gallant. "Goblins. But not the normal dark underground goblin. These are more devious than even a band of orcs. If you chance to run into the snow goblins, you will find yourself in another land with a whole new set of troubles worse than before."

"Another land?" Mexia asked.

"Nobody makes it back from a trek to the mountains."

"Why would anyone attempt them then?"

"For the diamonds. We never hear of the gem seekers again."

"Then how do you know they end up in another land with a new set of troubles worse than before?" Mexia asked, not believing the man at all.

He narrowed his eyes at her. She smiled. He was a great storyteller. Probably scared the kids to death with his tales.

They turned to see Gallant running his finger over a scroll.

"Well, what do ye, women, think? Am I to do all the work over here?"

The ladies joined him. "This one says they need a man to retrieve a runaway goat...last seen in the direction of the mountains of Monrovia." Kersta folded her arms.

"Right direction," Gallant said.

"Doesn't sound like a really gallant cause," the princess said, then smiled as Gallant raised his brows at her.

The princess read another. "This one states a young man ran off with this man's daughter, and he wants her returned."

"Sounds like a family dispute," Kersta said.

"I've never heard of adventurers being so picky over where the money comes from," the guild master scoffed.

Mexia read the next one. "Baby stolen from its cradle. Reward for its speedy recovery." She turned to her companions. "We have to find the baby."

The guild master chuckled. "First, the goat is owned by an old man who lost his whole family due to a sickness. The goat is all that's left of his family now. Secondly, the young man ran off with the butcher's four-year-old daughter because of a dispute over payment on a pig. And thirdly, the woman who claims her baby was stolen, never had a baby."

"Then why is it posted here? And why don't the other cases give better details?"

"Most everyone in these parts know the cases already. No need to give a lot of details. As for the young woman who claims her baby was stolen, we have to post these notices, even if we believe they're fraudulent."

Mexia fisted her hands on her hips. "Why? Because there may be some truth to the matter?"

"The woman never had a baby."

"Where does she live?"

He laughed. "At the end of the village, southeast corner."

The princess folded her arms. "The man whose daughter was taken?"

"The butcher, four houses down, right side of the road."

"And the old man who's missing his goat?" Kersta asked.

"Near the base of the mountain."

Gallant snorted. "Ye do not think we are going to solve all the quests the guild has posted, do ye now?"

"Do you know anything about this Boras, a reputed thief?" Mexia asked.

The guild master wrinkled his brow. "You would do best to leave that one alone."

Not shaken from the quest, Mexia added, "We need to return a sword that he stole."

"Whose sword? No one has turned in a guild quest for such a thing."

Mexia took a deep breath. "I doubt Sir Farrington would have posted such a quest."

"The knight who died," Cirrus said, pausing to rub his bearded chin, "some months ago?"

"How did he die?"

"A dispute over a woman." His whiskers rose as he smiled. "The same one who's looking for a baby who doesn't exist."

"It is getting dark," the princess said. "We will seek lodging for the night, and then conduct other business at first light."

"You appear to be ladies of some means and the tavern here does not allow women to stay there. The only other place you would be able to stay is Lord Cramer's castle at the south end of town with a mountainside view."

"Or here," Gallant reminded him. "As adventurers we have the right to stay here."

The man shifted his gaze from the dwarf to the ladies. "Not women. Women don't stay here. But you are welcome to."

"We have no letter of introduction to visit with this Lord

Cramer though." The princess folded her arms. "Or is this not a necessary form of protocol here?"

"You can tell him Cirrus sent you, but I do not really think it will be necessary."

"All right." The princess lifted the point of her staff from the floor. "Come, let us meet with Lord Cramer."

The party headed out of doors, then walked at a quickened pace toward the castle, its four spirals looming in the distance. Torches lighted each, the flickering flame whipping in the breeze, casting ghostly shadows on the white stone.

Mexia yawned. "I shouldn't be that tired, but I'm exhausted."

"We've walked our legs off today," Kersta said as she stretched. She turned her head back sharply to look in the direction of the adventurers' guild and narrowed her eyes.

Mexia looked back that way, too, but not seeing anything said, "What is wrong, Kersta?"

"That boy of a thief just entered the guild."

"If the guild master is in league with the thieves in this town, could he steer us wrong in sending us to the castle?"

The princess nodded. "I had a vision we would have trouble when we arrived here, but I thought it pertained to the sewers. Now I am not so sure."

"What was it, princess?" Mexia asked as they approached the castle. "What have you seen?"

"We are trying to find a way out. I cannot tell where we are... just sense our frustration. And Gallant is not with us for some reason."

"I will not abandon ye," Gallant said.

"No, of course not."

"Not like that Derek," Kersta added, her tone bitter.

"He has more important things to do, like graduate from the wizard school in two more days," Mexia said, her voice also on edge.

"What do you think, ladies? Gallant? Shall we try to stay here the night, or try somewhere else?"

The portcullis creaked open and a guard stepped outside dressed in golden armor, the same kind of tunic gracing his chest just like the knight's in the tomb.

"Sir Farrington must have been a knight working for Lord Cramer," Mexia said.

"You knew Sir Farrington?" The guard motioned for them to enter. "Anyone who was a friend of his must be a friend of Lord Cramer."

The princess spoke, "We seek lodging for the evening, and understand the tavern will not allow women to sleep there for the night."

He eyed them suspiciously. "Who sent you?"

"The guild master told us to seek lodging here, but we can attempt other accommodations if necessary."

"In the cemetery perhaps? No one allows outsiders to sleep in their abodes if they have no introduction. Who are you?"

"Princess Talamaya, and her lady companions, Lady Kersta and Lady Mexia."

The man's eyes widened in surprise.

"And our good friend Gallant, of the adventurers' guild of the village of Kern. We seek to aid those in need here, but require a place to sleep for the night, then we'll attempt to solve the quests."

He motioned for them to enter, but Kersta took the princess aside. "I fear for our safety here, princess."

The princess looked back at Mexia and Gallant who waited to hear her decision. She turned to the knight. "We will find other accommodations, thank you."

His mouth dropped open in surprise, and he stuttered, "No, no, my lady, you must come inside or my lord will be frosted to hear that I turned you away. There is no other place for you to stay. I beg of you, come in and enjoy the meal and accommodations for the evening."

"Thank you, we have changed our minds and do not wish to disturb his lordship."

The four headed back down the road away from the castle.

"What do we do now?" Kersta asked.

"Gallant may stay in the guild for the night or even the tavern for that matter."

"I told ye already, woman, I stay with ye. Ye may need my protection. I agree with ye that something is not right. Did ye see how shifty his beady black eyes were?"

They all looked at Gallant as he shifted *his* gaze from one to another. They burst out laughing.

"What?"

A bell rang in one of the castle's towers, and the princess shook her head. "I don't like this at all."

"What about the woman who lost her baby? Maybe we could ask if we could stay with her overnight." Mexia asked.

Nobody had time to answer as horses' hooves struck the cobblestone road behind them with such a clatter, Mexia's heart beat out of bounds. They all ran to get out of the way, but the knights who rode the horses, effectively corralled them before they could escape.

CHAPTER 10

A black-haired, clean-shaven knight spoke with an authoritative tongue to Mexia and her companions. "Lord Cramer wishes to make your acquaintance, ladies."

"We appreciate his kind offer but are unable to accept his hospitality," the princess said.

"Filled with undesirables, the town is no place for ladies of such distinction to stay." He dismounted. "Allow me to introduce myself. I am Baron Fitzwater, at your service."

"I am Princess Talamaya of the house of Sal in Damar."

"From the continent of Inherian?"

"Yes."

He glanced over at the other ladies.

"Lady Mexia and Lady Kersta, also of Damar."

"Ladies from such a noble house must stay with Lord Cramer. No other place here would do."

"We must decline."

"Where will you stay?" He walked around the ladies as they stood holding their staffs firmly in their grasp. "We've had problems with the thieves here of late. The mountains to the south are a treacherous journey in and of themselves. Occasionally the undead roam about the streets from the nearby cemetery. We are effectively cut off from Barston because of the mist surrounding the swamp, not to mention the problem with the undead and the fatal fireballs that shoot out of the water at intervals."

"We made it through the swamps just fine," the princess said, keeping her eye on the baron. "And we have taken care of the problem with the undead, not to mention the fireball traps have all been...sprung."

The man's black brows lifted in surprise. "Really? Well you must dine with us and tell all about your conquests, and about your home of Inherian as well. Our lord will insist."

Mexia waited for the princess to give them the order to fight the knight and his men, but when the princess didn't, Mexia stepped closer and whispered to her, "My lady, what do you wish us to do?" Her voice was filled with impatience as she tapped her foot on the stone road.

"We will join the baron as he asks it of us so kindly."

The princess glanced back at Kersta who nodded. Mexia didn't know what was going on, but she figured Kersta read the princess's mind, and they had something worked out.

Gallant grumbled under his breath.

The baron walked beside the princess as Gallant, Kersta, and Mexia followed behind and the other five knights rode their horses after them as if to ensure none of them stole away.

Mexia whispered to Kersta, "What is going on?"

"The princess does not want to create a scene. We could fight these knights, but it is not what we were meant to do here. We will see what must be done, inside the castle."

Having already experienced the fear of being locked in a castle that she had to find a way to escape from, Mexia didn't like the notion of entering this one. She tried to curb the growing anxiety rising in her system as the iron portcullis creaked its way to the ground, then closed with a grating bang, giving her a start.

She glanced back. The men smiled at her, sending a shiver up her spine.

The companions quickly were chauffeured through the outer courtyard, then into a great hall where tables situated like teeth in a comb stretched out from the spine, the head table elevated slightly above the rest, all clothed in white linen.

As they walked into the room, several were quickly relocated from the head table as everyone in the hall stood from their bench seats. A man wearing regal gold robes standing before a golden throne centered at the head table, motioned for the women to join him.

"Lord Cramer," the baron said to them as he escorted them to the table.

Once they reached Lord Cramer, the baron quickly made introductions.

One of the knights who followed them to the table offered to take their weapons. The princess shook her head. "Thank you, Sir Knight, but we travel light and keep everything with us at all times."

He looked over at Lord Cramer for his word on the matter.

The golden-haired man, his face cleanly shaven, nodded his approval. "Sit," Lord Cramer said to the ladies. "And enjoy the meal."

"Black beady eyes," Gallant grumbled under his breath.

Mexia glanced over at Lord Cramer as the princess sat to the left of him. He did indeed have black beady eyes as beady as Gallant's.

The baron positioned himself between the princess and Kersta, and the knight who wished to take their weapons sat next to Mexia. One more kept her separated from Gallant. Was it done to provide more sociability, or to keep the companions from speaking to one another privately? Mexia was sure it was for the latter purpose, which unsettled her.

Soon pewter plates piled high with rice, corn, and pork ribs were served. Mexia breathed in the spicy aroma of the meat, and her stomach growled in response.

With tankards clanking and forks jabbing at the food on the metal plates, the conversation returned to the hall. Mexia glanced to see if Kersta was eating. She smiled and waved at her to get started, but motioned to her flask.

Mexia nodded. She would have to slip her flask to Gallant so that he could share Modi's tea with him.

"I am Sir Randon," the redheaded knight between Gallant and Mexia said to her. "What brings you to Cramer?"

She didn't believe that she should mention her wishing to attend the wizardry school. In fact, she assumed that keeping her skills secret might benefit them, if they needed them later. She smiled sweetly. "We have never been to Albion before. The princess intends to write a book of our journeys here. But also, we are members of the adventurers' guild in Barston, so we wished to see how we could aid those here in Cramer."

"Women?" He chuckled as he lifted his wine goblet off the table. "I have never heard of women being members of an adventurers' guild."

Mexia tamped down the urge to hit the next man who said that to her. "We rescued children and returned them to their home in Barston. The guild master felt this was enough to prove us capable of being members of the guild."

"Ah, then you need to clear the rabble out of the sewers once and all for us."

"The thieves?"

"Yes. They have a stranglehold on the citizens here."

"Can the knights not do anything about it?"

He shook his head, a deep wrinkle etched across his forehead. "They are like rats, disappearing into the sewers, knowing their way through every inch of it and every way to escape from there. We have tried everything."

"Have these people some other work they can do? I mean, if they have no other skill, no way to feed themselves…"

The knight snorted. "The town has come under hard times what with our being isolated from the village of Barston and further from Langdon. But Lord Cramer feeds any who are of need of food. No one starves here."

"We have cleared the cemetery of the undead and the fireball traps. We only now need to free the cemetery of the perpetual mist that cloaks it. However, in the meantime, perhaps we can help you with the sewer problem you have."

The man's mouth gaped open. Then he quickly clamped it shut as he stared at her in disbelief.

She buttered a slice of bread. "Why did Lord Cramer wish us to stay with him?"

Sir Randon glanced at the knight sitting on the other side of Mexia and seeing he was busy talking with Kersta he whispered to Mexia, "He was told he would get a great reward for one of you women that traveled here in a group of three accompanied by a dwarf."

"Why do you tell me this?" she whispered back to him, her heart pounding in her ears.

"I believe if you have already done as much as you say, you could be of great help to us in ridding us of the plague of thievery. Several of us will help you in your cause."

"Who was this man who approached your lord?"

He shook his head. "Nobody from around here."

She stared at her meal, then looked up at the knight. "Which woman did this individual offer a reward for?"

"I don't know for certain. He said he was betrothed to the lady and wished her and her companions kept here until he returned two days hence for your own safety. Said he couldn't have her attempting to tackle the mountains of Monrovia."

"Derek? Prince Derek?" Mexia's shrill voice caught Kersta and the knight's attention sitting between them.

Sir Randon whispered, "Shh, my lady. Please, if Lord Cramer knew I warned you of this—"

"I will kill him." Mexia stabbed her meat with her knife.

The knight's blue eyes widened. "Lord Cramer?"

"Prince Derek, I mean."

He smiled. "You are the one he is betrothed to then."

"I am no such thing."

He chuckled. "Oh. Well one of the other ladies then?"

"None of us. He has some notion I shall marry him to fulfill some fantastical prophecy of his. But he is wrong."

"Why is it that you intend to go to the mountains? Surely you do not mean to seek the diamonds there."

"No. I must…" She stopped speaking, realizing it wasn't in their best interest to give away her abilities to this man or any other who worked for Lord Cramer. "So what does he intend to do with us?"

"Lord Cramer?"

"Yes."

"He will entertain you, ply you with drink and food, and be a perfect host. Nothing more."

"For two days' time?"

"Yes."

"All right. If you and the men escort us, will we be permitted to fulfill the quests the guild has posted?"

"I may be able to persuade Lord Cramer to permit such an endeavor. What about the thieves?"

"We must find Sir Farrington's sword and return it to him. In return, he may be able to help us with the fog that cloaks the path through the swamp."

"Someone stole Sir Farrington's sword?"

"A thief named Boras."

"How do you know such a thing?"

"Sir Farrington told us."

Sir Randon's eyes grew big. "Before he was killed? I thought he was laid to rest with his sword, shield, and battle axe, too."

"We met him in the crypt. He was pretty incensed Boras would steal his sword. Can you tell me how Sir Farrington died?"

"A dispute over Lila. She's a lovely lass, but just a poor farm girl. Lord Cramer didn't want one of his knights marrying a peasant girl." The knight leaned over to Mexia and said for her ears only, "He told me he married her secretly." He shook his head. "Truly, he loved her."

Mexia's heart was sickened with the notion that Lila lost the knight so soon after their commitment to one another. "Did they have a child?"

The knight cleared his throat. "Some say so. She posted a quest requesting the return of her baby. Some say she's crazy... only wishful thinking she'd had his baby."

And yet Mexia couldn't shake the feeling Lila had told the truth. "Who killed Sir Farrington?"

"A boyhood friend of Lila's. He felt she should have been his. That from birth their families expected the two to marry when they were old enough."

"And did both the families truly feel this way?"

"Lila's family wanted her to marry the knight. He would have made their lives so much easier. As it was, he gave most of his salary to Lila and her family. The boy's family felt that Lila and her parents betrayed them."

She took a deep breath. "What happened to the boy?"

"He escaped to the mountains of Monrovia. Everyone assumes he is dead."

"What about the baby? Could he have taken it with him?" Her

voice was as anxious as she felt. She wanted to rescue the baby more than anything, even more than attending the school in Langdon.

"If so, it would definitely be dead."

Mexia's heart sank with the notion. "And Lila?"

"She's brokenhearted of course. She's lost her husband and if she'd had a child, that, too."

She stared at the table, running her spoon over the white cloth trying to imagine how she could rectify Lila and the knight's lives. Then she turned to Sir Randon. "Can you take me to see her?"

"Just you? Alone?"

Her spirits rose. "Would it be easier for you to get permission to take just one of us or could you ensure we're all able to go?"

He rubbed his smooth chin. "I will obtain permission for you. If Lord Cramer has the others still in his...well under his roof, he will be reassured that you will not try to slip away by yourself."

She relaxed slightly in her seat, having won a small victory. Derek would have no say over her life. "Of course not, Sir Knight. It would be way too dangerous for one woman traveling alone."

"All right. Following the meal, Lord Cramer wishes you and your companions to speak about Inherian and the kingdom of Damar to his courtiers. But I will get your release and take you to see Lila."

~

*A*fter the meal, Gallant was taken to a room on the other side of the castle, while the ladies were escorted to the women's wing, where the single women stayed. The bedchambers set aside for them for the next couple of days sported a massive bed draped in wispy white sheers and a spread of rich burgundy velvet. Pillows of the same color, trimmed in gold tassels, nestled at the head of the bed while a wrought iron bench cushioned in velvet, rested at the foot.

White sheers covered a single narrow window, the green glass allowing only a glimpse of the full moon. Next to this, wrought iron hooks rested against the wall for the ladies' garments. Two humpback chests to store their possessions, sat beneath these.

Mexia spoke with her companions, "I'm going to speak with Lila, the woman whose baby was stolen, but they won't let us all go together." She pulled off her pack and set it on a table next to the bed.

"What's going on, Mexia?" Kersta asked, her voice filled with concern. "I couldn't hear your conversation with the knight, but got glimpses of his thoughts when the other knight wasn't distracting me with conversation. But this other thing, our confinement here, has something to do with Derek, does it not?"

"Yes, he wants Lord Cramer to keep us here until after he graduates, then he will come back for me and…marry me, so he says."

Kersta groaned, collapsing on the grand bed taking up most of the room. The rope holding the mattress up, swayed slightly, creaking with her weight. "She cannot do this, Princess Talamaya."

"What are you thinking, Mexia?" the princess asked, her voice fraught with concern.

Mexia sat on the bed next to Kersta and patted her shoulder to reassure her. "I only wish to speak to Lila and learn about her baby. Sir Randon said he would obtain permission for one of us to go to help solve the quests. But only one of us will be allowed to go. Once we have solved all the quests we're able to, we will be on our way.

"The knight said they want the thievery stopped. It's like the circle of misfortunes in Barston. If we return the sword to Sir

Farrington, he will help us stop the mist in the swamp. The people from here will again trade with those of Barston. The poor will no longer have to turn to thievery. There will be no need. The knights will be grateful for our help. Once we've done these deeds, they will aid us to leave for the mountains. I am certain."

The princess sighed deeply. "But they work for Lord Cramer, and they will not want to earn his wrath."

"Still we have two days to solve the quests, and then we can leave before Derek returns here."

"Derek," Kersta said, her voice bitter.

"You will only speak to Lila then?" the princess asked. "You will bring word back to us, and together we will decide what to do next, won't you?"

"Yes, my lady. I have every intention of doing so."

"Against my better judgment, I will permit you to see the lady on your own." The princess pulled the scepter from her belt. "Take this to protect you."

"My staff and my spells will give me protection enough. You must keep the scepter with you always." She took the princess's hand and squeezed it. "Do you have any visions of what will come to pass?"

"Only that poor Kersta and I will have to entertain the courtiers here with tales of our travels. Gallant will add his own comments from time to time."

A knocking on the door made Mexia and Kersta rise from the bed.

"Yes?" the princess said.

A lady poked her head in the doorway. "Lord Cramer wishes you to speak with him now. And Sir Randon is ready to escort Lady Mexia to Lila's home, though his lordship is not really pleased with the request."

"Why?" Mexia asked.

The lady looked from the princess to Mexia, then cast her

gaze to the floor. "He feels you have no need to speak with the woman. She is crazy. Beyond this, he's concerned for your safety."

Mexia didn't believe a word of it. "We shall see, won't we?"

"Keep yourself safe, Mexia." Kersta embraced her warmly.

Mexia smiled, knowing her childhood friends would take her place in a heartbeat to keep her out of harm's way.

The princess hugged her with the same kind of enthusiasm. "Do not be long, Mexia. Get whatever word we need from the young lady and return at once. We will decide how to deal with it after we sleep tonight."

"Yes, princess." She nodded at Kersta.

They left the bedchambers and Sir Randon led Mexia down the hallway the opposite way from the princess and Kersta. For a moment, she wished she joined them and helped them to tell their tales to the courtiers, too. But in her heart, she desired more than anything to help recover Lila's baby.

⁓

*L*ater that evening, Sir Randon and another knight walked with Mexia toward Lila's house, the lanterns still glowing in two of the windows.

"Is it really so dangerous for the citizens to walk through the streets at night?" Mexia asked.

"Yes, my lady. Lord Cramer set a curfew for when the sky grows dark. Anyone caught on the streets after that will be imprisoned, unless they are escorted by a knight, as we now escort you."

When they reached Lila's small stone house, Mexia knocked on the door. There was no response. She knocked again, then called out, "Lila? I am Mexia, friend of Sir Farrington and a member of the adventurers' guild. I wish to aid you in returning your baby."

"Everyone believes it is a lie!" a woman screamed out.

Mexia touched the door with her hand, attempting to reach the woman. "I believe you, dear lady, and I want very much to help."

The door creaked open a crack. "How can you help?" The girl's red hair was in disarray, her eyes filled with unspent tears. Her worn dress was smudged with grime as were her face and hands. Had she given up all hope of life?

Mexia took a deep breath, resolved to help the woman, but not wanting to lie to her. "I don't know."

Lila began to shut the door, but Mexia blocked it with her foot. "I have an idea, but I will need your help."

The girl nodded. Mexia stepped inside. As the men tried to enter, Mexia shook her head at them. "Let me speak with Lila alone for the time being."

Sir Randon balked. "You were not to be out of my sight for even a second, per Lord Cramer's orders."

"I will sit by the window, and you can watch me."

He hesitated. "All right. But if you move out of my line of sight, I will have to come in to get you."

"Of course."

Mexia moved over to the window and sat down on a wicker chair as Lila closed the door. Sparsely furnished, the room contained only two chairs, a worn table and a tattered, stained rug beneath it.

"How can you help me, my lady?"

"I'm a mage apprentice, and I have an idea. A rogue wizard is separating the peoples of Albion and I wish to stop him."

"What has this to do with me? My baby?"

"He has a powerful spell book. If I'm right, I may be able to find a spell that can help me to locate your baby."

"But if he's dead? My baby? What if he's dead?" Lila's voice neared hysteria.

"I don't want to get your hopes up, Lila, but—" Mexia

paused. She wanted more than anything to return Lila's baby to her, healthy and happy. But her stomach muscles clenched with the notion the baby had long since died. She really didn't want Lila to think she could work miracles, but she'd heard there was a spell that could allow a mage to change an event in the past, but only for good. Would this not qualify? And yet what if the spell didn't really exist? What if all she did was give the young girl, who couldn't have been any older than seventeen or so, false hope?

Mexia took a deep breath. "I'm not certain, but there may be something in the spell book that could help."

"A spell to bring back the dead?"

What a morbid thought. The notion brought a chill to Mexia's skin. Bringing the dead to life...well, that's what she put to rest in the cemetery only two hours earlier. "No, Lila. Something better. But I will need everyone's help who can give it to me to destroy this monster named Rosenthal."

"Rosenthal?"

Just the way the girl said his name and her eyes widened in surprise, made Mexia realize she knew him.

"You know of him?"

"Why yes, of course. He is Lord Cramer's nephew."

"Oh," Mexia groaned. The situation grew more intolerable by the minute.

"You intend to destroy him?" Lila shook her head, then began to pace, wringing her hands.

"He intends to destroy all of us. He cast a spell to set the dead to walk among us...to kill us."

"That's who did that?" Lila shuddered. "But Sir Farrington? Not him."

"No. I visited with his spirit. He guards his crypt now, but does no harm to anyone."

The girl's green eyes nearly popped out of her head, her lips parted but no words issued forth.

Mexia took a deep breath, not wanting to upset Lila any more than she had to. "He spoke with us. He said Boras stole his sword. Sir Farrington wants it back."

"His sword?" Her voice was shrill. "Nothing about me? He asked nothing about me?"

"I'm sorry, Lila. At the moment, he was pretty incensed about his sword. I'm sure it has to do with a knight feeling vulnerable, unable to protect those he loves without his weapon in hand."

"Boras." Lila nodded. "Head of the thieves' guild. It would take someone like him to attempt to steal from the crypt while the undead are roaming about." She folded her arms. "And someone like him to do such a horrid deed as to steal from a noble knight's crypt."

"I must find the sword and return it to Sir Farrington. Once I have done that, I will speak to him about you."

"You will take me with you."

"I don't know if you'll be able to see him."

"You will take me and I'll help you to get the sword."

"How?"

"Without Sir Farrington's income, my family and I were starving."

"I thought Lord Cramer fed those in need."

"The rubbish everyone leaves behind on their plates from the feasts. Since the end of trade with Barston, many of us barely make ends meet."

"We have rid the swamps of the fireballs and the cemetery of the undead. Sir Farrington said once we return his sword, he may have a way to help us get rid of the mist. If so, trade can again resume and the thievery can stop."

"Boras will never stop. He likes being the king of thieves."

"What about the others?"

"Many would like to return to their homes. Living in the sewers is not really the best way to live either."

"You will help me then?"

"Only you. I do not want the knights killing or imprisoning my friends. They steal only to stay alive, not to just reward themselves with riches at the expense of others."

"I understand. When do we go?"

"Now."

"But if we try to leave, the knights will return me to the castle where my companions are imprisoned."

"Can you not cast a sleep spell on them or something?"

"No." Mexia stood, then noticed out of the corner of her eye, Sir Randon straightened his posture as he watched her. "I have an idea though, Lila. Do you have a mirror that I may use?"

"Why yes, my lady."

"Good. Fetch it for me."

When Lila returned from her bedroom with the mirror, Mexia concentrated on her reflection, then she smiled. Through the mirror, she cast an image of herself. She had the illusionary figure seat itself in her chair as she stood out of the view of the window. Then she waited.

Lila nodded at the illusion, then joined Mexia. "Yes, the knights think it is you. Very clever, my lady."

"I've only done it once when I wanted to take a stroll with a gent and my father forbade it."

"And?"

Lila led Mexia out a back window through the bedroom.

"I got caught."

CHAPTER 11

"But you see," Mexia said to Lila as the girl stared at her in disbelief, "my illusionary spell worked fine. Only my father happened to take a stroll that night with a lady friend. Imagine both our surprise to see each other."

Lila smiled for the first time. In the lantern lights illuminating the back alley, Mexia could see how pretty Sir Farrington must have thought the redhead was.

In the shadows, Lila stopped, then pulled at a sewer grate in the center of the road. She whispered, "You do not have any money on you? Anything of value?"

"I have only the cloak I wear, and my gowns. If I am accosted, I will strike the offender with my staff. It will knock him out for a time, but I will not hesitate to protect myself."

Lila wavered.

"I cannot permit a man to steal from me, though I have very little with me at this time to rob. If any attempt to take my staff, cloak or anything else from me, he will earn my wrath. I come here to help you and the others, not to harm any. But I will defend myself against any who seek to hurt me. I will not be a victim here."

The lady nodded, her face frowning with worry. "Then you may truly be the one to help us in our time of need."

She climbed into the sewer. Her boots on the metal ladder clicked all the way down. Mexia took a deep breath, fastened her staff to her back, and then cast her protection spell. If any should attempt to accost her when she was barely on her feet in the sewers below, they wouldn't be able to come close. Still, her heart filled with dread at what she would have to face in the sewers, alone.

At the bottom rung, she stepped off, somewhat relieved to see only Lila's face watching her, her brow wrinkled with anxiety still. Mexia pulled her staff from her back and held it at the ready.

Lanterns cast bits of flickering light into the dark. Water trickled down the moss covering the stone walls, and drips dropped into puddles collected at the edges. Uneven stone walkways led through the sewers, the smell so pungent from raw sewage, rotting food, and mold, Mexia's eyes, nose, and throat burned from the noxious fumes.

"You will get used to the smell after a while," Lila whispered, then led her down a passage.

Rats squealed nearby, sending a shudder down Mexia's spine. To have to live down here must have been anyone's worst nightmares.

Suddenly, voices spoken down another passageway made Lila stop Mexia, halting her with her hand on hers. They listened, Mexia's heart beating so hard she was certain the sound would soon echo off the walls.

She recognized the boy's voice that had spoken to them in the street. "Yeah, the knights from Cramer's castle took the whole lot of them in. But then a little while ago, a couple of knights escorted one of the women to Lila's house. I could see the woman speaking with her through one of the front windows. The knights stayed outside."

"She won't give us away, will she?"

"It's about her baby, the woman sees her. Cirrus said the women and dwarf are adventurers here seeking to solve the quests posted in the guild."

A man snorted. "Right. I've heard tell of the Amazon women of Inherian. Be they these?"

"Nah. They are ordinary-sized women. Only a foot taller than me."

The sound of boots pacing back and forth across the stone walkway followed. "And the quests are?"

"The three posted since a month ago, Boras."

Boras. Mexia cringed. King of the thieves, and not one who would easily bow to her whims.

"All right. Sneak into the backside of Lila's home. Keep out of the knights' sight, but find out what the woman intends to do."

"Yes, sir." The boy ran toward Mexia, Lila, and the ladder they had just climbed down.

Lila grabbed Mexia's arm and hurried toward the ladder and beyond.

Before they could reach the next passageway, the boy shouted, "Halt! Who goes there?"

His words were not only meant to confront them, but to warn the others.

Normally, Mexia liked children. But this one was worse than any pest she'd ever encountered, despite his youthful age.

The sound of boots tromping toward them down two of the passages effectively cut them off from any chance of escape. And Mexia's hopes to garnish the thieves' willingness to help her to retrieve Sir Farrington's sword was instantly dashed.

"Wait!" the man named Boras said to his men as they drew near the women, his black eyes studying Mexia as she returned his gaze. She thought it a shame to waste such handsome strong features on a man who wallowed in the sewers as the king of thieves.

She gripped her staff tighter. If she struck him, and he collapsed in front of his men, would they give in to her? She doubted it. They'd double their efforts to best her, she was certain.

"I have come here seeking to return Sir Farrington's sword to him," Mexia said, resorting to what she thought her best ploy, and one they would totally not expect.

"I thought you said they were to solve the guild's posted quests," Boras growled at the boy. His hand flew back to strike him, but Mexia cast a spell that made the man levitate for an instant, then he dropped to his knees.

The men who'd edged closer to her, quickly took a couple of steps away from her.

"A witch?" He swore between clenched teeth. "They are witches?"

"I am a sorceress," Mexia said, trying to keep her anger from boiling over. "I am here only to help you and your people."

"You will not take over from me here."

"I wish only to help these people return to their families."

"To what? To starve? Lord Cramer taxes these people to death even if they cannot afford to pay them."

"She's already gotten rid of the fireballs in the swamps, Boras," Lila pleaded. "She's very powerful. She promises to purge the mist from there. Then we can again trade with the people of Barston."

The men around her began to converse with one another. Boras, fearing mutiny, took a step toward Mexia, but her protection spell kept him away from her as if a glass case surrounded her.

When Boras couldn't reach her, one of the men found the courage to speak. "What if she's right? What if she can aid us to live with our families again?"

Another scratched his matted chin whiskers. "I would give anything to live with my wife and two daughters like the husband and father I should be, rather than living like a sewer rat down here."

"Then we must work together to make this so," Mexia quickly said, hoping to enlist their support before they faltered under Boras's rule. "I will do everything in my power to aid you."

"She lies. What can one woman do?" Boras scoffed. He pulled out his sword threatening to harm any who disagreed with him. The men backed away from him who stood nearby, but Mexia advanced toward the thieves' leader.

She sensed the men's interest in helping her, if she could only overpower their leader now. "You only wish to keep these men here to do your bidding. You haven't their interests in mind at all. They serve you and despite having only a castle of sorts amongst the sewers and stench, you want the power these men bestow upon you."

He swung at her with his sword, but the sharp edge of steel bounced off her protective sphere. She fought the urge to cringe, hoping her protection spell would continue to work. She took another step forward, while he stepped back.

"Give these men the chance to return to their families. Or do you only strive to control them, giving them only scraps of a life to live?"

"I have kept them from starving."

"Maybe in the past. But things can be different, if we work together." She could tell from his set jaw and hard eyes, he had no intention of giving up his kingdom of slime.

"Work with me, and all will be well."

"They hang thieves in the court square. Do you remember, gents? They hang the likes of us."

"No," Mexia said. "These men are from Cramer, born and raised here. Lord Cramer wants them to pay taxes as before. If trade resumes, the men will be able to return to their farms, or other trades. There will be no need to terrorize the citizens in town any longer with your thievery."

The boy ran off, his small boots echoing off the walls with his rapid pace.

Boras glanced back at him, then to Mexia and smiled. "He will bring the others. These yellow-backed lizards may wish to desert me, but the others won't."

The men seemed uneasy, their nervous glances flittering from Mexia to their leader, as if they feared the others would kill them for faltering under the thieves' guild credence.

She raised her staff slightly. Still concerned the men would revolt against her if she struck their leader, she wished to get Boras's compliance, but reckoned he would never give it. "It's now or never." She couldn't wait until reinforcements arrived either.

Even then, she heard more footsteps behind her, but her focus remained on the greatest threat that stood before her.

"What's going on?" one of the new arrivals asked.

"The woman is a sorceress and she's going to make it so we can go home to our families," one of the men said.

"Lies!" Boras shouted, his cool being lost instantly. "The woman seeks to destroy us. She'll have us all hanging from the gallows."

Grumbled men's voices ensued.

"She wants to return my baby to me," Lila sobbed.

Everyone grew quiet as Mexia's heart ached for the young woman.

"She wants to help all of us."

"Here!" the boy shouted, this time he appeared behind Mexia, sure to stay far away from their leader. "Here is Sir Farrington's sword."

She smiled. "Thank you—

"Davin, my lady." He held out the sword to her and bowed.

Boras swore, then ran off down the passage, darting into another at the junction.

"What now, my lady?" Davin asked as the men hung close to hear her orders.

"We shall return this to Sir Farrington." She studied the ruby tongue and emerald eyes of the handle of the sword as the light reflected off the gems. "I will need an escort to take me to the cemetery, and from there, we will find the source of the mist, and end it. Afterward, the trade route must be resumed."

"At once, my lady," one of the men closest to her said.

"This isn't a trick, is it?" another asked.

"No, though I must warn you, Rosenthal is behind all of the evil that has come to this region. I vow to put an end to his devil's work."

Silence followed.

"He must be destroyed before he destroys all of us."

A man, his hair streaked gray, appearing older than the rest nodded, then knelt on one knee before her. "I will aid you, if it means I will return to my life as it was before."

"And I," another said.

Soon, the whole lot of thirty or so men knelt on bended knee, warming her heart.

She motioned to them to rise and smiled. "Come, we must hurry and return Sir Farrington's sword."

The worry now gnawed at her mind…what if Sir Farrington didn't know how to get rid of the mist? He'd only said he'd help if he could. And would he break poor Lila's heart all over again if she was able to see him at all? Would he recognize her? Show her that he still cared for her even in his present form?

She turned to the boy, Davin. "Can you carry the knight's sword for me? It would be a great honor."

His smile couldn't have stretched any farther across his grimy face.

Some of the men led the way, others followed after the two women and the boy as if protecting them in the center. After much maneuvering through the tunnels, one of the men motioned to a grate up above. "This is the closest exit to the cemetery, my lady."

She nodded.

After several of the men exited the sewers through the hole, they helped the two women up. The boy had to give up the knight's sword briefly to climb the ladder, but once he was on his feet again, the sword's grip was tightly locked between his fingers.

The men again made a circle around the women and the boy as if protecting them from unseen forces. But only the sound of the crickets singing their nightly chorus and an owl sitting on top of the crypt hooting at them, stirred in the darkness.

Several of the men carried lanterns, their eyes shifting nervously, studying the lay of the land, sure they would encounter the undead soon.

Lila, too, shivered twice, and looked about her, though under her breath she said, "See, she has done as she told us. The undead have been returned to rest." And yet her words were spoken low, as if speaking them any louder would bring the undead into the open again.

Even Mexia worried an undead creature might still stir somewhere in the dark, but none came forth, and when she reached the crypt, she took a deep breath and pulled the door open.

She motioned for only Davin and Lila to join her. "We will return shortly. Thank you for helping us," she said to the men.

With the door still partly ajar, they entered the cool, damp room. Sir Farrington hurried forward, and Davin nearly dropped the sword as Lila screamed out and fainted.

Three of the former thieves rushed into the room at the sound of Lila's scream, then stood staring at the ghostly form, their mouths agape in shock.

"You brought, you…" Sir Farrington knelt before Lila and ran a whisper of his fingers through her hair.

"She loves you very much," Mexia said, kneeling beside Lila, pulling her head into her lap. "The man who killed you, stole the baby you and she had. I want to return things the way they were before so many bad things happened."

"We had a baby?" He looked up at her, disbelief evident in his wispy wrinkled brow.

His gaze turned to the boy who stood nearby, his slight body shaking.

Davin quickly handed the sword to him and nearly dropped it when the knight smiled, then reached out his fingers for the jeweled handle.

Sir Farrington shook his head as his fingers couldn't quite grasp the metal. "Please, return my weapon there." He pointed to his sarcophagus.

Three of the men hurried to slide the stone lid aside.

Standing on tiptoes, Davin laid the sword beside the knight's body. "May you fight all of your battles well," he whispered.

The knight smiled. "You would have been my page, had I lived."

Lila groaned. Mexia and one of the men helped her to stand. She leaned on their arms as tears dribbled down her cheeks. "Harnon."

"My love." Sir Farrington leaned over to kiss her, but she sobbed aloud when they couldn't touch.

Mexia's heart clenched. She gripped Lila's arm tightly, trying to give her some of the strength she needed to see the man she loved, now only a shadow of his former self.

They stared at each other, the longing still in their unbroken gaze.

Mexia, not wanting to break the spell, but anxious to help the others said, "Sir Farrington, we need your help to end the mists that blanket the swamps."

He didn't seem to hear her as he reached his fingers to Lila's cheek. She twisted her head to nestle her face in his hand, but couldn't.

"You are a knight who has done much good for the people here. They respect you and would do anything to help you regain your former life."

The knight turned to her.

"I must have your help, and in return, I will do everything I can to aid you once again. You and Lila and your baby."

Still, he waited to hear more.

"The men will trade with Barston once the mists have evaporated." She took a deep breath. "I must find a way to kill Rosenthal."

Muttered words from the men escaped their lips.

The knight nodded. "Deep in the swamps there is a hot spring. Cap this, and the mist will no longer form across the swamps."

"Where in the swamps? Can you be more specific?"

"In the northeast corner. You will find a mountain ridge where the swamps end. The same ridge continues all the way to Barston."

"Ah, the same one that Dragonmage's castle sits upon."

"In the far north, yes."

She turned to the men. "Are you game? Or will you wait for me here?"

"We will go with you."

"Lila? Will you wait for us here?"

"Oh, yes, my lady. I wish to speak with my husband further."

Mexia ran her hand over Lila's hair. "Stay here, then. Once we have accomplished our task, we will return here for you." She turned to Davin. "Will you stay and protect Lila, if she needs your protection?"

"But I wished to go with you."

"Perhaps, you could serve Sir Farrington as his page, even now."

Davin looked up at the knight who nodded.

"I would be honored to have you serve me now and help to protect my ladylove."

Mexia gave Lila a squeeze, then headed out of the crypt with the three men.

"Can you stop the mist?" the one asked her as she considered the path into the swamps.

"I do not have the map through this maze," she said, realizing that the princess had drawn it, but kept the map with her.

One of the men pulled out a piece of leather parchment. "We used to come this way frequently, my lady. But even with the trails marked, we cannot see for the thick fog."

She drank from her flask, then passed Modi's tea around to the men. "It will aid you to see more clearly in the mist."

Considering the shortest route to the mountain ridge, she pointed at the path. "Advise me which way to go as we head for this point on the map. I will walk in front in case any of this takes us on paths I have not already passed over."

"You mean because of the fireballs?"

"Yes, one of my lady companions has the map she drew of the region, but I would not know for certain if I have passed this way before."

"But the fireballs will kill you, my lady."

She smiled. "They give me strength."

But could she cap the hole that caused the steam to rise and cloaked the area in the dangerous mist? Maybe through their united strength, she could.

Then the owl she'd seen sitting on the crypt flew overhead, screeching in the darkness as if it'd found its prey. The sound sent a trickle of fear down her spine. What if it was Rosenthal's familiar? Sent to spy on her?

Would he lie in wait for her, not pretending to be wounded this time in the form of Derek, but something much more deadly when she reached her destination?

CHAPTER 12

Mexia walked forward, urging everyone to stay behind her. For several minutes, they maneuvered through the swamp maze path without incident. Except for the bugs' noisy night conversation and the men and Mexia's footfalls, nothing else made a sound. Then the light glowed softly on her belt buckle, warning her of impending danger. She motioned for everyone to stop.

When they did as she asked, she took a step forward. Despite knowing the belt would protect her, she still clenched her teeth and tightened her stomach muscles in dreaded anticipation. Her belt instantly took the impact of the heated flame as several cries were heard from her newest companions. For a second, she breathed in a couple of breaths to calm herself.

Silence followed.

She turned back to smile at the men as they waited, their mouths dropped in surprise, then waved at them to continue. Now she knew she hadn't been this way before though, and the same worry she'd be too reckless gnawed at her mind.

The looks on her companions' faces, too, gave her pause. Most were mixed with awe and disbelief. If they'd been unsure as to whether she was more powerful than Boras, they'd probably be convinced by now.

The mist grew thicker and she assumed it was because they drew nearer its source. Her heartbeat grew more rapid. Would Rosenthal be there, too? Or was he busy elsewhere creating more havoc?

"There!" one of the men shouted.

Mexia nearly jumped out of her skin as she'd been so tense, concentrating so hard as she searched for the source of the mist. She glanced back at the mountainside and had an idea. She'd been able to move boulders in Inherian when need be. If she could create an avalanche from the rocks teetering on the slopes above, could she then maneuver them toward the crater? Sure, on solid ground she could, but could she manage them over the swampy water and into the hole?

Concentrating on the rocks, she worked her spell. A rumbling followed. Several small stones rolled down the hill. Then suddenly a whole slew of them careened in a giant waterfall of debris with a thunderous roar.

She and several of the men coughed in the wake of the dust sent flying. When the particles settled, the rocks sat at the front of the ridge. She began to move them across the swamp, but as she did so, the men gathered up smaller rocks and tossed them toward the crater. The rocks clunked against each other, then splashed into the crater, hidden partially by the moss-blanketed water.

For two hours, they worked at it, until all at once the mist which had decreased to a trickle, stopped completely.

Mexia smiled and wiped her hands off on her skirt. "I believe you should ready your wagons for trade with Barston, gentlemen."

"You have done a great service for us, my lady. How can we repay you?"

"Only do what is right from now on. Take care of your families."

"What about Lila? You cannot mean to promise her the return of her baby. He would most likely be dead by now."

Her stomach knotted with the notion she might not be able to return Lila's baby to her, but she had every intention of trying. "I will do everything in my power to aid Lila in reuniting her with her baby."

"If you ever need our further assistance, you only have to ask."

The men all kneeled before her. She smiled. "I only did what any adventurer would have done for you."

"No, there have been none who would have concerned themselves with our plight since all we were to them were just a pack of thieves."

"You are no longer thieves. I must return now to Lila's home before the knights discover we're missing."

As they made their way back to the crypts, a breeze had already begun to clear out the remaining mist from the swamps to Mexia's relief.

But when she entered the crypt, she was surprised to find only the boy and Lila.

"Where is your husband?" Mexia asked.

"Asleep," Lila said, her eyes shimmering with tears. "He is resting."

"He told me some of his knightly tales," the boy said with enthusiasm.

Mexia smiled at the boy. "Good." Then she quickly turned her attention to Lila. "We must return to your house before the knights find us missing," Mexia urged, certain Lila didn't want to leave the sacred place where her husband remained, but afraid the whole lot of them would be caught running through the city during curfew. Then what would happen? She didn't even want to think of that scenario.

The men escorted them back to the town, then disbursed quickly to their homes before anyone saw them roaming about while the area was under curfew. Davin remained with Lila and Mexia.

"Where are your parents?" Mexia asked him.

He shook his head. "They died last month."

"Will you take him in, Lila?"

She nodded.

Before they could make it down one of the alleys that led back to Lila's home, they heard horses' hooves pounding the cobble-stone path.

"Lord Cramer has sent out the guard," Lila said. "He does it when several are sighted, disobeying his curfew."

"Or they have discovered us missing from your home." Mexia's stomach tightened with worry that the men had not had time to make it to their homes. Had the men caused the alarm to go off? She figured she and Lila could talk themselves out of whatever situation they found themselves in much more easily then the men could if they got caught.

Still, she hoped to make it back to the house before they realized she and Lila weren't there, if they didn't already know it.

A knight shouted in their direction as they turned a corner. The boy ran off and Mexia's heart lurched for him.

"He will make it back to the house," Lila said as she grabbed Mexia's hand and ran her down another alley.

"The two women ran this way!" a knight yelled.

The horses' hooves again clattered on the stone as they turned direction. They grew closer to Mexia and Lila who darted down another alleyway.

"Are we getting closer to your house?" Mexia whispered, her breath short.

"No, my lady. We are getting farther from there. They're effectively blocking our way to my place."

"We'll be back in the cemetery before long." Mexia took a deep breath trying to calm her disquiet as they hid behind barrels next to a shop. "Should we slip back into the sewers?"

Lila hesitated. "Boras is probably still down there. Since you have turned his men against him, he would be a deadly adversary."

"Can you take me to the man's home who has lost his goat?"

"Pemlican? I might be able to get you there, but why?"

"I need to help him return his goat."

"Everyone says the goblins have taken it. You will never get it back."

"Why? Do they eat them?"

Lila frowned at her. "No, my lady. But if you run into them, they send you to another place."

"How can they do this? They have no magic, do they?"

"The mountains are magical. Anyone who goes there never returns."

Old wives' tale.

"What about the family whose young daughter was taken? The butcher and his wife?"

"The other quests. You are thinking of taking care of the other quests, even though Lord Cramer wishes to have you locked up in the castle."

Mexia smiled. "I have several jobs to do. Lord Cramer will not keep me confined. But I do need to free my friends as well."

"My lady," a small voice whispered. "Where are you?"

"Davin?" Mexia whispered back.

Silently, he crept forward on little cat paws. "I thought they caught you. I got to Lila's house and there you were...only it wasn't you. And one of the knights was talking to you, but you didn't speak. Then he grabbed your arm, and his hand slipped right through you. Then he hollered out in fright. The others are looking for you now. One was left behind in case Lila or you returned. We cannot go there now."

"Do you know how to get into the castle?"

"But they will lock you away," the boy said, his voice tinged with surprise.

"I must free my friends so that we may continue with our quests."

He smiled. "Will you take me with you?"

"I must first see the butcher and his wife, and the man who lost his goat. If you can get me there—"

"She is attempting to solve the quests," Lila said when his eyes widened.

"The butcher's house is not far from here." He looked beyond the barrel, then motioned for them to come.

The three dashed into the street, sticking to the shadows as the sound of hooves against stone resounding down the next street, met their ears. Shouts of the soldiers made Mexia's skin crawl as Lila's eyes grew wide with fear.

"They cannot have gotten that far!" one of the knights called out.

"It'll be our heads if we lose her," another responded, his voice desperate and on edge.

"Here." Davin pointed to the butcher's shop as they ducked behind two crates. He pulled out a set of keys. "I'll unlock the back door, and once I have it open, you both run for it."

Until now, Mexia had never assumed knowing a thief could have been good luck. "Go, then. We'll be right behind you."

Davin darted for the door, struggled for a few seconds, then opened it with a creak. He waved vigorously for them to follow, then shook his head quickly and shut the door.

Three knights rode by. "I swear I heard something over here."

"Rats."

The horses clip-clopped on their way.

Without waiting for a second more to slip by, Mexia ran for the door. Lila followed on her skirt tail, the two of them making hardly a sound, except for their rapid breathing.

When they reached the door, Mexia grabbed the handle. Twisting with a jerk, she discovered it locked. Fear trickled down her spine.

More shouts nearby nearly gave her a heart attack as her heart leapt in her chest. Then the door handle twisted in her fingers.

With a creak, the door opened. Before Mexia could enter, a man-sized hand reached out from the darkened house, grabbed her arm and yanked her inside.

She stifled the scream that attempted to escape her lips, her heart beating at twice its normal pace. Lila was jerked into the house beside her, her scream stifled by someone's hand, Mexia assumed. The door shut behind them. The lock clicked close after that.

From the blackness, a gruff voice said, "The boy says you're here to find my daughter. But I say you're nothing but a pack of thieves and liars."

"I am Lady Mexia of Damar in Inherian, a mage apprentice of the house of Sal. But I am also a member of the adventurers' guild in Barston."

"Women are not members of adventurers' guilds."

Mexia rolled her eyes and she folded her arms. "I am here to help find your daughter."

"She has already done much for us, Gandon. She has cleared the swamps for our people to once again trade with the people of Barston."

A flame flickered in a lantern, casting eerie shadows on their faces, the butcher's thick brown hair disheveled as if he'd just fallen out of bed. Nearby, a slightly younger man held Davin still, his brown hair in the same disarray.

"I told them," Davin said, "but they wouldn't believe me."

The younger man held up the boy's keys. "And why should we, when you have tools of the thieves' trade?"

"She wants to help return Pemlican's goat to him. And she wants to get my baby back to me." Lila's words were choked with tears.

"Your baby and the goat are dead," Gandon said, dryly.

"And your daughter? Maybe she is dead, too." Lila glared at the butcher.

Fiery embers burned in the man's black eyes. He released Mexia's arm. "What do you propose to do?"

"I need to know what happened, first. But Lila requires a place to rest for the night and so does Davin. Then you and I must talk."

"I must help you, my lady," the boy pleaded. "I will show you the way into Lord Cramer's castle."

"Yes, you will. But later…after we have all had some sleep."

"Why do you wish to enter Lord Cramer's castle?" the man asked, his voice lowered with suspicion, his eyes narrowed.

"My friends are being kept there against their will."

"More thieves?"

"No. We were being detained because a wizard has some misconception I am to be his betrothed."

White teeth shown in a bed of brown whiskers as the man smiled at her. "It seems he shall have a time making that come to pass."

"Yes. He will."

The butcher waved at the younger man. "My brother. Take Lila and the boy to the loft." Turning to Mexia he said, "Why would Lord Cramer detain you and your companions?"

"Prince Derek offered him a reward to keep us as Lord Cramer's guests until Derek graduated from the wizard's school.

In two days' time he shall return, so I must attempt to solve the quests posted in the guild before this happens."

Again the butcher smiled. "He will have to pay a pretty price for you, no?" He motioned to the common area. "Sit, and we shall talk."

Mexia sat on a wooden chair padded with a goose down pillow. "What happened between you and the pig farmer?"

"We had agreed on a price. I was to butcher the pig for Caron and he was to pay me four goldens. After I had cut up the pig just like he wanted, he said I had stolen some of the choicest parts and refused to pay me the agreed upon price. I wouldn't let him have the pig until he paid me in full."

"Had he paid you at all?"

"No. He offered me half of what we had agreed upon. I wouldn't accept his money."

"Did Lord Cramer not help to decide the matter?"

"Caron stole my daughter before a trial could start."

"Why did he think you had taken some of his pig?"

"The man was crazy. How do I know what ailed him?"

The butcher shoved his hands in his pockets and avoided her gaze. Certain the butcher hadn't been completely honest with her, she assumed Caron had a legitimate grievance. But could a pig farmer win in a trial against a successful merchant? Maybe not. Still, stealing the butcher's daughter was unforgivable.

"Are you certain Caron stole your daughter? That it wasn't someone else who would have done such a deed?"

"No one else would have done anything so hideous."

"Has he fled the town then?"

"Yes. And gone into the mountains of Monrovia."

"Where no one returns?

The man's eyes filled with tears and Mexia's own puddled up.

"May I rest a while? I'm very tired. In a few hours, I will leave here and return to Lord Cramer's castle. I must free my friends, and we will go to the mountains. If we have any luck at all, we will return your daughter to you."

"You will be like the others…never returning."

"I have to risk it."

He nodded, then escorted her to the loft.

"I will sleep for four hours. Can you wake me after this? We must be on our way."

"I can do this."

"Good. Thank you for helping us."

"It is I who should be grateful for your attempting to return my daughter."

"I only pray that we shall be successful."

Mexia lay down next to the boy and Lila, both who snored softly in their sleep. She hoped when the boy helped her into the castle, they'd have no difficulty, but she worried before this, a house to house search would soon be performed. Would Lord Cramer lock her away in a tower to keep her from escaping him again? That's what she worried about more than anything as she attempted to clear her mind of such notions and drift off to sleep.

$\sim$

*B*efore the butcher could wake her, banging on the door downstairs made her bolt upright.

Davin wiped the sleep from his eyes. Then jumped up from the mattress. "They've come for us," he whispered.

Lila opened her eyes. "What's going on?"

Mexia peered out a window from the third level of the house. "The soldiers are doing a house by house search. I feared they might."

"What are we to do?" Lila asked.

Mexia knew she had to leave Lila behind, but when the soldiers questioned Lila, would she give Davin and Mexia's plans away? Certain Lila would, Mexia had to give her different plans to throw the men off.

"It is too dangerous for Davin and me to attempt to go to Lord Cramer's castle now. We will go to Barston instead where I have made several friends. They will aid me for having helped them before."

"And me? What shall I tell them when they ask me?"

Mexia smiled. "Tell them the truth. I will return in a couple of days. Lord Cramer has no business holding my friends' hostage. And Prince Derek will not pay for their release either. He only wants me."

Mexia embraced Lila. "I will return as soon as I am able." Turning to Davin, Mexia said, "How do we get out of here without being seen by the soldiers?"

The butcher had tried to keep the soldiers from entering the house, but now, they could hear the men tromping through the rooms while the butcher yelled at them. "What is wrong with you, men? There is no one here other than my wife and baby."

A howling baby cried some distance away followed by a woman's distressed voice. "What is wrong, love? Why are these men here?"

Davin looked out the window and pointed to a trellis attached to the wall. The last time Mexia had climbed one of those, she fell. She took a deep breath and nodded.

"I will go first, my lady."

"And you will catch me if I fall?" she teased.

He smiled at her. "Yes, my lady. As a page to a knight would do."

Within seconds, he had scrambled to the ground. She pulled at the trellis, then as she heard the sound of boots tromping to the second floor, she hurried down the vine-covered sticks laced together.

Before they could move, Lila began the climb down. "Go! I

will run the opposite direction away from you, and that will give you more time to get away. Plus, the butcher will not be implicated for hiding us."

As soon as her feet touched the ground, she took off running. Davin grabbed Mexia's hand, but she said to him in a hurry, "Take me to the castle."

"But you said—"

"Yes."

He smiled at her. "Of course, my lady. This way."

When he motioned to a sewer grate, she hesitated. "Boras."

"Yes, my lady, but you have powers. Come. It is the only way. Besides, he will not expect us to return to them."

They pulled the grate aside. Voices grew near, and Davin said, "Go! Follow the path that leads directly south. Never stray from the southern passageway. Good luck."

"But—"

"I will give them a run for their wages."

Mexia took a deep breath and nodded. "Thank you, Davin."

With heavy heart, she slipped into the sewer tunnels as the grate slid with a groan back in place overhead.

Pulling her staff from her back, she held it at the ready then ran south, hoping the path would remain clear until she reached her destination...Lord Cramer's castle. Then what? Would she find a doorway, another sewer grate? How could she get in without a key?

Other than her footsteps padding along the moist walkway, the dripping of water, the blood rushing through her ears, and an occasional squeal of a rat, she heard no other sounds.

Still, she strained to listen for the echo of men's voices or footsteps in the event Boras, or even some of his most stalwart thugs who remained loyal to him, attempted to stop her. Then she wondered what she would do once she sneaked into the castle.

Where would the path lead her? How could she get the ladies and Gallant out without being seen or heard?

Her thoughts reverted to the tunnels as she heard rough male laughter followed by a couple of curses, all coming from the juncture to her path. She eased up to the connecting east/west passageway, hoping the men were well out of view at a bend, maybe, in their path.

Before she could peek around the corner, the splashing of boots in the water behind her made her turn, while her heart pounded like thunder.

CHAPTER 13

Mexia didn't have time to react as the bearded, smudge-faced man ran his fist into her cheek.

The next thing she remembered, smallish fingers tugged at her hand. "My lady," Davin whispered, repeating his words over and over.

Her head hurt like the devil. She opened her eyes, fearing the worst.

"What happened?" she whispered, as she attempted to sit up on the cot her body reclined on. Wincing, she touched her face, her cheek, swollen and sore.

"I followed you down here after I made the soldiers chase me for some distance. I wanted to make sure you found your way to your friends once you were inside the castle. But then I saw Bear hit you before I could warn you. I tackled him, and they brought me here with you. As I hoped they would. Together, maybe we can figure some way to get out of here."

She lay back on the cot and stared up at the stalactite-decorated ceiling. "What do we do now?"

"They took my keys from me. Said if I wasn't going to be a thief any longer, I didn't need the tools of the trade." He pointed to the door. "Besides, I could have unlocked the door if they'd let me keep the keys."

Mexia narrowed her eyes as the side of her head burned as if it was on fire. "What did they leave me with?" She couldn't raise her head again without inflicting more pain. For the moment, her heart pumped unsteadily, filled with defeat.

"They took your staff, my lady. I'm truly sorrow. They didn't take any of your clothing though. If you'd been a man, they would have. But being a woman, they wouldn't. Bear only hit you because he was afraid you'd cast a spell on him first. Otherwise, he'd have never hit a woman."

"That doesn't endear him to me. Sorry." She slipped her hand into her cloak pocket and smiled. Boras's key that had lain next to the sarcophagus. Pulling it out, she showed it to Davin. "What does this unlock? Do you have any idea?"

His eyes widened as his mouth gaped wide open. "Where did you get that, my lady?"

"In the crypt. Sir Farrington said Boras dropped it beside his sarcophagus when he stole the knight's sword. I guess he was in a hurry to get out of there."

"It's a skeleton key. It'll open any door, anywhere. Boras had Rosenthal make it for him with his magic. For days, Boras has been roaring around the place, furious, thinking that someone stole his key." Davin smiled. "And now you have it."

"Can it unlock the door?"

"Yes, truly it can unlock anything."

Though the notion gave her some comfort, she could barely move. "I cannot even sit up without my stomach rocking like a boat on unsettled seas." She reached into her pocket again, then pulled out a healing kit. "If my head didn't hurt so, I'd heal myself with a spell, but alas, I cannot. Lay this across my cheek, will you, Davin?"

"Oh, yes, my lady. A page should know some healing skills as he serves his knight, should he not?"

She smiled. "Yes, Davin, he should."

The cool patch eased the ache, but before she could fight the effects of the medication, she drifted out of consciousness.

Much later that morning she heard voices, men's harsh voices speaking in muffled tones on the other side of the room.

"She's been out for hours. What the hell did you hit her so hard fer, Bear?" a man asked.

"She's got magic. What did you expect me to do? We were all warned to take her down before she cast a spell on us."

"She didn't cast one on us before, you imbecile. She only used one fer her own protection."

Mexia lay still, trying to think of a spell that she could use on the men to aid Davin and her, though she hadn't heard his voice once. Her stomach clenched with worry instantly. What if they'd removed him from the room? Or worse, had harmed him for helping her?

"What's Boras going to do with Davin?"

"Send him to the mountains. He won't last long there. He knew what would happen, if'n he ever turned on us."

She had to peek at the men if she was going to manage a spell. A love spell. No. Mind control. She lifted her lashes slightly. The men faced each other. Good.

The one man turned to face her. "She's awake."

"Good. You're coming with us, young lady." The man named Bear grabbed her arm.

She began her incantation. "No longer free on water, nor on land, you will do as I command."

Bear instantly dropped his grip on her arm. "We will take you to the castle." His words were spoken in a slow-paced, monotonous monotone.

The other, red bearded and as grungy as Bear said, "Davin is sleeping in the room next door. I will get him for you." He sounded just like Bear.

She smiled, thrilled her spell worked so well. "Good. Go now. And hurry."

She slid from the bed, her face healed, her head and stomach back to normal, to her relief. As she took a step toward the door, the verdigris-coated brass handle twisted with an ear-shattering squeak.

Taking a calming breath, she waited.

Davin pulled the door open, then ran to her. "What is going on?" he whispered. "Red is acting really strange. Smiled at me and everything. That's not a good sign."

"They are escorting us to the castle. Have you got the key, or have I?"

"You do, my lady."

"Come, then, let us get out of here before we have more trouble," she said with urgency.

Davin glanced over at Bear who smiled back at him. He shook his head. "I don't know what you did to them, but," Davin said, then laughed, "it sure is funny."

They stepped into the passageway with Bear leading the way and Red following behind them.

"If anyone asks, Bear, you are escorting us to see Boras."

"Escorting you to see Boras."

"The same for you, Red. You are escorting the lady and Davin to see Boras."

"To see Boras."

"Yes."

Davin shook his head again, the smile tweaking his lips upward. "I wish I could be a mage."

"A page is what you will be."

He smiled at her. "Thanks for helping me, my lady."

She ran her hand over his tawny blond hair. "You deserve a better life."

They traveled east for quite a way, and she realized then that if she'd freed herself, she'd have been roaming in the sewers underneath the city for ages, totally lost. Davin truly had been a godsend. She squeezed his hand as he smiled up at her again.

Then they turned south.

When she looked down at Davin to confirm their path, he nodded. "Are we getting close?" she whispered as the sounds of men voices echoed in the distance, the concern returning as her heartbeat quickened.

"Yes, my lady." Then he grabbed her hand and pulled her forward. "Run!"

Bear stepped out of their path, his face confused.

She turned back to him. "Don't let anyone follow us, Bear, Red. Stop them if they try to come after us. Stop them!"

"Stop them," the two men said, blocking the path behind Mexia and Davin as they retreated in haste.

Shouts followed and then the fists flew as she looked back. Bear and Red fought the men who attempted to run after Mexia and Davin.

Curses filled the air as Davin took the key from Mexia, then inserted it in an iron grate door. Once on the other side, he quickly locked it back up.

Then he slipped the key into her cloak pocket and took her hand. "No one but Boras could make it through that gate. And now that you have the key, even he cannot follow us."

"That is good to know," Mexia said, sighing deeply as she glanced back to see two of the men get by Bear and Red. Both bared their yellow teeth in a menacing growl and though she assumed they couldn't reach the boy and her, she still hurried her pace away from the gate.

Davin pulled her through a narrow passageway soon afterward. "The kitchen is off this passage. Boras would sneak in here to get food for us. But he often kept the best stuff for himself."

He motioned to a ladder. "It's still early. The meal won't be prepared for another half hour or so."

She grabbed the first rung of the ladder.

He took her hand. "Let me go first. Make sure there's nobody about. I'm smaller."

Feeling protective, she shook her head. "I can cast a spell."

Smiling at her, he said, "You sure can, my lady." He hurried up the ladder as she waited.

Her heartbeat still pounded faster than normal after their narrow escape, and now, they were back in the snake pit where Lord Cramer wished to keep them prisoner in the first place. She'd kill Prince Derek when she saw him again.

Davin opened the grate, then motioned to her. "No one here yet."

She hurried up the ladder as fast as she was able, but regretted leaving her magical staff behind. It had saved her life more than once before in her journeys across the continent of Inherian and now Albion. The notion she had lost her staff made her feel as though she'd let the soothsayer, Modi, down. But beyond that, she wasn't certain she'd be successful fighting her way through the rest of their perils without her weapon in her grasp.

"Where did they take my staff?" Mexia asked Davin, not able to shake loose of the worry over it.

"My lady, Boras was carrying it around like a trophy for a while. But we cannot go back for it now."

"It was a gift to me, Davin. It is part of me. I cannot explain."

Davin shook his head. "It is too dangerous, my lady. Maybe when your companions are with us, we can return for it."

Then she considered their situation. Yes. She could use the princess's staff in the meantime while the princess used her scepter. But Mexia would return for her staff. What if Boras could yield it against others like she could? He would use it for no good. She would have to return for it, as soon as she was able.

After Mexia and Davin replaced the grate, he led her through the massive kitchen where stacks of firewood already rested beneath the black cauldrons.

"They'll be fixing the morning meal soon." He motioned to a hall. "Your dwarf friend would be staying with the servants. We'll have to try to get his attention without him getting too loud about it. The only thing is, this is the male servant's wing, and the men will be sleeping without any...well, a lady shouldn't be in there."

She raised her brows.

He ran his fingers through his hair.

"I'm afraid if you try to wake him, he'll grouch and wake the whole place up. He might even say you're a thief or something. Then we'll be in real trouble. Can you locate him first for me? Then I can come in afterward and go straight to where he's sleeping? I'm not sure I can wake him without him being loud, but he'll know I'm not a thief at least."

Davin took a deep breath. "All right, my lady." He slipped into the room where bedding was scattered all over the big hall.

Snores drifted to her. She yawned and stretched her arms, not having quite had enough sleep herself.

Two voices conversing in the hallway behind her made her duck quickly into the men's sleeping quarters. Nearly tripping over a man sleeping on his bedding on the floor, she clasped her hand over her mouth to keep from crying out.

He stirred.

She moved away from him, looking for signs of Davin. Then she saw him halfway across the hall next to the wall on one side. Being used to watching for danger on his treks, she imagined Gallant slept with his back to the wall as a precaution.

Davin looked up, then motioned for her to join him.

Tiptoeing, she tried to maneuver through the bodies without

stepping on anyone. Then to her surprise, a hand reached out and grabbed her ankle. Again she squashed the scream of surprise that nearly broke free of her lips.

"Whatcha doing in her, sweetie?"

She cast a spell, making him forget what he was doing. He turned his back to her and began to snore.

A sleep spell. That's what she needed to learn in addition to the vanishing one she had to master.

Continuing forth, she noticed some of the men stirring, their blanket shifting over their bodies. One suddenly rose from his bedding with his back to her, his lean body as naked as the day he was born. She quickly averted her eyes.

When she reached Gallant, she leaned over him and whispered, "Gallant, it is me, Mexia. Be very quiet."

His beady eyes popped open, then his mouth did the same. "Woman!"

"Shhh," she warned him.

He grabbed up his bedding, stuck it under his arm, then hurried with her out of the hall while the room began to stir before the bell rang, waking everyone for morning chores.

As soon as they were away from the room, Davin said, "Do you know how to get to the women's floor?"

"Yes."

"I will stay here with the dwarf."

"Gallant," he corrected the boy, his voice gruff. "What's he doing here?"

"I'll explain later. Where will we meet you?" Mexia asked.

"In the courtyard…the gardens. There is a sewer grate near there."

"How do you know so much—"

"My father was one of the gardeners."

She nodded. "I will meet you as soon as I get the ladies."

Mexia hurried to the stairs that led to the women's quarters, hoping that the princess and Kersta wouldn't have a guard posted.

But as soon as she reached the landing, she knew she was in trouble as she heard Lord Cramer's voice from beyond the curve in the hallway.

"What do you mean the women escaped? There was no sign of Lila?"

"No, my lord. We're still doing a house-by-house search. But there's no sign of either woman or the boy, Davin."

"Have they returned to the sewers then?"

"We fear so. But another development has arisen. Several of the villagers have headed out of town toward Barston with wagons loaded with merchandise. When asked what they thought they were doing, they said, 'Lady Mexia has cleared our way to begin trade again. And in doing so, she has ended the thievery in the city, except for a few diehards.' Do you not think, my lord, that keeping her companions prisoner is not entirely civil when she has helped our townsfolk so?"

"Prince Derek is a powerful mage. I would not wish to see what would happen if he does not find his bride-to-be here when he returns tomorrow evening after his school graduation."

Mexia fumed as she folded her arms. Powerful mage. Next time she had a chance, she'd show that powerful mage a thing or two.

Footsteps began to approach her. Mexia ducked into a ladies' chamber. A lady screamed out, sitting naked in her bath, while two others who attended her cried out in surprise also.

Mexia smiled at them. "Hello."

Then she dashed to the window, her heart thundering again as she tried to figure out how she'd get out of this predicament, knowing full well the soldiers would investigate quickly.

Two knights barged through the door, slamming it with a thunderous bang against the wall. The lady in her bath and her companions screamed out again.

The bell for morning chores rang throughout the castle, adding to the ruckus while Mexia scrambled down a trellis beneath the window.

"She went out the window!" one of the ladies in the room said.

Mexia looked up to see the knights peering out the window at her.

Then Lord Cramer's head poked outside. "Blasted! Get her before she injures herself, or gets away again!"

As soon as Mexia's boots touched the ground, she ran for the gardens. Then a different bell rang, the warning one. Soldiers hurried out of the barracks into the courtyard.

Dashing into the flower gardens, Mexia hoped the sewer grate would be nearby.

"Over here!" Davin waved from behind a shrub, then pointed at the ground.

"I didn't get the ladies," Mexia cried out, her voice nearly breaking.

"They've already gone down there with Gallant, my lady."

She climbed down into the sewer, her heart still unsettled. Davin followed her and pulled the grate back in place.

"Princess, Kersta," Mexia said as she reached the floor, then hugged them both. She still couldn't believe they were together once again.

They wrinkled their noses at her, and she smiled. "We will all need baths after this. You'll get used to it after a while."

Davin pointed the way. "We must hurry. The soldiers will most likely follow us."

"Where is my staff?" Mexia asked him.

"Oh, my lady, if Boras does not have it on him, it will be in his room."

"Then we must go there."

"It is not the way we wish to go."

"It is the only way that I wish to go."

"All right. Adults always know better."

Mexia smiled. If she had a son, he would be like Davin.

He ran as fast as his short legs would carry him, down one passageway, then switching to another. They heard the sound of the soldiers entering the sewers afterward, clomping down the metal rungs, their boots stomping on the stone walkway after this, and muffled shouts.

Davin said, "They do not know their way around down here. But Boras and the rest of his men will."

"Just take us to his room."

After several more minutes, Davin pointed to a door at the end of a path. "His room is there. A staff isn't his usual weapon. A dagger is, so he might not be carrying the staff around…too cumbersome."

Mexia ran to the end of the path with Davin while the others kept watch. Listening at the door, she heard no sounds inside. With a twist of the handle, she found the door locked. Mexia turned the key in the hole, then Davin pushed the door open. She smiled.

Her staff lay on Boras's ratty, patched and torn quilt-covered bed. So much for being the king of the sewer rats…not much luxury here.

Rushing across the room, she hurried to retrieve her weapon. As soon as her fingers touched the smooth wood, they heard shouts. "Curses!" Mexia cried out, her stomach knotting.

She and Davin ran back toward the door. Before she could leave the room though, Davin called out to her companions, "Come in here, this way!

"What, Davin?" she said, her voice incredulous.

"There's a secret way out of here. Boras figured if he needed, he would leave everyone behind and escape."

The princess and Kersta sprinted for the room as Gallant

attempted to catch up.

As soon as they were in the room, Davin locked the door, then bolted it. He pointed to the bed. "A tunnel is located underneath there."

"Do you know where it leads to?"

"Beyond the city. We have to do a fair amount of crawling though. I sneaked in here once to see where it led to."

"They're in there!" a man shouted outside of the room.

"Break it down then!" another added.

"Soldiers?" Mexia asked.

"Yes," the princess said.

The companions moved the bed away from the wall and uncovered the tunnel. Davin grabbed the lantern sitting on a crooked table situated next to the bed while Kersta pulled out the fairy wand.

Mexia crawled into the tunnel after Davin, the princess following her, while Kersta argued with Gallant about going last.

Finally Gallant growled, "Go, woman, now!"

"What made you enter the gardens?" Mexia asked the princess.

"Gallant tossed a rock into our open window. When we looked out, we saw Davin and Gallant waving for us to come at once."

"We didn't hesitate," Kersta said, "figuring they knew where you were."

"Yeah, I was attempting to rescue you, but ended up narrowly escaping from the bedchambers next to yours instead."

The tunnel smelled earthy, but better than the sewers. After crawling for several minutes, Mexia said, "By the time we leave here, we will really need a bath. Is there any place we can go to get cleansed up before we travel into the mountains, Davin?"

"Hot springs, but I've heard something lives there...something evil."

CHAPTER 14

Mexia climbed out of the hole after Davin and squinted her eyes in the bright sunlight. At once her heart skipped a beat as relief washed over her to be free from the dank, dark hole.

Blue-green needled fir trees clustered at the bottom of the mountains and to the east, a neat little stone house stood. Smoked curled from the chimney located to one side of the home and the smell of pork drifted to them.

"Pemlican's house," Davin said.

"The man who's missing his goat?"

"Yes. He's a hermit."

Mexia's stomach grumbled.

The princess motioned to the house. "Perhaps we can buy breakfast."

Mexia studied her companions, their faces and garments all smudged with dirt. She smiled. "We look a sight."

"Perhaps he will let us bathe in the horse's trough," Davin said. "Though I do not see that any of us look that bad."

They strode quickly to the house, in case the soldiers broke into Boras's room and discovered the tunnel.

The princess knocked on the door while the others wiped their hands on their clothes. Mexia looked down at her palms, her fingers remained dirty.

A gray-haired and bearded man pulled the door open, his bright blue eyes examining each of the companions. "What are you here for?"

"We've come to help find your goat."

"Isabelle? She's gone. Just like my family." He began to shut the door, but the princess stopped him with her foot blocking it.

"We are here in Cramer to help those in need. We wish to help you also. But first, we seek a meal that we will pay good money for, then be on our way."

He opened the door. "You look like you are chimney cleaners. Why would any that look as grungy as you, go on such a difficult quest?"

"We made a narrow escape through a tunnel to get here." The princess smiled to see the man's mouth drop open in surprise.

"And why would you be needing to escape from any?"

Mexia cleared her throat. "I do not wish to marry a man. My friends helped me to escape him."

"Oh." Pemlican motioned to a table. "Have some seats. I will feed you."

"Can we wash up somewhere?"

The man turned to Mexia. "Out back. There's a waterfall that cascades over the mountain. Water's a might cold, but it'll get you clean."

"I'll wait for the hot springs," Gallant said. "Don't like cold baths."

"I can't wait," Mexia said, and headed outside with Kersta and the princess following on her heels.

When Gallant and the boy joined them, Mexia turned to face them. "Where are the two of you going?"

"I will watch for trouble while ye bathe."

"I'm not going to be left behind," Davin answered.

Mexia pulled off her cloak and backpack. "You run into the house and talk to Pemlican. See if you can find out anything further about our journey. And don't come back until we're through. Gallant will stand guard while we wash."

The boy grumbled under his breath all the way back to the house.

The princess pulled off her cloak and laid her weapons on top of them. "We cannot take the boy with us on our journey."

"He is an orphan. I'm afraid he will be imprisoned for helping us to escape, Princess Talamaya. What else can we do?"

"It will be too dangerous for him to continue with us, Mexia."

Kersta slipped out of her skirt, then blouse. "I agree with the princess. We cannot take the boy."

Mexia took a deep breath. "Perhaps he can stay with Pemlican, if he will. Davin's helped me an awful lot. I wouldn't want any harm to come to him." She quickly unbraided her hair, then slipped under the waterfall with her vial of soap in hand. Immediately, she cried out as the icy water hit her skin, goose bumps trailing down every exposed inch.

Gallant whipped around, his war hammer in hand ready to do battle.

"Turn around!" Mexia shouted as the other ladies covered their underdresses with their hands.

He shook his head as he faced away from them. "Ye will give me a heart attack from all the screaming ye do for no good purpose."

"The water is frigid," Mexia explained gruffly as she scrubbed off the dirt in a hurry. "You would have screamed out too if you had not expected how cold it was."

Gallant shook his head again. "I would not scream about such a thing."

Kersta stepped into the water next to Mexia. "Yes, right, and that's why you would not join us. You'll wait for the hot springs instead. You and the boy will have to eat your meal outside and downwind from us."

Gallant unfastened his cloak and tossed it to the ground.

"What are you doing?" the princess asked, her eyes growing round.

"I will eat with ye at the table. Not outside, nor downwind of ye."

"You cannot join us while we are washing."

He grunted as he removed his shirt. "I have seen plenty of ye. It doesn't bother me if ye see plenty of me."

Mexia hurried to get a change of clothes out of her pack. "I, for one, will not be explaining how I bathed with a man."

He chuckled under his breath as he pulled off his boots.

Kersta grabbed up clean clothes and hurried to put them on over her wet underdress. "Cold, cold."

Mexia glanced over to see Gallant in some kind of loincloth as he slipped under the waterfall while the princess ducked out of it.

"Ahhh," he said running his hands through his thick beard. "Have any of ye women some of that sweet smelling soap ye wear?"

Kersta tossed hers to Gallant. He smiled at her and waggled his dark brown bushy brows. "Thanks, love."

She groaned and turned away, then attempted to dry her dark curls.

Mexia wrung her hair out, squeezing as much of the water from it as she could manage. When she began to braid it, the princess interrupted her. "Leave it down for now, Mexia. We need to dry our hair and clothes by the fire. If we go into the mountains while our hair is still wet, we'll all catch our death."

"All right." Mexia pushed the thick strands behind her back, not used to having her hair down and in the way. "I'll be inside then while you ladies…" She glanced over at Gallant who scrubbed under his arms with gusto and sang a raspy tune under his breath. "…and Gallant finish up."

He winked at her. Her cheeks burned. She turned away and grabbed up her cloak, staff, and pack.

Upon entering the house, she found the boy sitting beside the fire drying his wet hair. She smiled. "You took a bath?"

"In the horse's trough, my lady. I couldn't have you wrinkling your nose at me over the meal. My momma taught me to always wash up before meals. Besides Pemlican told me to do so."

She smiled, then turned to Pemlican who watched her with suspicion. "We have a dangerous journey before us. I wonder if I might ask you to watch over the young man here, to ensure his safety."

When Davin began to object, she silenced him with a sharp look.

Pemlican nodded. "I could use some young hands around the place."

"I am going to be a page," Davin said, proudly, his small chin stuck up in the air.

"Yes, and to become a page, you must help others," Mexia agreed. She ran her fingers through her hair to dry the strands more quickly while standing beside the flames of the fire.

Pemlican straightened his back. "Who is this young man who wishes to wed you? Will he be looking for you here?"

"Actually, he has offered to pay Lord Cramer to keep me here so that I cannot journey into the mountains. Because of that, Lord Cramer's men may be here looking for me soon enough."

"That's why I must go with you," Davin pleaded, pacing back and forth across the floor. "Otherwise they'll imprison me for having helped you to escape."

"I'll keep Davin safe," Pemlican said.

Mexia smiled. "Good, then it is settled. You will stay here with Pemlican and I will return when I can."

"I should not have posted the notice about Isabelle," the man said. "You will never be able to return her. The way is too dangerous."

The princess and Kersta walked into the house.

The man smiled. "Everyone looks so much cleaner."

Kersta shook her head. "You were right. The water is cold."

Seconds after the ladies sat down for the meal with the boy, Gallant walked inside. "Ye were eating without me?"

"Not that you would do that to us, now, right, Gallant?" Kersta asked, pulling a piece of bread from a loaf.

He chuckled. "I could not help it you were so slow in coming down to the meal in Langdon."

"Or that you continued to eat the meal when the soldiers attacked us."

Mexia noticed Davin soaked up Kersta's and Gallant's words with interest. She imagined he wished he'd been with them from the beginning on all of their adventures. The next words out of his mouth confirmed this.

"I want to go with you and learn to be an adventurer." Davin directed his comment to Gallant as if a man would take his side more quickly than the women.

Gallant shook his head. "Ye are only a lad. The women are right. Ye must stay here."

Mexia patted Davin's hand, noting the militant look on the boy's face. "I promise I *will* return."

The princess set the pork rib bone on the clay plate. "The food is very good."

Gallant had already devoured four of them.

Mexia ate another slice of bread, but when she heard the

sound of horses' hooves pounding the dirt in the distance, she jumped up from her chair. Her companions did likewise, each grabbing up their packs and weapons in haste.

The man motioned for the princess to put her money pouch away. "Return my Isabelle, if you can. *That* will be payment enough."

"Thank you, kind sir. We will do our best."

They hurried out of the back door of the house while Davin scooted in front of them. "I can show you the trail that leads to the hot springs. Beyond that, I have never been. No one comes back who goes that way. The soldiers will not follow."

"You will return to Pemlican's house after this, won't you?" Mexia said, her voice scolding, meant to ensure he did what she wanted him to.

"I just want to show you the way. Quickly, before the soldiers catch up to us."

He ran between pink stone boulders, then up a narrow path lined with rusty-colored pine needles. Mexia and her companions ran single file after him, the needles cushioning their step.

The air heated and turned humid from the steam rising from the pools next to the path. But the sound of men shouting back at Pemlican's house made the party continue on past the springs.

"You must return, Davin," Mexia urged, reaching for his shoulder.

"A little way further, my lady. I'll lead you a little way…" He paused his speech as a portal of green swirling lights appeared on the path before them.

"Do you think it might be a portal to the mage's castle, Mexia?" the princess asked, peering over her shoulder.

"I don't know." Mexia studied the width of the portal. The sides touched the rounded boulders next to it. "If we are to continue along the path, we will have to try and climb much higher to get around it."

"Can we not walk straight through?" Davin asked.

"No, it would take us somewhere. But where, we have no clue."

Gallant cleared his throat. "Make a decision quickly, woman. The soldiers are headed this way."

Davin dashed into the portal and disappeared.

"No!" Mexia screamed, her heart pounding so hard in her chest, she feared it would give the soldiers their location soon. "I cannot forsake Davin." She ran into the portal after him.

Seconds later, she stood inside a room where gold and ivory enameled ceilings vaulted twenty feet high. Fluted pillars surrounded her in a circle and the floor beneath her feet was painted in gold and royal blue symbols.

"Psst," Davin said from behind a pillar. "Where are we, my lady?"

"I have no idea, except these symbols—"

The princess bumped into her, then grabbed her arm for reassurance. "Oh, my where in the world are we?"

Mexia and she moved out of the swirling light. "I'm not sure. But it only seems to go one way. It didn't seem to wish to return me to where I had come from, though I stood in it long enough for it to take me that way."

Kersta appeared, then raised her brows to see the ladies. "You don't know where we are, don't tell me."

Gallant followed her into the light. "Well, woman, now where have ye taken us?"

"I'm afraid I have no idea." Mexia looked over at Davin. "But if I could return you from whence we came, I would. You, young man, have to learn to obey."

"Sorry, my lady. I wanted to get us free of the soldiers."

Next, they heard feminine voices speaking to one another in casual conversation. The party hurried to one side of the room where they could see a doorway leading into a great hall, but they themselves were hidden by the pillars.

An older woman in a peach-colored silky gown stepped in front of the doorway with another similarly dressed but much younger. Both had golden hair piled on top of their heads in satiny curls, tied together with braids of peach ribbon and pearl-decorated combs.

They stopped for a second at the doorway and peered into the room toward where the portal light had been.

"He said he would bring her here soon. Why are the guards not posted in the event she arrives earlier than him? He said she behaved as mischievously as a snow sprite and might come here without him."

"There was some disturbance in the south side of the castle. But you are right, my lady mother. The guards should never have been pulled from here."

The older woman took a deep breath. "Do you not sense something?" She shook her head and turned to her daughter. "I wish your brother was here."

"He will be, my lady mother. He will be."

The two sauntered off.

"Where are we?" the princess asked.

"I thought we might be in the mage of Monrovia's castle." Mexia pointed at the symbols on the floor. "This place is a royal wizard's home."

"Was Parenkin a royal wizard?" Kersta asked.

"I don't have any idea."

Mexia examined the symbols on the walls. "Look and see if there is some kind of a button or indention in the wall that we can push. Maybe we can reactive the portal so that we can return to the place where we entered it."

The ladies, Gallant and Davin searched the walls for some such device. Finding none, Mexia finally said, "All right, we must get out of here before we are found trespassing. Perhaps we can find out if we are high in the mountains, or something else to indicate this place is Parenkin's abode."

"Yes, we must leave the portal room before the guards return to their posts," the princess added.

Mexia peered through the open doorway. The hallway appeared clear, and she waved for her friends to join her. They walked down one hall, then hearing male voices as they spoke, growing closer, Mexia grabbed a doorknob nearby and twisted. The room wasn't locked and she opened the door, her heart thundering with anxiety.

Inside, the room was dark. She and her companions hurried into it. Kersta used the fairy wand as Gallant shut the door behind him.

The floor was tiled in more wizardry symbols and half columns butted against the walls surrounding the circular room. Mexia touched them. "It's like the portal room, only a smaller version."

"What does it mean?" Kersta asked, looking for buttons or switches like Mexia was doing.

"I think it's a portal to take you somewhere else in the castle."

"Oh." Kersta withdrew her hand from the wall. "Then we'd better not touch anything in…"

"Oh!" Gallant jerked his hand away from the wall.

The room swirled in lights. When the lights quit flashing, Mexia took a breath of air and chuckled. "Scared me there for a second. Let's get out of here."

She opened the door and peeked outside of the room. Instead of a hallway, she saw a veranda decorated with hanging clay pots dripping with purple flowers.

"We've transported to somewhere new," she whispered. They all stepped out of the portal room and onto the veranda. Forty feet up, they looked out over a city bustling where vendors sold everything from clothing to fresh produce. "We're not on the mountains." Seabirds flew overhead squawking and the air was thick with the odor of fish. "We must be near the seacoast."

"Langdon?" the princess asked.

"No, this palace can't be in Langdon. Langdon castle was the only large place there. This one," Mexia said leaning out over the balcony, "appears to have about half the number of towers, but it seems to have more courtyards and gardens."

A boy looked up at them from one of the courtyards, grabbed a woman's hand, and pointed to the veranda. Mexia and her companions leaped out of view. "Shoot, nobody's dressed the same as we are here."

The princess added, "And if you hadn't noticed, everyone's blond-haired."

Gallant tugged at his beard. "And there are no dwarves here."

Mexia hurried toward the portal, but her heart stopped when a bell rang out across the castle. "Sounds like a warning bell."

Davin said, "Perhaps I could slip around the castle and find a way out for us? I am dressed similar to the boy down there and have blond hair."

Mexia shook her head. "More than likely everyone will know everyone in the castle. You'll be a stranger as much as we are."

"What are we to do then?" Kersta asked.

"Somehow get out of the castle. If we can get to the city, we should be able to blend in better with other outsiders."

The lights in the portal room swirled and Mexia shook her head. "Not that way. Someone's using it to come here, I think."

She ran through a hall until she came to a marble stairway. Halfway down, they heard the clomping of boots on the stairs below them. Turning, they found guards dressed in purple tunics emblazoned with the image of the silver moon behind them at the top of the landing. Looking down, they found the same, more of the royal guard, she assumed.

No one said a word for a moment as the men stared at the companions. Then Mexia uttered an incantation, "No longer free on water, nor on land, you will do as I command." She paused to see if her spell had any affect. The men waited. She nodded. "Escort us to the city outside your castle. Allow none to delay us."

One of the men smiled. "Your spells will not work in his lordship's castle, my lady." The man bowed slightly.

The ladies readied their staffs for a battle.

"You are a day early," a woman said, her words parting the men who stood on the stairs below Mexia and her friends. "My son said you might get here early. Come, I will show you to your rooms."

"You are mistaken, my lady," Mexia said to the woman who had been speaking to her daughter outside the portal room when they first arrived. "We came here by accident. We beg your forgiveness for intruding, but wish only to be on our way. Where is here, by the way?"

"Malar."

The place Derek had spoken of? Suddenly Mexia's stomach grew unsettled.

"Prince Derek would be upset with me to say the least, if I didn't take good care of his sweet bride-to-be."

Mexia's head began to spin.

"Come, dear." The woman, undoubtedly Derek's mother, motioned to her. "We must get you and your friends cleaned up and dressed properly. Entertainers are ready to provide some entertainment for you."

Her words brushed Mexia's ears, but didn't sink in.

"Your gowns must be made for the wedding. Such lovely gowns they shall be, too. Much must be done to prepare for the big event. Your betrothed will be home tomorrow night after graduation. You've worried him senseless though with your desire to attend the school. You have no need to graduate from there, you know. Ruling as the new queen here will be all that's required of you."

The whole world spun about and before Mexia could stop the spinning in her head, she collapsed.

CHAPTER 15

Mexia opened her eyes. Above her head a canopy of blue silks was tied to the ceiling with a ring of gold centered in the middle. For a moment, she stared at the sight. Then Kersta said, "She's awake, princess!"

"Oh, Mexia, how do you feel?" The princess crossed the floor to the bed.

"Where are your traveling clothes?" Mexia reached out to the ladies. Their peach-colored silk garments shimmered in the sun-drenched room. "You cannot travel in gowns as fine as those." Immediately, her stomach knotted with worry.

Kersta sighed heavily. "They have confiscated our packs, staffs, and even Gallant's weapon."

The princess patted her scepter, still secured at her waist. "They figured a princess who had a scepter couldn't be separated from it."

"They don't know how powerful it is," Mexia said under her breath.

"No, but when Derek returns, he'll know."

"We have to leave before he gets here. We mustn't delay." Mexia sat up. "What in the world happened to me?"

The princess sat on the bed next to her. "Davin said you hadn't had enough sleep, and had been hit by one of Boras's men earlier."

"Yes, but I healed myself. How long have I been sleeping?"

"Four hours. It'll be time for the afternoon meal soon."

"Where are Gallant and Davin?"

"In the men's quarters, for now."

They froze as the door to the room opened with a slight creak. The blond-haired woman they had seen at the portal peeked in. "Ahh, so my brother's bride is awake now. One of you ladies should have told the guard the news. I would have come right away. My name is Alinas."

"Derek is mistaken about me." Mexia rubbed her temple, trying to clear the fog from her mind. "I'm not the one who has been prophesied to marry him."

Alinas smile stretched across her face in delight. Pretty and perky, with a small chin, powder pink lips, and big blue eyes, the woman must have caught many a man's eye. "He said you would say this. When he returns, this ought to be most entertaining. I always assumed the woman who would marry him would wish to do so. Nay not just wish to do so, but would be begging to be queen as he becomes king. He's a very popular man amongst the populace here. Many of the ladies would do anything to be his wife."

Mexia groaned in annoyance.

The lady quirked a blond brow. "I can see now, this shall not be the case with you...most intriguing. I will be right back to have the maids dress you for the noon meal. That traveling underdress will not do, not do at all." Her smile was as impish as any pixie's.

What had the woman in mind? A gown to impress her brother? Mexia had no intention of trying to please Derek.

"Oh, and the royal captain of the guard told me that you

attempted to use a mind control spell on the men. You will not be able to use any of your spells here. My brother rules this house of Mendon. Only he can cast spells here."

Folding her arms, Mexia scowled at the woman. "Derek will not rule over me."

Alinas laughed. "I will enjoy being your sister. He does not rule over me either, though he often makes the mistake in trying."

For an instant, Mexia had hope. She truly liked the woman who seemed to have it in for her brother, too. "Then you would help me to leave here before he arrives?"

She laughed again, dashing all Mexia had hoped for. "No, you are too funny. I will have much more fun with you being here with me. I can see you will not be easily persuaded to do what you do not wish to do. We may very well be able to give up our court jester at mealtime if you and Derek entertain us instead."

Before she retreated from the room, she paused and turned. "Oh, and by the way, a message was sent at once to my brother, telling him of your arrival here. It took half the time it usually does to get a response from him. I've never seen him get so worked up over a woman. But he was extremely concerned that you might attempt to leave here before his arrival.

"Double the guard is posted at your door. You will have the royal guard escort wherever you go. And my brother has stated he will return here tonight, to eat the evening meal with you. Of course, he will have to return to the school sometime following that so he can graduate tomorrow. But at least you will not have to wait until then to see him."

She hurried into the hall while one of the guards shut the door.

Mexia took a deep breath, trying to calm her irritation and shook her head, her mind muddled with discord. "I've really gone and done it this time."

"All is not lost." The princess patted Mexia's hand to reassure her.

Kersta walked to the window and peered out. "They put us in a room that appears to be above the veranda we stood on earlier."

"The women's wing of the castle, don't you imagine?" Mexia asked.

"Yes and as such, it appears they've been careful here to ensure there are no trellises available for gentlemen suitors to reach their ladyloves."

Mexia crawled out of bed, then headed for the window.

She breathed in the ocean air, then looked into the sky as a shadow drew over the window. A dragon. She smiled. Brown scaled unlike the green dragons where Dragonmage resided or the blue ones in Inherian…could it aid them?

She lifted her skirt, then climbed into the windowsill as Kersta grabbed her hand.

"What are you doing, Mexia?" Kersta asked, her voice exhibiting her fear.

"I'm wondering if I can call him."

"Can you?" the princess asked, joining them at the window.

The door creaked open and Princess Alinas screamed in surprise, startling Mexia and her friends.

Kersta helped Mexia from the window as the guards rushed into the room. Quickly, Mexia covered her underdress with her hands. "Leave here at once!"

The men looked to Alinas for counsel. She seemed unsure as to what to do as she still attempted to catch her breath at the fright she'd had. Her own ladies-in-waiting stood beside her with gowns for Mexia.

Finally a guard said, "Princess Alinas, shall we remove her to the tower?"

"Under lock and key?" Mexia asked. "My, will you have me locked away always?"

"I…I…" Alinas crossed her arms as she narrowed her eyes. "You should not have done that."

"What? I was attempting to see the ships in the harbor. Did you think I intended to jump? Why would I do a foolish thing like that?" Mexia wrinkled her brow at the men who stared at the light dress she wore. "Would Prince Derek not be concerned his men viewed his bride in her undergarments?"

Alinas motioned for the men to leave with a flick of her wrist. She still frowned at Mexia though. "What were you really doing?"

"I wasn't planning on jumping. It is not that I do not care for Derek." The words lumped up in her throat. Mexia couldn't hide the deep-seated feelings she had for the mage, but his attempting to stop her from completing her mission irritated her to no end. Her skin prickled as she glanced over at Kersta and assumed she read her mind. Normally it didn't matter, but when she thought about her feelings for Derek…

She attempted a calming breath. "Derek knows very well I have a mission to perform and cannot think of marrying any until after I have completed it."

"He has already said this…that you feel you have something you must do before you can wed. But he has also said when you are wed, he will take care of it. You will remain here where you will be safe."

"That is very sweet of him." But Mexia wasn't giving up her mission for anything. Somehow, she'd find a way to see Parenkin in the mountains and attend the school as she intended. Somehow.

"Dress her," Alinas said, her mouth turning up slightly.

Mexia considered the silky, ice blue gowns.

"The color is what Derek wishes you to wear. Do you approve?"

The color was fine. The style and material would never suffice on their trek into the mountains however. Mexia lowered her head, then raised it in agreement.

After the maids dressed her, she and her companions were

escorted to the great hall for the meal. It appeared they would not be allowed out of a royal guard's sight.

Gallant and Davin were seated at a lower table, while Mexia sat next to Alinas. Princess Talamaya was given the seat on the other side of the queen and Kersta sat to Mexia's left.

But shortly after the companions sat at the elevated head table for the meal, the conversation died to nary a whisper.

Suddenly a man entered the room, his royal blue cape flowing in his wake. He nodded to the queen, then stepped aside. The queen motioned for all to rise.

Alinas laughed and leaned over to Mexia. "Your betrothed has arrived early for the meal. Most of the courtiers placed bets on whether he would. Some knew his schooling was more important than anything. But I knew he had lost his heart to you at once. No way could he stay away a minute longer than necessary."

Mexia folded her arms. Great. She'd had every intention of finding a way out of the castle before Derek arrived for the evening meal. She never figured he'd arrive in the afternoon several hours earlier instead.

Derek strode into the great hall, his demeanor kingly as he stood straight and tall, his chin held high. His broad shoulders seemed even broader. He headed straight for the high table...a man with a mission. He nodded at his mother in greeting briefly, but his gaze quickly shifted to Mexia as a smile tugged at his lips.

Her body heated in response. Just that little smile and every resistant bone in her body turned to liquid all at once.

A hush of voices filled the hall. Alinas whispered to Mexia, "I do not believe I've ever seen him strut so. He truly wishes to impress his ladylove."

Derek joined them, and kissed his mother on one cheek, then the other. Afterward, he turned to his sister and did the same. When he stepped around her to see Mexia, the room grew silent again.

His dimples shown as his smile broadened. "Lady Mexia, how good of you to drop in on me like this."

Before she could respond, he took her hand and raised a glass of wine for a toast. "To my bride!"

"Here, here!" the courtiers responded in chorus.

Then after everyone drank their wine, Derek kissed her cheeks in greeting. "Sit," he urged his people, "and enjoy your meal."

He took his seat between Mexia and his sister as one of the courtiers moved from the head table to a lower table.

Though irritated Derek would assume she'd marry him, she remained curious about his family. "Does your mother rule when you are away?"

"Most certainly."

"And your father? Is he deceased?"

"Yes, for ten years now, I'm sorry to say."

"I'm sorry to hear this also. Do your mother and sister have your abilities?"

He smiled. "No. Not many females do. What about in Damar?"

"No. Not in Damar either. My mother had no magical abilities, though a great aunt did."

Derek took Mexia's hand and kissed her fingers with a tender touch, sending a spiral of warmth cascading through her body. "Tell me. How many golden leaves do you see this afternoon?"

Six. Two more than the last time she saw on his cloak, but she wasn't about to tell *him* that. "I see none. Perhaps you are the imposter, Rosenthal, playing Derek's part again."

He raised his brows at her, his mouth quirked in a smile. Then he turned to his sister and said, "How many gold leaves does she see?"

"Six, my dear brother."

"Ah, six." He smiled. "My, my, trying to keep secrets from me already?"

Mexia's heartbeat picked up its pace and her eyes widened in disbelief. Could his sister read minds like Kersta? What else had Mexia given away? Whatever she did now, she had to keep her thoughts to herself when Alinas was nearby. Mexia's whole world collapsed with that one little question and Alinas's correct answer.

"She loves you, too, Derek, though she fights the feelings." Alinas raised her wine goblet off the table. "It seems she feels her duty is to her home of Damar and killing the rogue mage, Rosenthal, first and foremost."

"Yes, well, I will take care of him soon enough." Derek smiled as he took Mexia's hand in his and squeezed it. "She will stay her, safe from the evils of the world."

"Over my dead body," Mexia said, her words caustic.

He chuckled.

"I knew the two of you would be entertaining." Alinas laughed. "Really should be interesting. I'm so glad you found her as soon as you did and brought her home. Ever since you told us you'd discovered her, we've been waiting with horrible expectancy."

Mexia glanced over at Kersta. Tell the others about Alinas. Kersta nodded. She would pass the word to the others that Alinas could read their minds.

"Your friends must stay for the wedding, and then I'll make certain they're returned safely to Inherian after this." Derek sighed. "Everything is falling into place as it should be."

"And what of my father? Does he not get an invite concerning his only daughter's marriage? Surely you cannot leave him out."

He gripped her hand with a tight squeeze. "If I allow this, you may convince your father to aid you in leaving here."

She jerked her hand away as the blood rose to her cheeks in anger, filling them with heat. No way was Derek going to dictate to her what would or would not be done in her life.

Lilting flutes and harp music played in the background as the first of the food was served. Lobster, shrimp, scallops, and some kind of a pink fish she didn't recognize were delivered on gold platters to the tables. Loaves of brown and white bread, white and orange cheeses, and bowls of rich green sea kelp followed this. A pleasant aroma of well-seasoned fish scented the area mixed with the sweet fragrances the women wore.

And even Derek smelled heavenly of some kind of a spice scent.

Mexia lifted the tail of a shrimp in her fingertips, then pulled the succulent meat from the shell with her teeth, her lips wrapped securely around it. She looked over to see Derek watching her with interest, his lips turned up at the corners. His attentiveness made her cheeks burn.

She discarded the shrimp's shell, then lifted another off her gold-rimmed plate. Before she plucked the meat from its shell, she faced Derek, raising her brows. "I'm very hungry, but if you watch every move I make, I'll feel I'm way too glutinous."

He smiled at her. "From all I could gather of your shenanigans in Cramer, you have need of a good healthy diet. I've been told, due to your help, the villagers of Cramer are again trading with those in Barston as we speak. Dragonmage and our mage friends are attempting to clear a path for the two peoples to make it safely through Darkland Forest to trade in Langdon as well."

"I'm glad to hear it." She finished three more shrimp, then picked up a fourth.

He chuckled. "I can see shellfish are your favorite. We will have to ensure we never run out of the food."

Though Mexia attempted to couch her thoughts to avoid Alina's reading of them, her mind drifted to the notion Derek might have some spell books she could learn from. She patted his thigh, bringing a smile to his lips as his eyes darkened with desire.

"Do you have a library here? I'm a voracious reader."

"Yes. Not only do we have quite an extensive collection of

books and materials from other regions, but several of my courtiers have written their own."

"As it is in Damar."

Alinas tugged at Derek's sleeve. "But is it not that library she wishes to see, my lord brother."

His lips twitched into a smile. "Ah, pray tell what do you mean then, Mexia?"

When Mexia tore apart a lobster tail and didn't respond to Derek's question, Alinas chuckled. "She wishes to see your spell books."

"I see. All that I have is yours, Mexia. You only need ask."

"You will show them to me?"

He smiled. "What is she contemplating, Alinas?"

"She wishes to be as powerful as you."

"Ah." His hand settled on Mexia's thigh, sending heat coursing through her body. "Everything of mine is yours."

Torn between wanting him to kiss her and kicking him for keeping her hostage, she nearly died when Alinas said, "She wishes you would kiss her."

Mexia's skin prickled with embarrassment. She fought the urge to tell him she also wanted to kick him.

"But kick you at the same time," Alinas added, then chuckled.

Derek laughed out loud. "If you hadn't added the latter thought, I would have figured she was hiding them from me."

Mexia shoved his hand from her lap.

He leaned over and whispered in her ear, "We will stroll through the gardens following the meal, and you may have that kiss from me."

"I will give you all the kisses you want, after I fulfill my mission, first."

"She is like you, Alinas, totally stubborn." Derek took Mexia's hand. "But you are cleverer and more resourceful than any woman I have ever known. I will show you my spell books, but know this…in my castle, no one who can use magic is able to do so."

"I only wish to learn all I can, Derek. I have an insatiable appetite for knowledge."

He looked over at Alinas who nodded. Turning back to Mexia, he said, "And for shrimp."

~

*W*hen the meal ended, Derek led her out of the great hall and into the courtyard. "Your companions will be entertained while I spend this time with you."

She glanced around her. Though several men and women watched their actions, none followed them. "Am I not to be properly chaperoned?"

He nodded. "When you are in the company of other gentlemen, yes."

Grateful Alinas wasn't chaperoning them and listening in on her thoughts, Mexia switched topics, hoping to learn something more about what Rosenthal was up to. "Have you heard anything about Rosenthal's whereabouts?"

Derek paused, a glimmer of amusement in his eyes, most likely for her abrupt change of subject. "Rumors have it he spent some time in my own village, pretending to be a sailor."

"Then it is not safe for me here either. What if he comes here posing as you?"

"You will be able to recognize him. He won't have six golden leaves on his cloak, for one."

"Eight." She reached out to trace each one of them.

His eyes grew as round as the loaf of bread they'd had at the noon meal. When she smiled, he cleared his throat. "Following my graduation, we *shall* wed."

"Will your family attend your graduation?"

"Yes, but you will remain here. It is safer. Rosenthal knows every part of Langdon Castle. I would fear he might try to get to you there."

Derek's family would need a royal guard escort. Fewer left behind to watch Mexia and her companions. Hmm, when the family left for the graduation, perhaps, that was the best time to plan their escape. "And then what will you do?"

"After we're married, I'll hunt Rosenthal down myself."

"All right."

He smiled at her, then pulled her onto an isolated garden path. "You say all right, but I don't trust you one bit, my dear."

"How can our marriage succeed if we cannot trust one another?"

He chuckled under his breath. "I have told Dragonmage what fun you are. He will be sorely disappointed to hear I have you at my castle, locked away for safekeeping."

"Do you intend to play your wizardry games with me here then?"

"I do not intend to play games with you at all. My business with you is totally serious."

They strolled along a stone path, the edges trimmed in ruffles of blue and purple flowered petals. Blooming in profusion, the sweet fragrance of honey sifted on the light breeze.

Mexia took a deep breath of the heavenly fragrance, the odor of the sewers and earthy tunnel, swiftly fading into a distant memory. "It smells heavenly here."

The sound of gurgling and splashing caught her ear, and she pointed to the path that held the secret. He nodded and walked her, arm in arm, down the new path. It led to a fountain where crystal blue water spilled from three wide-mouthed fish into a shell basin. The fish and shell were sculpted in green marble, striated with streaks of white and black, the shining stone catching the filtered rays of the sun.

"It's lovely."

"We have many all over the gardens...all different sculptures. We are fortunate to have many artists who live among us."

"When are you leaving?"

He hesitated, seemingly surprised to hear her switch the subject so abruptly, and then smiled. "You are ready to be rid of me, my dear? Is it that you are contemplating taking an excursion from here?"

"How can I do such a thing? I only wished to know as I wanted you to show me your library that holds your spell books before you leave."

"There will be time enough for that." He strolled with her onto another path, then suddenly pulled her into a hedge maze.

"What had you in mind, Derek?" Her words were suddenly wary.

"To give you what you wished for."

"I did not wish to be alone with you, at any time."

He walked with her in silence for several minutes, then said, "I would not marry you against your will."

"Then let me do my quest."

"We are at an impasse. I cannot in good conscious let you loose on the world. You are prophesied to be my wife. What happens if I lose you? I cannot allow it. It is not that I...well that I'm controlling. I just cannot lose you." He glanced over at her. "Do you not think of me, Mexia?" He shook his head and took a deep breath. "I cannot get you out of my mind. I think of you day and night. Even my studies have suffered because of my thoughts of you."

He pulled her through the fine-needled leaves of the fourteen-foot-high yew. She looked around at the four walls of greenery. "My secret room," he said, motioning to a marble bench. "Would you like to have a seat for a moment in my special garden?"

The entrance where they had entered seemed to have disappeared. Except for the fragrance of wintergreen, a wisp of white clouds drifting by overhead, and the sound of an owl screeching as it soared close by, the whole world seemed to vanish. Only Derek, standing before her in his royal blue silk shirt, and suede-like breeches, his cloak still covering his broad shoulders, existed. His blue eyes watched her with intrigue, waiting for her to give her permission to what? Kiss her?

"We shouldn't be here alone like this. A man shouldn't be with an unmarried lady alone." She could face anything—the undead, dark elves, rogue mages…but her feelings for Derek.

"You will be my bride tomorrow."

"It doesn't matter. We shouldn't be unchaperoned."

"You wanted me to kiss you."

"Kick you. Your sister got my thoughts wrong."

He chuckled. "She will be amused to hear you say so." When he took a step closer to her, Mexia stepped back. "How can I kiss you if you keep backing away from me?"

"Why did you leave us to fend for ourselves alone in the cemetery? Why didn't you help us?" She crossed her arms in irritation.

"Our headmaster has a way of recalling us when he senses we are in danger. I'd been injured by one of the undead. The next thing I knew, I was back at Langdon Castle. He had me on lock-down. Which means, he would not permit me to come to your aid any further. I managed to send a message to Lord Cramer to keep you in his village though, until I returned after graduation. Seems he wasn't able to keep you under lock and key any more than Dragonmage was able to."

"Doesn't that give you any clues about how long you're going to manage to keep me here? That your efforts are futile?"

He smiled. "It means you will be thoroughly watched by my staff at all times."

"And now?"

"You're being watched by me."

"What about the portal that appeared on the path? How did it come to be?"

"I erected it in the event you happened to slip out of Lord Cramer's castle somehow and managed to make it to the mountain passage. I should have realized you'd get free from his castle before I graduated."

He stepped closer to her. She stepped back. Her legs touched the bench held up by two dragon statues, the heads were turned, their teeth bared as if they growled at the other for not holding their own weight.

Derek smiled. "You are not going anywhere."

Her heart pounded. She didn't want to go anywhere, not at the moment, not with his body heat warming her. She wanted him to kiss her like he'd done before, despite her mind telling her she had to keep her distance.

He shouldn't have been alone with her, not like this. And yet the thrill of them being together, just the two of them, in a room as secluded as any bedchambers, made her skin prickle with anticipation.

CHAPTER 16

"Tell me you don't want to be kissed, and we'll continue to stroll through the gardens," Derek said, his hands cupping Mexia's face with tenderness.

She fingered the silk ties on his shirt as her heartbeat quickened. Her gaze focused on the v-cut exposing his tan skin, lightly covered in blond hair.

"Mexia?"

Her gaze met his.

His mouth turned up, and her gaze shifted to the curve of his lips and the incredible power they held...like magic. She parted hers to speak, then reconsidered. Closing them shut, she swallowed hard.

He nuzzled his face against her cheek, the hair from his beard tickling and scratching at the same time. She wanted to run her fingers through his blond hair confined in a knot at the back of his head and give him permission to kiss her without reservation, but...she had more important things to do, like save Albion and Inherian from the mad rogue mage, Rosenthal.

Derek's eyes turned from vivid blue to nearly navy with desire, and she wondered if her own had changed from green to black. He considered her eyes for a moment, then another smile dawned on his face. "We will not be wed soon enough."

Did he know then she had no backbone to fight him? Or did he realize she felt the same way for him as he felt for her?

She tilted her chin up, pursing her lips in annoyance, ready to tell him if she were to marry him, it would be on her terms, not his. But as soon as she lifted her mouth to him, he interpreted her actions as an open invitation.

Without hesitation, he commandeered them. She gasped in surprise at the suddenness of his action. His warm lips touched hers, pressing hard, claiming her as if he'd won a strategic battle, and the territory was more precious than any he'd ever possessed.

Her traitorous body burned with longing for his love, his touch, to fulfill the raging desire he felt for her. He leaned his hard body into hers. She realized at once how important it was for them to be chaperoned as her fingers moved from his shirt to his waist. She pulled him close, when she'd fully intended to hold him at bay.

His hands grasped her shoulders as if she were his finally, their tongues tangling in a memorable dance, their bodies molding together as one. Then their breaths mingled, and lips touched again, pressuring one another for more.

Derek wrenched away from her and groaned. "You are too sweet, my love."

Mexia couldn't respond. Her heart warred with her mind. No way could she give in to him. Her back stiffened as she attempted to distance herself from the man who encouraged the animal instincts sleeping deep inside her to surface.

Noticing her withdrawal, he lightened his hold on her, then kissed her lips more gently.

In response, she nipped his lower lip playfully, bringing a smile to his face. With renewed gusto, he kissed her hard.

Light footsteps on the maze path beyond the secret garden

sounded, distracting them. Mexia tilted her head to the side and listened. Derek paused.

"Derek, are you here? Mother will be sorely peeved with you if you have Lady Mexia alone in your secret garden. You know what she said about your being with her without chaperone."

Derek smiled as Mexia looked up at him.

"Derek?" Alinas's voice was high pitched and scolding. "I can't read your mind because of your infernal magic, but I can read hers. She feels I have come in the nick of time to rescue her."

Mexia almost laughed as Derek quirked a brow and smiled. He waved his hand at the direction of Alinas's voice, then waited while her footsteps padded off down the path.

He kissed Mexia long and hard as she responded with gusto. Then he touched her braided hair. "We will continue to stroll along the path, before I forget that you are not yet my wife."

"What about Alinas? Will she tell your mother?"

"She has had a convenient memory lapse."

Mexia chuckled. She knew Derek was truly the one for her, only he would learn soon he could not dictate to her like he thought he could.

He sneaked her out of his secret garden, making a lady and her gent squeal out in surprise. They both quickly showed their respect. He chuckled under his breath as he slipped his arm through Mexia's. "I guess the word will soon get back to my mother that we shared some time in my special garden."

"No memory lapses for them?"

He laughed. He pointed to two more courtiers half hidden behind a yew. "I believe someone will reveal this, if they have not already. The secret garden is my place to get away from everyone. It appears several have checked to see if I had brought you here."

"So are you often found alone with women at your beck and call here?" She raised her brows.

He shook his head as his smile stretched across his face. "To read. Often when I am in my bedchambers, I'm interrupted."

"It kind of makes for a difficult situation, if you wish to be alone with your wife, doesn't it?"

"The rules will change. Once we are married, unless the castle is under attack, no one better disturb us."

"About your library…"

He looked down at her. "I'm wondering if I should only allow you to look at it after we are married. What goes on in that clever mind of yours?"

"A thirst for knowledge. If you will not permit me to attend the school at Langdon, I wish to see what it is you have learned, and I will learn what I can on my own."

"Ah. You need no tutor then?"

"You can tutor me."

"All right."

"And teach me how to make a portal and how to vanish."

"Only after we're married."

"Have I told you how impossibly controlling you are?"

"Have I mentioned how stubborn you are?"

They paused before a cluster of rosebushes as Alinas hollered, "There you are! I've been looking all over for the two of you. Mother wants a word of you about tomorrow, my lord brother."

"All right. Will you take Mexia up to my library? I will join you in a little while." He kissed Mexia's cheeks, then squeezed her hand.

Mexia tried to hide her enthusiasm despite the added spring in her step as she hurried away with Alinas. She tried to keep her mind a blank though, figuring Alinas was busy trying to read it.

When they reached the third floor of one of the towers, Mexia's mouth dropped open to see the books shelved from the floor to the top of the ten-foot ceiling. "Has he read all of these?" she asked, her voice whispered in awe. "All of these?"

Alinas chuckled. "He will be pleased you are so impressed with his collection. No one else is."

Mexia ran her hands over the bindings. "I could live my whole life in here."

Alinas laughed. "I'm sure he will wish you to spend some time with him, too."

Mexia sank to her knees, her eyes filled with tears.

"Are you all right?" Alinas crouched down next to Mexia and took her hand. "Mexia?"

She sniffled. "Yes, I've just never seen such a wondrous sight."

Alinas smiled. She turned and quickly rose as Derek walked into the room.

"What's the matter, Mexia?" He hurried to pull her from the floor. The concern on his face made Alinas laugh.

"She is so awestruck by your library, my dear brother, that I believe you will have a time getting her interested in much else."

"Good, for now anyway. It'll keep her out of trouble." He smiled at his sister.

Mexia pretended not to hear them as she ran her fingers over the titles. They could think that his library would distract her from her business all they wanted. And in truth, she had it in mind to read all she could...and learn how to escape the castle at the same time.

"I must take care of some business. If you get bored here, be sure that a guard is posted at the library's entrance. She may go anywhere she wishes, as long as she has a guard escort."

"Inside the castle, you mean."

"Of course."

He kissed Mexia's lips. "Enjoy your reading. I will see you later."

"Yes," she said, but her gaze shifted from his beautiful blue eyes to the books' titles.

Chuckling under his breath, he made his way out the doorway.

For a while, Alinas sat at a small table, but finally she grew bored as Mexia read through several books. "Are you getting anything from those? I mean, from the way you are going through them, I cannot imagine you are learning anything."

"Just fascinating."

"You have been saying that for well over an hour every so often. What is so fascinating?"

"Just everything."

Alinas yawned. "Well, reading and libraries make me sleepy. If you need to leave here, the guard will take you where you wish to go. I'll be in the sewing room for a while."

"Yes, thank you, Alinas."

"You're welcome. I think." Alinas left the room.

Luckily, Mexia's speed reading must have seemed like just scanning page after page of words to Alinas, who Mexia figured was reading her mind the whole time. But what Alinas couldn't decipher was Mexia's ability to memorize everything so quickly. Having used a memory spell to help her memorize potions for a test once at home, she hadn't realized it would last forever.

And now she had been through at least thirty books already, though there must have been a thousand on the shelves. She still hadn't found one concerning vanishing, sleeping, or portals though.

The guard poked his head into the room. His hair, beard, and eyes were a nondescript brown. If she saw him in a crowd again, she'd have never recognized him. Nothing seemed at all remarkable about him. "Are you looking for anything in particular?" he asked.

She eyed him suspiciously. How would a guard know where a specific magic book would be in the prince's collection? "Do you read from the prince's collection often?"

He smiled at her.

"All right. Do you know where one would be on sleeping?"

"I would think you would want something more useful than this."

She tilted her head to the side slightly. Guards wouldn't have been in the least bit interested in magic books. Only mages. "Like?"

He shrugged a shoulder. "Maybe, how to move yourself from one place to another? Prince Derek does it often."

"I can already do this."

His brows rose slightly, then he smiled. "I see. Then you would not have need of this knowledge."

"No. But perhaps there is something other than that in this book I could read, that would be useful."

"It is under lock and key in his room."

"Will you take me there? His sister said you would take me anywhere. And he said all that he has is mine as well."

"Then if that is the case, yes. Follow me."

A guard who wouldn't question her authority when she was under house arrest, sounded like one who either needed further training, or didn't belong here in the first place.

Her skin prickled with worry. What if Rosenthal was no longer playing the role of a sailor in the village, but had infiltrated the castle and now acted the part of one of the royal guard?

If Derek was powerful enough, Rosenthal couldn't use his own powers in the castle. If Derek was powerful enough.

Mexia on the other hand was power*less*. The knight had a broadsword, and she had no weapon whatsoever. And now her magic wouldn't even work.

The knight took her up to the fourth floor. "This is the royal suite. Only the royal family members live here. No others are allowed, except for the staff to clean and the like."

"And the prince's chambers?"

"Here." The man motioned to a room.

She stood before the door, then shook her head. "It is protected by a spell."

"I thought you could enter it because of your being his wife."

Why wouldn't the man know Derek hadn't married her yet? She assumed he wanted in Derek's room, but couldn't get in without an unwitting person gaining entrance for him first. And then said person, would be killed at once, while he, most likely Rosenthal, absconded with the prince's spell book.

More than anything she wished to kill Rosenthal before he hurt anyone else, but she was certain the battle couldn't be played out here, certainly not without her having some kind of a weapon.

She tapped her foot on the floor as she considered the door. "If I knew where they took my garments and other items, I might know of a way to get into the room."

The man smiled. "And how would you be able to do this?"

"I have to see if all of my things are there."

"I will take you to the room at once."

"Where is it?"

"In the cellar."

The idea of going down into the bowels of the castle with the man who was sure to kill her as soon as he knew how to get into Derek's room didn't set well with her at all as her skin freckled with perspiration. Plus, she was certain that if he knew she realized who he was, he would not hesitate to end her life. He probably figured being only a woman, she wasn't bright enough to consider that.

She smiled. "Take me there, then, Sir Knight."

"Have you still a mind to..." He grabbed her arm and pulled her down a back set of stairs as they heard voices coming from the staircase they had previously taken.

"I'm certain I saw a knight leading the lady this way, Princess Alinas."

"It is off limits to anyone, unless Prince Derek, my mother, or

I approve. Everyone knows that." Their footsteps paused. "There is no one here. If she is not here with the guard, where are they?"

When the knight reached the second level, Mexia said, "Have I a mind to do what?"

"See Parenkin still?"

Either the knight was Rosenthal in disguise, or he worked for him, and was trying to find out what her next move was.

"I guess not, as I am confined here. So it appears I'll be staying here as Derek's happy little wife."

The knight stared at her for a moment, then hurried down to the first floor. "You didn't seem to be the type that gave up that easily."

"I have done much for many in the world already. It is time to settle down and have some children…be a wife and a mother."

He shook his head. "That is why the school doesn't allow for sorceresses to attend it."

"Ah. Is that the reason they give? And if my children have magical abilities, then what? I cannot teach them any of my skills?"

The man *was* Rosenthal. How else would he know why the school would object to training female mages there?

When they reached the cellar, she was surprised to see no one guarding the room. But then she figured no one would ever have told them their clothes and other essentials were down here. It would have taken her companions and her way too long to search the whole castle for their things otherwise, and by then she and Derek would have been married, if he had his way. Besides, they were always to be chaperoned.

"So what did you have in here that might help with the prince's door?" the knight asked.

She walked into the room. Would her staff have its magical power still, or not? Fear crawled through her stomach. No way could she fight his broadsword with a simple staff.

She lifted her staff off the floor and ran her hand over it, trying to sense if the power still remained. Normally she could tell if an item was magically enhanced. All mages could. But she couldn't sense anything. Was it because her abilities in the castle wouldn't work?

He didn't suspect what she had on her mind at all as he drew close. His weapon remained sheathed to her satisfaction.

She pulled her worn leather belt off the floor then slipped it around her waist. If it still had any power, maybe she could use it, even if she couldn't use her own spells.

"What do you have that can help us open the prince's door?" he asked again.

"Let's see if any of this works," she said and motioned for him to leave the room where he blocked the door.

"Tell me first, what do you have that will aid us?"

Us. He'd used the term twice. Why would he need aiding? If he wasn't the mage Rosenthal? And what need had he of using Derek's spell book? He'd been a fourth year student also. He must have known everything that Derek did. But then again, he hadn't graduated. Still he had Grimoria's spell book and Rosenthal was supposed to have been extremely intelligent. So what did Derek have, that Rosenthal didn't?

"Have you seen Derek's book?" she asked.

"I know of it."

"What spells does it contain that are so important that I would find them useful?" She nearly made the slip to say that he needed them.

His eyes narrowed slightly.

He was suddenly onto her. She swung her staff at him and screamed out, hoping to attract attention and bolster her own bravado.

He jumped back, and she charged him.

Even if her staff wasn't magic enhanced here, she could hurt him before he managed to unsheathe his weapon. Maybe enough, so that she could escape.

The element of surprise threw him off balance. She slammed her staff against his hand as he reached for his sword, and she screamed out again seeking attention.

He cried out in pain as he grabbed his hand, the staff having struck him so hard, she was certain she heard a bone or two crack. She knew though, he'd quickly heal himself once he was free of the castle, and he'd want to kill her with a vengeance.

Somebody would surely be looking for her now. Though she didn't want any to know she'd found their weapons and clothes and move them again. She twisted her staff and struck his arm as he attempted to use his other hand to grab his sword.

Again, he cried out in agony. He backed up toward the stairs, and she lunged at him, striking his leg with a swing. He stumbled as a slew of curses spilled from his lips.

Suddenly, the warning bells rang out, and for the first time, her heart cheered to hear them.

She concentrated on her training and thrust with her staff at his belly. He managed to move out of its deadly path and rushed up the stairs, grunting in distress.

"Know this, Rosenthal, your end is near!" she yelled, again hoping someone would hear her and come to her aid, her blood pumping through her veins at an accelerated rate.

"You'll never succeed in reaching Parenkin," he snorted, still attempting to beat a hasty retreat from the weapon she wielded.

Again, he reached for his sword with his uninjured hand. She struck his fingers so hard, she knew this time she heard some of the bones snap. He cried out as the sound of boots tromping on the marble floor drew closer.

"Rosenthal's here!" Mexia screamed.

"You will be mine," he said under his breath, and made a break for the side door.

She chased after him, but despite his injuries, his six-foot stride made him outdistance her. As soon as she was outside, the guards rushed to apprehend her.

One quickly pulled her staff from her grasp, as two other knights grabbed her arms.

"Not me, you imbeciles! Him!" she screamed at them, her voice nearly hoarse. "Let go of me!" Her whole body burned with rage as she attempted to twist her arms free, kicking and screaming. "Rosenthal is getting away! Let go of me!"

Derek suddenly appeared. "What's going on here?"

"Rosenthal is getting away! Tell these men to let me go!"

He motioned for them to release her.

As soon as she was free, she jerked her staff from one of the men's grasp and dashed after Rosenthal who'd managed to get beyond the castle gates.

"Grab her!" Derek shouted.

The men ran after her and took her into custody again, their hands grasping her arms as they nearly lifted her off the ground.

"Troll's dung, Derek! These men let him get away!" she screamed at him.

The men walked her back toward the castle. She squirmed, attempting to wrench her arms free, striking at them with the toe of her boots, trying to kick them solidly in the shins.

Derek ran his hand over her face. "Calm thyself, my lady."

Immediately, she collapsed, as one of the men lifted her in his arms. In a foggy state, she heard Derek say, "What happened?"

"She struck one of our knights with her staff. He ran out of here for dear life. It appeared she'd broken his fingers."

"How did she get to her weapon?"

She shook her head, slurring her words. "He escaped, you fools. Now he will get me."

"Carry her to her room. Have two guards posted."

Princess Talamaya and Kersta ran into the courtyard, their own guard escort dashing outside with them.

"Mexia, are you all right?" the princess asked. "Did he hurt you?"

She sighed deeply. "He will."

The princess glared at Derek. "Rosenthal was able to get into your castle. It is not safe here for Mexia." She folded her arms when he didn't say anything. "I had a vision, Derek. He posed as a knight, and she had to fight him. He attempted to draw his sword. Would a knight of yours pull a weapon against the woman you're betrothed to if he truly worked for you?"

"You tell 'em, Tala," Mexia drawled.

The princess raised her brows to hear Mexia call her that.

Mexia pointed to the princess. "You tell 'em."

"Take Lady Mexia to her room," Derek said. "I want to see the captain of the guard at once."

"At once." Mexia saluted Derek with a sloppily placed hand to her brow.

The women followed her back up to her room as the guards escorted them.

When she was in her bed, Kersta touched her cheek. "What happened?"

Mexia frowned. "It was Rosenthal. I could have…have…have killed him." Her thoughts were muddled, frustrating her.

"Not without your powers, Mexia," the princess warned. "And not without our staffs being magically enhanced. I don't even know how you could have hurt him as much as you did, but I can see your training paid off."

Alinas ran into the room and joined the other ladies at the bed. "Are you all right?"

Mexia shook her head. "He'll kill me if I…" She sighed deeply. "Don't get him first."

"The word is all over the castle already. Nobody can believe Rosenthal could have sneaked in like he did."

"Troll dung," Mexia said, then closed her eyes.

Alinas gasped to hear her swear. Then she took a deep breath. "Did he hurt her?"

"No." Kersta touched Mexia's arm. "I think she's been drugged."

"Spell," Mexia corrected her. "Sluggish spell."

"Calming spell," Alinas said. "My brother's used it on me before."

Mexia hmpfd. "I'll use it on Derek next, once...once I learn how to do it."

"What's that, dear Mexia?" Derek asked as he walked into the room. "What do you propose to use on me?"

CHAPTER 17

"Okay, Derek, you let that creep get away," Mexia moaned as she gazed at him. Her eyes felt droopy and barely responsive, to her utter irritation.

Princess Talamaya said, "What are you going to do to ensure Mexia's safety? Rosenthal could pose as a cook next and poison her food."

"You tell 'em, Tala."

Kersta frowned.

Derek held Mexia's fingers to his lips and kissed them. "I will let no one harm you."

"He wanted your…your spell book."

Derek's eyes widened. "He said this?"

"He hadn't killed me because he wanted me to get into your room. He thought we were…" She took a deep breath, losing her train of thought, then closed her eyes.

"Mexia?"

"Can you not undo the calm spell?" his sister asked, her voice highly agitated.

"You know I cannot."

"I thought you only said that so you wouldn't have to return me to the way I was before *you* used the spell on me last month, my lord brother."

"No. There's no spell I know of that counteracts this one." He ran his hand over Mexia's braided hair. "Mexia? What did he want the spell book for?"

She opened her eyes. "To vanish?" She gave him a lopsided smile, making him shake his head.

"He already knows how to do that."

"I figured as much. There's something else...something in there he wanted. I asked but he...he...his sword. He went for his sword."

"When you asked him, what did he say?"

She smiled. "I wasn't so dumb...not so dumb after all."

"What did he say, Mexia?"

"Ah, Derek, he got away. Why did they stop...stop me?"

Exasperated, he took a deep breath, his hand still holding hers securely. "I cannot take you to the school, despite wanting you there by my side. It'd be too dangerous. He knows every inch of it. You will stay here and wait for me."

"He wants me."

Derek raised a brow. "What?" His voice changed from soothing to deadly.

"Dead."

Kersta touched Mexia's shoulder. "He didn't say that, Mexia."

"Dead." She nodded.

Derek turned to Kersta, but she shook her head. "He said he wanted her or would have her or something to that effect. Her thoughts are muddled." She folded her arms as she creased her brow at him.

"She wounded him...hurt his pride. She intends to kill him. Why would he not wish her dead as well?"

"Great." Mexia sighed. "I could have killed him... and now he wants me dead."

"If he could take her away from you and was able to harness her power…there are not many female mages around, you must realize, wouldn't she be the ultimate conquest for him? Perhaps he wishes companionship. Just capturing her untamed spirit could be something he'd desire, don't you agree?"

"No," Mexia said, wrinkling her nose.

Derek stared at Mexia. "He cannot mean to have her."

Kersta huffed in annoyance. "You've imprisoned her here against her will, have you not? What difference does it make if you keep her, or he does?"

"I love her with all my heart. That's the difference."

"You tell 'em." Mexia smiled.

"If you hold her here, all of us here, she will not be able to defeat him when next they meet."

"She has no need as she will not see him again." He rose to his feet. "I *will* kill him." He leaned over and kissed Mexia's lips. "It will be my honor. Sleep for now, Mexia. I will return later."

Derek stormed out of the room.

Alinas turned to the guard posted. "Shut the door."

He bowed his head and closed it.

She faced Princess Talamaya. "I fear for Mexia's life. My brother is too lost in his love for her. He cannot see that she may have the abilities to fight Rosenthal and win. I've never seen him afraid of anything before, like he is of losing Mexia. It's affecting his judgment."

"Judgment." Mexia nodded.

The ladies all looked over at her as she smiled back at them.

"What do you propose to do, Alinas?" the princess asked.

"Tonight, after the evening meal, Derek will return to Langdon Castle. The ceremony and demonstrations of magical skills will be held all day tomorrow. My mother and I and our escort will take us to the castle before dawn breaks. That is when you will leave here for Parenkin's castle."

The princess sighed. "But our staffs, our clothes...we will need these."

"I will bring them to you after Derek leaves here this evening."

Mexia waved her hand as if she was in school. "The spell book?"

Alinas considered Mexia. "Yes, I can get you into his room to see his spell book."

The princess sat at the foot of the bed. "How do we get out of here?"

"I will activate the portal you first came here in so you can return to the mountain pass."

"But Derek will know you have done this, won't he?" the princess asked.

"More than likely I will have to confess, as I will not allow any other to take the blame for my actions."

"And then?"

"He will banish me from here."

"To where?"

Alinas shook her head.

"You can come with us to Damar," Kersta said.

"And if you and your companions do not survive? The way to Parenkin's castle is fraught with danger."

Mexia pulled her amulet free from around her neck. "You will wear this as a gift from me. My father will take you in. You...you will be most welcome."

Alinas glanced over at the princess and smiled.

Assuming Alinas had read the princess's mind, Mexia said, "What?"

"The princess had a thought. Her twin brother is unattached," Kersta said.

"Ah," Mexia said. "I want to see Derek's spell book."

"Tonight," Alinas offered, "after Derek has left the castle. If we do it before this, we will get caught."

Mexia closed her eyes.

Alinas patted her hand. "She needs to rest. The calming spell makes you want to sleep more than anything. When she wakes, she will be back to her normal self. Would you ladies like to come with me to play a game of cards in the meantime?"

"Yes," Kersta said.

"I would," the princess agreed.

Their light steps crossed the floor. Then the door opened, they exited the room and the door closed.

Mexia lay quietly for some time, her mind drifting between the images of fighting Rosenthal and kissing Derek. She smiled, then opened her eyes.

The spell book. She had to find out what Rosenthal wanted.

Rolling off the bed, she slipped her feet to the floor. Then remembering the guards posted at the door, she walked to the window instead.

To her distress, an owl flew close to the window. Rosenthal's familiar? Was he keeping an eye on her through the winged fowl?

"Be gone, owl!" She waved her hand at it as it alighted on the veranda roof below, its eyes fixed on her.

After lifting her gowns, she climbed onto the windowsill. Again, she saw the brown-scaled dragon, this time farther in the distance. Could she will it, despite not being able to use her mage skills in the castle? Then realized, yes. Kersta could still read minds. The princess could still have visions. Mexia undoubtedly could call the beasts to aid her.

But if the dragon helped her, would the owl fly back to Rosenthal and tell him she'd escaped from the castle? And if so, wouldn't the rogue mage be a bigger threat to her as he could use his powers against her?

Still, she had to get to Derek's room somehow.

She willed the dragon to her.

The speck in the sky grew closer, its expansive wings alternatively gliding on top of air currents, and beating the breeze with sophistication.

Grabbing hold of the window-frame, she called out to it with her mind.

He turned in her direction as her heartbeat increased with expectation. Glancing down at the owl, she noticed he'd twisted his head around to see the dragon's approach. Well, she hadn't wished Rosenthal to know she could summon a dragon, but it was done now.

The dragon coasted in close to the building, and she jumped, hoping she wouldn't slide off his scaly body and fall to the veranda two stories below. After she made it and got a good grip, he flew around to the top side of the floor where the royal family resided.

She had him maneuver to Derek's window. Seeing only a large bed and wardrobe, she urged the dragon to the next window. Here was his office, a desk, a stack of books lying in one corner of it, and another resting on a stand. With her heart racing, she leapt at the window and landed half on and half off the narrow sill. Struggling, she finally managed to crawl into the room, then thanked the dragon. With her urging, he soared safely away from the building.

She looked down into the courtyard to see three boys, one who held a ball, staring up at her. She dashed back from the window and fell against the stand holding the book.

Before it crashed against the floor, she grabbed the stand, but the book hit the floor with a bang, the sound reverberating into the next room.

Or was it a door closing that had made the noise?

"Your Majesty, the Grand Wizard has sent word three times already requesting your return to Langdon Castle at once."

The sound of the man's voice nearly gave her a heart attack. Derek was now in his bedchambers?

"And I have said I will go after I have dinner with my betrothed, no sooner."

If he found her here, then what? She stood still, trying to figure out where they were heading, but they seemed to remain in one spot.

"He wants you to help with setting up the ceremony for tomorrow. Normally there are 45 of you to do the job, but with just the three of you seniors this year…"

Mexia picked up the book and set it on the desk, then turned to the first page, trying to ignore the conversation in the next room so she could absorb all the spells she could before she got caught.

The page showed several generations of kings who had passed the book down to their mage sons. Derek's name was the last entry.

She ran her finger over the letters which immediately resulted in a tingling that occurred in her fingertip, then quickly extended all the way through her body.

Suddenly, the pages flipped back and forth as if an invisible force attempted to find the right one in haste.

She stared at the page that the book had opened to. The sleep spell. She quickly memorized it. Then the pages turned, and she smiled to see the calm spell.

Again, she concentrated on memorizing the spell. As soon as she had it down, it was as though the invisible page turner knew, and flipped through the pages again for her. This time the spell on transportation appeared.

If one wishes to transport one's self, he must think of the place he wishes to be and he will go there. When one has this ability learned, he may attempt to take another with him, two at the most.

She wanted to test it out later, find the spell that Rosenthal wanted, but she couldn't turn the pages, though she attempted to. She grimaced and concentrated on the transportation spell, hoping she wouldn't end up someplace bad, or unable to return again to Derek's office.

Where could she go that would be close so that she could just walk into this room? Another room off this one. His bedchambers? His voice came from another room.

Three doors led out of his office. One most likely to the bedchambers. One perhaps a sitting area. The other into the hall?

The men's conversation had stopped. Her skin bristled with worry. She hadn't heard the door shut upon their exodus. Were they still in the room?

She peeked into the bedchambers. No sign of Derek or the other man he'd been talking to. She shut the door, then returned to the book. Concentrating, she imagined herself in the bedchambers, only the image of the bed came into mind with its pale blue satiny sheets and comforter, all trimmed in gold. Instantly, she found herself standing in the middle of it, surrounded by the partially closed curtains of the bed.

"Have you closed the castle gates so that no one can come in or out of it?" Derek asked, pulling the door open to his bedchambers. "I don't want anyone to leave or come in until the lady and I are married. This should ensure Rosenthal doesn't get back into the grounds again."

The wardrobe door opened, then closed.

Mexia's head pounded with fretfulness as she thought of being in the office in front of Derek's desk. Immediately she transported from the bed to his desk, just where she envisioned.

She stared at the pages, but they wouldn't turn. What had she done wrong? Transporting another person. She still hadn't learned that spell yet. How in the world could she manage that without setting off all the alarms in the place? As soon as she transported some poor soul…

Boots pounded on the floor next door and a man cleared his throat. "Your Majesty, I beg your forgiveness at interrupting your bath like this and I know this has to be completely unfounded, but you said to tell you if anything unusual occurred. Anything unusual at all."

"Yes, yes, what is it?"

"Three boys in the courtyard said one of the ladies from Inherian was in your office moments ago, looking out the window. They said a dragon carried her there. I know this is preposterous but thought you should be made aware…"

Hurried footsteps headed for the office, filling Mexia's stomach with dread. Immediately, she transported herself to her guest chambers. Again, she stood in the middle of the bed.

She quickly lay down and closed her eyes, a smile stirring on her lips. She tapped her fingers on the bed as no one came to check on her. Would Derek discover the pages turned in his spell book…shoot, she'd left the book on his desk not on his stand where it'd been.

He would know then. Wouldn't he?

Forever it seemed, she lay in the bed waiting, attempting to remain patient, sure they'd check to see if she was in the chambers.

Finally, the guard opened the door. "Yes, my lord, she is still sleeping here."

Derek chuckled. "I bet she is."

The door closed and Mexia frowned. When she chanced to open her eyes, she found herself alone in the room still, to her relief.

She sat up in bed, then wondered, if she could do the spells from the book, had her powers returned? Had the magic from the book recognized she would be Derek's wife and given her powers back to her?

She ran over to the mirror and formed the illusion of herself, then bade it lie in her bed. Concentrating, she transported herself back to Derek's bed, hoping he wouldn't have laid down for a nap. Certain he wouldn't, she had to find out where he was now. Had he returned to his office, waiting for her to learn some more spells?

The chambers were deathly quiet. Dare she peek into his office?

She couldn't chance getting caught. Instead, she had an idea. She returned to her bedchambers, then opened the door.

Only one guard stood there instead of two now, and he turned to her and tilted his chin up. "Yes, my lady?"

She reached out and grabbed his wrist before he could say a word. Instantly, she transported him into her chambers. Then she cast a spell, making him lose his memory of the instance.

"What do you want, Sir Knight?" she asked him as he stood staring at her.

"I...I..."

"You checked on me and found that I was fine. Then you wished to return to your post."

"Yes."

He shook his head, stepped outside her room, and shut the door.

She looked up at the ceiling in the direction of Derek's chambers. Did the spell book's pages turn to the next spell she wished to learn once she completed her learning of the last spell? And was Derek watching the book in anticipation of her returning to his office? She imagined he was, just like the owl.

She hurried over to the window. Yes, just like the owl who still watched her goings-on from the veranda below.

She paced across the floor. Somehow she had to get into his

office again, but first she had to get him out of there, if he indeed waited for her next move. Then she thought of Kersta's invisibility cloak. Would their magical items work now in her grasp?

She glanced back at her image still sleeping in the bed. Then she transported herself to the cellar where their things were still stored. Grabbing Kersta's cloak up, she quickly pulled it over her shoulders, situated the hood over her head, and clicked the gold clasp shut.

Totally pleased with herself, she smiled. Now she could have some real fun.

She materialized inside the prince's office, only this time on the other side of the desk, and totally invisible.

Derek paced across the floor, then sat down at his desk. His intense blue eyes studied the book as he breathed in deeply. Was he trying to maintain his serenity?

She leaned over the desk, trying to peer at the book to see what page it was on now. A new spell. She chuckled. How to make a portal.

He frowned. She straightened her back. Taking another deep breath of air, he leaned forward into the desk.

Did he get a whiff of her fragrant waters? She stepped away from the desk.

He shook his head and leaned back in his chair, then steepled his fingers as he studied the book.

She drew close to the desk. Either she'd have to turn the book around and give him a real start, or she'd have to try and memorize the spell from reading it upside down.

Of course, the other choice was standing next to him, but her body heat and fragrance would probably give her away.

After reading the spell slowly to ensure she got it right, she then attempted to make a portal in his bedchambers. The book's page flipped over one.

He jumped from his chair. She stifled the chuckle that nearly burst from her lips.

"Mexia? Love?" He smiled broadly, making her smile in return. "You are very good at these wizardry games." Reaching his hands out, he tried to touch her. She stepped away. He tilted his nose up and smelled. "You smell heavenly. You were concerned about not being chaperoned, but what about now? Here you are, in my bedchambers with me all alone, no less. What will everyone think?"

She smiled and was dying to respond. And he knew it.

He moved to where she'd stood, while she maneuvered around the desk and read the next spell. It turned out to be another portal spell, but one that would end the journey this time where she could go from one into the other. She formed the second portal in the kitchen.

The book flipped several pages, and she quickly moved away from it as he hurried around the desk, reaching, grabbing at the air, amusing her no end.

"Dragonmage will be sorely disappointed to find out how much fun you are and that I'm the one who gets to enjoy your antics. You and I can pair up at the next of his wizardry games. It'll be most enjoyable."

She was dying to tell him, thanks but no thanks, she'd do better on her own.

He lunged forward as she stood against a far wall. She clasped her hand to her mouth to keep from laughing out loud.

He smiled. "I'm afraid we're going to have to have a change of plans, however."

Now what?

"If you know all of my spells, and your own have returned, I can no longer keep you safe here."

"Locked up here, you mean."

She chuckled as he ran for her. She knew she couldn't avoid responding to him one of these times, the way he aggravated her.

Instantly, she materialized in the hall outside his bedchambers. She waited for a few seconds, then returned to his office.

He stuck close to his book still. Clever mage. He knew she'd come back to see what else she could learn from his book. She attempted to read it upside down again, but he leaned over the desk toward her. His heavy breathing made her realize he was still trying to tell whether she was there based on her fragrance.

She looked down at the book. A reverse time spell. Wanting to flip the book around, she desired to read it as quickly as she could. If she could only use that to go back and save Sir Farrington from getting killed...

So engrossed was she in reading the spell upside down, she hadn't noticed Derek maneuvering around his desk until he touched her shoulder. She cried out in surprise and he laughed.

Wrapping his arms securely around her instantly, he said, "Okay, Mexia, I have you now. Try to get free from me this time." He attempted to kiss her lips, but his mouth met her forehead instead. He moved his mouth lower when two of his royal guard burst into his office.

One of them said, "Your Majesty..."

"I've got everything under control..."

Mexia kissed Derek's cheek, then transported herself to her bedchambers.

Kersta and the princess cried out as Derek materialized in the room with his arms wrapped in a circle around something none of them could see.

CHAPTER 18

Mexia squirmed to get free of Derek, not realizing when she transported to the women's quarters, she'd have taken him with her. "Let go of me, Derek!" she finally yelled.

The princess and Kersta laughed, finally realizing what had happened as they could hear her voice while Derek struggled with the invisible force. Mexia's stomach clenched with annoyance at her friend's joviality. Luckily, Alinas wasn't there to read her thoughts, though she wasn't sure Alinas could do so when Mexia was invisible.

"I want to know how you made yourself invisible. Why didn't you use that spell before? Show me how you did it!" His words were spoken in wonder, mixed with fun. He tightened his hold on her, evidently feeling she was slipping away.

"No! Let go of me!"

This was one thing she hadn't planned for, not being able to free herself of Derek…a simple thing like that. She just couldn't fight his strength, her own body grew weary from the struggle, and her skin perspired from the combination of their body heat and workout.

He wiggled her to the bed and managed to get her down.

Unmistakably, he'd tired, too, and the only way he could keep her in his grasp was to pin her to the bed.

She imagined being in the gardens, instantly transporting them into the shell basin of the fountain where one of the three fish poured water on top of them.

In his surprise, Derek released her, and she quickly materialized in his office, and read his spell, being careful not to drip water on his book. Then he grabbed her again. She squealed out in alarm.

The pages of the book rippled, opening to a new spell, but Mexia couldn't see what had appeared as Derek's fingers slipped under her cloak, tickling her waist.

She laughed. "Quit it, Derek!"

"Tell me how you do it!"

"No!" she gasped between laughing as his fingers worked over all of her ticklish spots beneath her ribs.

"Tell me!"

She laughed out loud. "Derek, quit it. My stomach hurts from laughing so much."

He maneuvered her into his bedchambers and pinned her to his bed this time, both dripping wet.

"You will have a devil of a time sleeping in a wet bed."

"I will be returning to the school tonight. But my servants will wonder why they have to dry out my bed when I give the order."

His hard body rested against hers, growing harder by the second. She tried to unsettle him without success.

"You are only making things more tenable, my love. How can I let you go to see Parenkin when you stir such desire in me?"

Her breath came quickly as she tried to settle the feelings that he stirred in her. Though she should have been cold and wet from the dip in the pool, her skin felt as though she just bathed in the hot springs.

He leaned over and kissed her lips this time and smiled when she kissed him back. "Wizardry games have never been this satisfying." Then he grew serious. "I can see I will never be able to keep you here though. As much as my heart breaks to have to release you, I will."

His fingers caressed her cheeks. "I cannot think of any way to keep you here against your will…though know this, I only have done this to keep you safe, not because I am a tyrant." His voice was spoken firmly, but with kindness and his brow furrowed with concern. She knew he meant every word of it.

"I love you, Derek."

"Oh, Mexia, now you say the words I've so wished to hear from your lips."

"I couldn't say it before until you gave me my freedom to pursue my quest."

"Do you realize that what I say about the prophecy is true? None other than my own betrothed who is a mage like me or a mage descendent of mine can learn the spells from the book. Not even Rosenthal could read them. He would have to have used you to get to the book. I want you to wait for me after I graduate and we are wed. Then we will journey to see Parenkin together."

"I cannot delay what I must do, my love. You know it is so. Rosenthal will continue to grow more powerful if he can. I cannot wait for your return."

He sighed deeply. "I understand."

She unclasped the fastener on her cloak. His eyes instantly darkened as she lay beneath him. He shook his head. "You are more beautiful than any woman I have ever known…and the most clever."

"I bet you say that to all of the women who swim with you in your fish fountain."

He laughed and kissed his fill of her. Only the sound of a woman clearing her throat at his bedchamber's door made him stop. He rose from his bed, and quickly pulled Mexia up. "My lady mother."

"My son." She raised her brows at Mexia.

Mexia's mouth curved up, then she transported herself into Derek's office, only he still had hold of her hand, and she moved him there, too.

She chuckled under her breath as he smiled at her.

"Pixie," he whispered to her.

She smiled at the reference to being mischievous and glanced over at the book. The new spell showed on the page.

He frowned. "The book has never opened up to this page for me."

"I am more powerful than you," Mexia teased.

"Derek?" his mother said in his bedchambers, apparently expecting him to return to her at any moment.

The door shut on her way out.

"Sorry, Derek. I didn't think I'd have taken you here with me when I used the transportation spell. I figured if anyone had some explaining to do to your mother, it was you, not me."

He laughed. "And none of it was truly my fault."

"Ha! Who held me hostage here?"

He kissed her cheek and pulled her close as they studied the page.

Time Stopper Spell.

Mexia cast the spell before Derek had finished reading it.

With his arms still wrapped around her when she transported back to her bedchambers, he went with her. The room was empty, and they pulled the door open, then entered the hall.

"I didn't have time to cast the spell," Derek said.

"I did."

She walked past the guards who didn't even seem to notice them. Derek paused and waved his hand in front of one of the men's faces.

Mexia smiled. "I think the spell worked. They are stopped in time while we are still moving. They can't see us."

"I was going to lecture him for not greeting me with respect as he should have."

She laughed. "I believe this may have been the spell Rosenthal was after. He could create such havoc, while no one could react."

"But I hadn't even completed reading the spell."

"I'm a fast reader." She winked at him, then pulled him through the hall. "Take me to the kitchen."

He led her down several flights until they were on the main floor.

She shook her head, her smile couldn't have stretched any farther. "Couldn't you have transported us there?"

He chuckled. "I figured if you had wanted to, you would have taken us there."

"I haven't been to the kitchen before, therefore I couldn't transport myself there."

"Ah, a slight technicality I hadn't remembered."

"But now that I have been, I will be able to."

They found Gallant with a leg of griffin wedged between his teeth as he ate the fowl.

Derek laughed out loud. "Seems your companion got hungry between meals."

She pointed to the man who was supposed to be guarding Gallant. The guard had a goblet raised to his lips. "Drinking on duty?"

The prince pulled the cup from the knight's grasp and smelled the liquid. "Water."

Mexia sighed. "Good. I would not wish to think I got the man in trouble because of a spell I cast."

He took her hand and returned her to his office. "I have to finish reading the spell. Though this does give me an idea."

"What's that?"

"We could return to my chambers and no one would ever interrupt us."

She smiled. "Now you are being mischievous."

He chuckled. "I met my match when I encountered you, Mexia." Then frowning, he considered that the page had already turned. "To undo the spell. It didn't give me time to learn the spell."

She leaned her head against his chest as they read it together. Once she finished the spell, she cast it.

The bell rang for the supper meal, startling them.

Derek shook his head as he continued to read the spell book. "You will have to teach me how to read that fast." When he was done, he looked over at her. "And how to cast the invisibility spell."

"It is not a spell, Derek."

She fastened the cloak at her throat and vanished.

He reached out for her.

She unfastened the clasp and reappeared. "An invisibility cloak. We found it in the Cave of Sorrows, but it is Kersta's. I borrowed it."

A knight knocked at the office door. "Your Majesty, the bell has rung for the evening meal."

Derek nodded. "Yes, we shall be right there."

He pulled Mexia close as soon as the knight hurried away. "I don't want to let you go. It is the hardest thing I've ever done."

"Believe me, Derek, I don't want to leave you. But nothing will be right, until I have done what I must do." Her stomach muscles tightened with concern with the thought of leaving him.

He kissed her mouth with pent-up frustration as she plied his with the same kind of pressure. "I will come for you at Parenkin's castle. Wait for me there, then. For now, we share a meal, then I must return to Langdon Castle."

She nodded, and he took her just outside the dining hall using his spell. He escorted her into the hall, her hand in his. Everyone bowed as they passed the tables. When they reached the head table, his mother's face remained stern.

He walked over to her, then kissed her cheeks in greeting. She whispered to him and he nodded.

When he returned to Mexia and pulled her chair out for her, she said, "Pray tell, what was said."

He sat beside her and placed his hand on her thigh and squeezed.

She laughed. "Quit it, Derek. You're tickling me and I shall spill my wine."

He chuckled. "She told me I need to marry you soon or we'll create a scandal."

"And you said?"

"It was all your fault."

"Great."

"She also said, she never thought I'd meet my match as I've done in you."

Mexia noticed all of the courtiers, though they worked on the meals set before them, watched the couple who would soon be wed.

She pulled apart the breast meat of a griffin. "I'm sure my father will be pleased when he meets you."

"Ah, you do not think he will be upset with me for holding you hostage?"

"I'm sure he'd have a word or two with you about the matter. He's pretty powerful, despite being just a country-trained mage. Therefore, I have no intention of mentioning it to him."

Derek looked over at the boy, Davin, who was busily tugging at a wishbone with another boy. "You will leave him here, won't you?"

"Yes. I would not wish the young man injured on our journey."

"I take it all of the rest of your companions will go with you."

"They will not be dissuaded."

"I cannot persuade you to take some of my knights?"

She paused. Then shook her head. "If I could, I would go alone, to limit our losses."

"I wish you would wait for me."

"I will, at Parenkin's castle."

"You have all the knowledge you need, Mexia. Why do you persist in going to the school when the headmaster and other boys do not want you there?"

"Partly, it is the principle of the thing. But can you not see that I also wish to have the title? My own people have never had the distinction of being school trained."

He nodded. "But you are cleverer than any mage I've even encountered. I think your simple ways have made you more resourceful, more determined, so to speak."

"Simple ways? Hmpf. Truthfully, I figured you'd say I was more stubborn." She raised her brows as Derek's mouth turned into a smile.

"Yeah, definitely that."

When they finished with the meal, Mexia and Derek said their farewells in the gardens. Tears filled his eyes making hers tear up as well. "I cannot bear to leave you, Mexia, knowing the dangers you shall face."

"You have given me the opportunity to learn many new spells. I'm sure they will help to keep me safe."

He kissed her fully, their tongues touching, their lips pressuring, their bodies melding together as one. "If I do not leave, the headmaster will transport me there himself."

She smiled. "I love you, Derek, and will see you at Parenkin's."

He kissed her one last time. "At Parenkin's, my love."

He bowed to her, then vanished.

Kersta cleared her throat. Mexia turned to see Princess Tala-maya and Alinas waiting for her, too.

"We are here for you, Mexia. We will always be here for you."

Mexia wiped a couple of errant tears daring to dribble down her cheeks. "Thank you, ladies."

"The musicians are waiting to entertain us," Alinas said as she took Mexia's hand. "My brother has told me he is returning your things to you and permitting you to leave the castle on the morrow."

"Yes, so you will not be in trouble when we leave, Alinas."

She smiled. "I would have done this for you. It would have only been right to have done so."

That night with harps and flutes playing a lively tune for their entertainment, Mexia and her companions sat with the queen and her staff, but Mexia's mind was on Derek. She knew now why Kersta saw him as a danger to Mexia. If she could not get her mind on the dangerous mission that lay ahead, they would indeed be in trouble.

Early the next morning, Mexia, the queen and Alinas said their goodbyes. Then dressed in their own traveling clothes, Mexia led her companions to the portal that would transport them to the mountain passage.

Only Davin was absent. They had purposefully kept their journey secret from him so when they reached the passage, Mexia nearly died to see him sitting on a boulder waiting for them.

"I shall be a page you said, my lady. I know you do not easily give your word, then take it away. Everyone placed bets on whether you would make it out of the castle to fulfill your quest. I knew you would." He patted a pouch of coins. "Many knew you wouldn't. But they assumed Prince Derek was much more powerful than you. I knew this wasn't so."

"Who will you be page to, Davin?"

He smiled. "To Sir Farrington. You promised."

She took a deep breath. "All right."

"What's wrong, Mexia?" Kersta asked. "You seemed concerned about the boy, but I couldn't read your mind as to why."

Mexia took her aside. "We didn't expect Davin to join us and here he is. I worried it was Rosenthal up to his old tricks."

Kersta nodded. "But I can read the boy's mind. I doubt Rosenthal would permit me to. Dragonmage, Derek, and their friends purposefully hid their thoughts from me."

"But I cannot. And even if Rosenthal can, he is very clever."

They both looked back at Davin.

Mexia walked over to him. "When we saw Pemlican about his goat, we thought the mountain water awfully cold to bathe in. Did you also?"

"Of course, my lady. That's why I used the horse's trough."

Mexia still wasn't convinced. What if Rosenthal's owl had seen the boy bathing there?

She fingered her staff with apprehension. His gaze shifted to the staff. If it was Rosenthal, did he worry she'd break his fingers again? "What was it we found by the sarcophagus in Sir Farrington's tomb?"

He smiled. "Boras's key."

She sighed deeply.

"Did I pass the test?"

"What test?"

"The one to see if I was Rosenthal? I am not he."

"But how can I be assured of this?"

"I hid in the loft with you and Lila in the butcher's house.

Bear hit you when we were in the sewers. I applied the healing patch to your face."

She nodded. "Yes, you did. And helped me to escape into the castle's library."

"Kitchen, my lady."

"All right, Davin. But I wanted you to stay with Pemlican. He said he needs your help."

"I will. Because you promised me I'd be a knight, and I must help others."

"Yes."

He gave her a hug. "Come back soon, my lady."

He ran off down the path, turning once to wave, then continued on his way.

Mexia headed up the path.

The princess said, "Did you not think it was Davin?"

Mexia paused as she watched the path behind them. "Wait here for me." She transported herself to the men's sleeping quarters in Derek's castle.

A young man approached her. "My lady, we were told you left."

"I have returned for Davin. Is he still sleeping?"

"I will check. Though most have arisen for morning chores."

A few minutes later, Davin appeared, still buttoning his shirt his hair mussed up from sleeping.

"We are leaving for Parenkin castle now."

"You will take me with you, will you not?"

"Yes, get your boots and cloak. But be quick about it."

Davin soon joined her, then took her hand. She transported him to where her companions waited.

Kersta gasped. "It was Rosenthal? Or this one is?"

Davin yawned. "I'm what?"

"The rogue mage, Rosenthal."

Davin frowned. "I do not look anything like him, from what I am told."

"Where did we first meet?" Kersta asked.

Davin looked over at Mexia. She nodded.

"I asked you for a coin. I beg your forgiveness. I stole because I had to."

Mexia squeezed his hand. "This is Davin."

"How do you know for certain?" Kersta asked.

"It is something I feel in my heart. I cannot explain. I met Rosenthal first in Inherian in Grimoria's castle and since then two more times. There is something about him that makes me naturally suspicious." She turned to Davin. "Will you stay with Pemlican and help him?"

"But I wish to be an adventurer like you."

"Not a page?"

"Well, yes a page, but until I have a knight to serve, I wish to be an adventurer like you."

"The lad is too young," Gallant grunted.

"You will take me with you, will you not, my lady?"

She glanced back at her companions. "You see Davin did not do as I asked."

The princess smiled. "I believe you have it figured out correctly."

"Then we must go to Pemlican's place and kill Rosenthal," Kersta said.

"I imagine he never went there."

Mexia pushed forward on the path growing steeper with every step she took. The air thinned, but still remained warm. The branches of the evergreens stretched their fingers outward, shading the path as the sun grew higher in the sky. Willow o' wisps sputtered and sparked around them. Just flashes of colored light dashing hither and thither. Birds chirping overhead grew quiet suddenly though.

Mexia cast her protection spell over her companions and her.

"I didn't think the dark elves lived in these mountains," Kersta remarked.

"They don't," Davin said. "Goblins do."

The scent of pinesap filled the air as it turned cooler and crisper.

"Had Derek ever visited Parenkin's castle before?" the princess asked.

Mexia paused in her footsteps. "I never asked. If he had, he could have transported me there." Her skin tightened with irritation. "If he had and didn't help us, he can forget my marrying him."

"He must not have, Mexia," Kersta said. "He let us continue on with our journey, but was extremely reluctant, fearing evermore for your safety."

"But you see, he had to go to his graduation. That was more important." Mexia couldn't help the ice that settled on her words.

Davin ran ahead all of a sudden.

"Davin!" Mexia cried out and dashed after him.

"It's another portal."

She studied the lay of the boulders. "It is the same one that took us to Derek's castle."

"What does it mean, woman?" Gallant asked.

"I wished to see Parenkin and get permission to attend the school at all costs. But I have failed to do the quests set before us, first."

"But everything that needed to be done led to the mountains," Kersta said.

"Everything that needs to be done must be accomplished in the past. Everyone gather close to me and hold tight. When did all of the problems occur, Davin? Sir Farrington was killed, Pemlican's goat disappeared, along with Lila's baby, and the butcher's daughter. When did it all happen?"

"The day of our great feast. Mae day, the third day of the month."

"Time?"

"Sir Farrington was killed in the morning right at dawn."

"Was this also before Rosenthal set the firetraps?"

"Yes, my lady."

"Then we must return there before the hour. Are we all ready? Remember, no one will know us. They have not met us before this."

"What about me?"

"Where were you during the feast?"

"Home sick. The same sickness that managed to kill my parents."

She nodded, her stomach muscles tightening with the notion. Had the people of Cramer no healer? "All right. Here we go."

CHAPTER 19

Mexia and her companions appeared in the town square next to the stone well that provided water to the community in the center. Immediately, she realized she should have made them appear in the cemetery, anywhere that would have given them a chance to blend in more.

Then she realized from the garments they wore, none of her companions fit in very well at all.

A woman screamed out as Mexia and her friends materialized.

"Mages," the woman said in disgust and hurried away.

At once, Mexia knew they were in trouble as a trickle of fear wound down her spine. Standing in a group, Derek, Dragonmage, their friends, and even Rosenthal and others she vaguely remembered from Grimoria's castle...the rogue mage seniors who had turned against the school, were there.

None of them would know her, and yet, she had to ensure none saw her now. She turned to Davin. "You didn't tell me Rosenthal and Derek would be here."

"I didn't know. I was sick in bed."

"I'll see to the sick," the princess said, and hurried off toward the castle of Cramer.

Davin's eyes grew big. "She will cure my parents?"

"If she can."

"We should kill Rosenthal," Gallant said. "Now, while he least suspects what we have in mind to do."

"We cannot. The spell only allows for one to go back to do good things, not bad."

"But killing something evil is good, is it not?"

"He hasn't done anything wrong yet. We would be worse than he, if we did anything to him now."

She considered the activities taking place. Two youngsters fought in a mock knightly forum, tables were piled high with a variety of foods from stuffed boar to cobs of corn, and a puppet show entertained the youngest of the crowd. Nearby, a group danced to a lively assortment of musical instruments, pipe whistles, drums, stringed quarters, and rattles.

Booths displaying special merchandise made for the festivities, stands for archery competition, and sack race games were all part of the day's activities. But the booth that seemed to hold the most interest was one where a lady offered her kisses for a price. Mexia smiled at the pretty blond who puckered her lips for the next man to stand before her.

Kersta grabbed Mexia's arm. "Derek just caught sight of you. In fact, because of the attention he has shown you, the others have turned to see you now."

"Orc's dung." Mexia started walking toward the butcher's shop. She had to go anywhere to get out of the mage's sight.

"He is following us," Kersta said. "He is drawn to you, like he was the first time he saw you. There is something about you that entices him like no other."

"Great!" She turned to Kersta. "Give me your cloak, if you would. I must vanish for the moment."

Kersta hurriedly switched cloaks with Mexia. "You will be nearby, though, won't you?"

"Yes." Mexia clasped the fastener shut on Kersta's cloak and instantly vanished.

"Wow!" Davin said. "Can I wear it next?"

"No word of this must be spoken," Kersta warned him.

"Ye best watch your words. The prince approaches with three of his friends."

Kersta turned to face them. Derek, Dragonmage, Rosenthal, and another she recognized from Langdon, but wasn't sure of his name.

"I am Prince Derek and these are my friends, Ros, Creighton, and Rosenthal. I wonder if I might inquire as to where you are from."

"Inherian." Kersta crossed her arms.

"And you are?"

"Lady Kersta."

He smiled. Mexia smiled. Kersta was giving him as little information as she could, and the notion amused him.

Davin tugged at Kersta's hand. "Can we go and see Lila now?"

"Wait a moment, young man. I wish to ask Lady Kersta where the other women in the party went to."

Kersta shook her head. "I have no idea. They wish to… mingle, I do suppose."

"One headed for the castle. But the other, just kind of vanished. I wish to know who the one is who…disappeared into thin air, so to speak."

"Lady Mexia," Davin blurted. He tugged at Kersta's hand. "Now please. We have to go now."

"Excuse me," Kersta said, curtseying to Derek. "I promised." She hurried away with Davin with Gallant running to keep up with them.

Davin glanced back at the mages. "They are watching us. Prince Derek is stroking his beard, deep in thought."

"He's determined to find Mexia and have a word with her," Kersta said. "His mind says so."

"Great. He will always pursue me."

Kersta glanced over at where Mexia's voice came from. She smiled. "Yes, Mexia. He cannot help himself. He is a danger to you and our mission, but not for the reason I first thought. Rather it is his inability to let you go, that causes the difficulty. Something binds the two of you together. Something magical."

Kersta turned to Davin. "Where are you taking me, Davin?"

"To where Sir Farrington is. Near Lila's house. That's where Benj killed him."

The party hurried to reach Lila's house, and when they arrived, a man somewhat younger than the knight held a sword at his throat. Immediately, Mexia cast a spell, causing the man to drop his sword.

Sir Farrington unsheathed his sword, ready to slay Benj, Mexia was certain. She cast the calming spell on Sir Farrington, then turned her attention to the other who shifted his gaze to the companions.

Kersta said, "Your lives will both be ruined if you further this grievance between the two of you."

Still invisible, Mexia grabbed Benj's wrist, causing him to cry out in fright. Her own heart beat way out of bounds, hoping she could change history, but only for the good of all.

In the next instant, she set Benj in front of the lady at the kissing booth. Before she could work her love spell on the two, the man who was standing next in line shoved Benj out of the way. "Wait your turn like the rest of us."

Mexia quickly cast her calming spell on the disgruntled man, then grabbed Benj's wrist and pulled him in front of the other again.

More grumbling ensued from the men behind the one she'd

calmed. Then she noticed Derek watching the situation. Could he figure out what was going on?

She cast a calming spell on each of the men in line, then turned to see Benj jamming his hands in his pockets as he searched for a coin to pay the lady. The girl folded her arms. "If you do not have the money to pay me for the kiss, step aside, Benj."

Working her love spell, Mexia cast the magic on the girl first, then Benj. The girl smiled sweetly at Benj and pulled him to her, their lips cementing together at once.

Then the girl quickly motioned to another to take her place, and the deed was done. Mexia sighed deeply as the man and his new love walked over to the dance, hand in hand.

Mexia transported herself to where Kersta, Davin and Gallant awaited her. She touched Kersta's arm, making her squeal out. "Mexia," she scolded, her voice hushed. "You shouldn't do that."

"Sorry, where's Sir Farrington?"

"He and Lila just walked inside their home. What about Benj?"

"Found a new lady to love and she, him."

"Okay, so now Benj won't steal Lila's baby and the knight shouldn't be dead, right?"

"Yes, hopefully not."

"And the butcher's daughter?"

Davin said, "They had an argument about the price, right over there, I was told." He pointed at the merchants' booths. "Everyone heard the row."

"When?"

"It was soon after Sir Farrington was killed. Almost like something evil was in the area at the time, causing all of the problems."

"Rosenthal," Mexia said. She hurried toward the butcher's stall as her companions followed her.

Already they could hear raised voices from thirty feet away. Mexia worked her calm spell on the pig farmer, Caron. Then for Gandon, the butcher, she cast the spell of obedience.

He smiled at Caron. "I was mistaken. There are two more selections of meat packaged here that are yours as well."

A little dark-haired girl played with a doll at his feet and Mexia assumed she was the one who'd been stolen away.

Caron gave the coins to Gandon, then took his sack of meat and bowed. "'Til next time."

Kersta said, "Well, that seems to have worked."

Before anyone could react, Rosenthal bumped into her. "Excuse me," he said, bowing his head slightly to her. He wrinkled his brow, his lips curved up. His long black hair was pulled back in a tail, and his face sported a thick curly beard. Blue eyes stared at her for a moment, then turned to consider Davin and Gallant. Facing Kersta again, he remarked, "You are not a mage…" He paused his words and smiled broadly. "But you read minds."

She folded her arms.

Mexia stood still, not wanting him to see that she was the mage who unraveled his wrongdoings. Now was not the time to confront him. For now, all she could do was accomplish the guild quests, then return to the present and continue on her journey to see Parenkin. There would be time enough to put an end to Rosenthal's evil ways.

"Hey, Rosenthal," Ros said. "We need to be getting back to Langdon."

"Yeah." He studied Kersta for a moment more, then looked around the area. His gaze rested briefly on Pemlican walking with his goat near one of the tables of food.

A smile brightened Rosenthal's face, then he vanished. Ros joined him with a flick of his wrist.

"Pemlican's goat," Mexia said just as Derek and Creighton

appeared next to her. She drew back as Derek reached his fingers out, pretending to swat at a nonexistent gnat, but she knew he was trying to locate who had spoken, but still invisible to the eye.

Kersta cleared her throat. "Did you want something more of us?" she asked Derek.

"My companions spoke to you for a moment. Did they say where they were off to?"

"The school."

Dragonmage shook his head. "Guess you ought to return, too, before the headmaster grows angry with you. Makes me glad to be a graduate of the school."

"You're not leaving the festivities?"

"No, think I'll hang around a bit more and see more of the lady you're itching to find. This Lady Mexia." He winked at Derek. "I imagine she will be joining her companions soon enough. I will be there when it happens."

The sound of footsteps in their direction made them turn to see the princess headed for them. She nodded to Kersta. It was times like these Mexia wished she had the ability to read minds.

"Are they all right?" Davin implored. "Did you cure them?"

"I was able to save your mother, but your father, he had already died."

"We must go..." Mexia clasped her hand to her mouth and transported herself two hundred yards away, her heart nearly stopping in fright as she hadn't meant to speak further in front of the two mages.

Derek and Dragonmage tried to find her as they waved their arms in the air. She chuckled.

"A mage," Derek said under his breath.

Kersta took the princess's arm and Davin's hand and hurried toward the mountain pass. Gallant ran to catch up as Mexia waited and watched for Derek and Dragonmage's response. They spoke to one another, then nodded and hurried after her companions to her dismay.

Judging by the direction they took, she figured they were either going to Pemlican's house, or the mountain pass. She would meet them there.

When they made it to the outskirts of town, she grabbed the princess's hand, making her cry out in terror.

Mexia whispered to her, "Everyone grab hold of me. We will go back to the present."

The princess and the rest grabbed the air in a circle as Mexia watched the two wizards slow their approach. She smiled, then cast her spell. The mages sprinted for them again, but Mexia and her companions vanished from the past and reappeared in the future.

Kersta took a deep breath. "Now what?"

"We didn't save Pemlican's goat," Mexia lamented.

They headed back toward his small stone home. From inside, they heard laughter. Peeking in through one of the windows, they saw Pemlican kissing an old woman while three grown men stood nearby smiling at them, every one of them resembling Pemlican, except for being younger versions.

"I cured his family," the princess said. "The goat doesn't matter now."

Mexia smiled. "Good. Then if all is well, we should be able to make our way through the mountain pass."

She turned to Davin. "You will now be a knight to Sir Farrington and must stay here."

"But how will he know—"

"He said so."

Kersta shook her head. "But what if we did not return his sword. If he wasn't a ghost in the crypt, Boras might not have stolen his sword. And if Davin's mother was still alive, he might not have been hiding in the sewers with the others, acting as a thief."

Mexia nodded. "Come will shall see Sir Farrington then."

The party headed back to Lila's house. When they knocked on the door, Sir Farrington opened it. He smiled. "I thought my new page had decided he'd rather go adventuring with you."

"No, Sir Farrington, he wishes to stay here with you." Mexia nudged Davin forth.

"Anything for the lad having helped me to retrieve my sword stolen by Boras." He patted Davin on the shoulder. "You have your mother and sisters and brothers to care for. You will work hard, but the money you earn will provide for them." He pointed to his armor lying in the main room. "My armor needs much work to shine as good as new."

"Yes, Master Farrington," Davin said. Then turning to Mexia, he bowed low. "Thank you for helping me. I shall always be in your debt."

"Do good always, Davin, and you shall be rewarded." She kissed his cheek.

"My prayers will be with you and your companions as you seek to meet with Parenkin."

The party said their goodbyes, then headed back to the mountain passage, the day already half over.

When they made their way beyond the portal, the air turned cooler and thinner. Fresh snow decorated most of the trees whose limbs remained shaded from the sun, the limbs drooping with the extra weight.

They hadn't gone very far when they heard a "mah-ah" from somewhere up ahead. "A goat," Mexia whispered.

"Pemlican's goat?"

They walked further, their footsteps hurried as they maneuvered around the boulder strewn path.

Mexia motioned for them to stop. "I hear nothing, other than the bleating of the goat."

"No birds singing, you mean," Kersta whispered.

"No. No sounds at all."

Mexia cast her protection spell, then moved forward.

As soon as they rounded a bend in the path, they saw the long-haired goat, only a kid, its eyes wild with fear. Mexia stopped her companions with a wave of her hand. "He is tied up to that tree."

"Who would have tied him there?"

Mexia took a deep breath trying to settle her disquiet. "Something that wishes us to help it? Something that will pounce on us as soon as we try?"

The princess pulled her scepter from her belt. With a well-aimed blast, she burned through the rope and the goat bolted free. Mexia used her charm on the goat, guiding it to return to Pemlican's abode. Instead the goat ran up the path.

Mexia frowned. "My ability to move animals to do my bidding has always worked. Even with the magical intelligent dragons. But why would a goat not do as I ask?"

"Why?" Kersta asked.

"Because he is not a goat?"

"Rosenthal?"

Mexia nodded and stuck her staff on the ground as she continued the climb. "He knew we sought to find Pemlican's goat. Even though the old man has his wife and sons, he must have still posted the note for the return of his goat. Rosenthal would know this, don't you think?"

She glanced up to see the same owl who tracked her movements the whole time she'd been in Albion, sitting in a tree higher up the mountain. His head turned. "Who?" he said.

She shook her head. "Rosenthal's familiar. He watches every move we make, that he can."

Figuring they'd have a fiendish time making their way

through the white devil wolves, goblins, and other creatures that were to make it tough on them, Mexia and her companions were surprised to find no resistance. Though the howling of the wind through the mountain passes, the ever increasing cold, and the lack of noise except for their boots crunching on the frozen ground, made Mexia shiver.

"What is so dangerous about this place?" Kersta asked. "Except for threat of frostbite, I can see no trouble."

"We are," Mexia said, then looked upward at the mountain, its peak hidden in a mass of thick, snowy clouds, "maybe only halfway there. But then again, perhaps my protection spell is aiding us more than usual."

Gallant pointed at a white furry foot, half hidden in the snow bank. "Perhaps someone has been here before us."

He swept away the snow. Underneath, lay a dead white devil wolf, but no wounds appeared on his body.

CHAPTER 20

Mexia looked to the path ahead of them. The firs' branches decorated in fresh blankets of snow, dripped toward the path as the
cold wet stuff piled up around them. Flurries of snowflakes
whipped in a frenzy as the air thinned and chilled. "Great. Do you
think Rosenthal killed the wolf?"

She glanced back at her companions whose noses and cheeks
wore a red blush as their breaths warmed the air in front of their
faces in puffs of smoke.

"Or perhaps Derek slipped away from the school again," the
princess said.

Mexia scoffed. "His graduation is way too important to him."

"And your attendance is not?" the princess asked, raising her
brows.

Mexia smiled back at her. "You are right, my lady. It is...as
I'm sure it is for Derek to graduate from, too."

They continued the trek forward, their breath growing labored
as the air thinned more.

Gallant's stomach rumbled. "I hope that Parenkin will feed us
when we get there."

"Did you not eat at the festivities in town at the Mae Fest?"

Mexia shoved an errant slip of hair loosened from one of her braids, behind her ear.

Gallant grumbled. "Ye say that when ye wouldn't give me a chance to wet my whistle. Solving the quests were all ye were after."

Mexia stopped in her tracks as a blue light came into view. "A portal."

Kersta groaned. "Not the one to Derek's castle again."

"No." Mexia approached the portal using caution. "We are much farther up the mountainside this time."

"Then what?" Kersta asked.

"Perhaps it is a way to Parenkin's castle. Wouldn't that be nice?" Mexia quickly skirted the twirling lights.

"Or into a dungeon of Rosenthal's," Gallant added.

"That's why we shall not bother with it." Mexia paused to catch her breath. "I hope the air does not grow much thinner."

They trudged on further, a light snow settling on their cloaks in a sudden flurry of flakes.

Despite the elevation, the trees remained thick. Gallant pointed at the side of a boulder. "Another body, only this one appears to be a goblin."

Mexia and Kersta stepped closer. The half-hidden body appeared gray, not like the normal brown skin of the goblin.

"How long do you think he's been dead?" Mexia asked.

"An hour or longer, for his skin color to change so."

"More of Rosenthal's work?" Mexia shook her head in answer to her own question. "Why would he aid us?"

"Maybe to make the game more of a challenge?" Kersta asked. "He could have attempted to kill us when he posed as Davin earlier, and yet he didn't. Why not?"

Mexia continued along the path again. "He is playing a game with us." Her words dripped with irritation, but she was ready to meet the challenge head on. Enough with the games.

"Yes. Well, I think so. When he was the goat, why did he not turn into something else and attack us?"

"It might have ended the game too soon."

"Yes. You said the other mages played wizardry games at Dragonmage's castle. Maybe this Rosenthal is fond of playing games, too."

"Great."

Three quarters of the way up the mountain, another portal appeared. Mexia lifted a brow. "Persistent, isn't he?"

"I am almost willing to take it if it will make me warm," the princess said, collapsing into a bank of snow.

"Princess Talamaya." Mexia ran back to her. Her heart pounded with fear. She hadn't realized until now how quiet the princess had been. Mexia rubbed the princess's mitten-covered hands, trying to get some warmth into them.

"Can you transport us farther up the mountain?" Kersta asked.

"No. I can only transport us to places I have been."

"Then take us down to the hot springs. We can revive her there."

"No." The princess shook her head. "Let's keep going."

They tried to lift her, but she was too weak.

"We have a problem. I can only transport two at the same time with the transportation spell."

"I will stay behind," Gallant offered. "Go. Take care of the woman."

"I will leave Kersta with the princess, then return for you."

"Aye, but be quick about it."

Mexia transported the ladies to the path where the hot springs were. "I'll be right back," she said after helping Kersta walk the princess over to the bubbling water, steam pouring off its surface and the slight breeze swirling the mist into playful whirls.

"I'll take care of her. Just go get Gallant." Kersta pulled off the princess's cloak.

"Yes. I'll be right back." Mexia quickly materialized back to the same spot where she'd left Gallant, but to her horror, she stood inside the portal. Rosenthal had moved it!

Before she could jump clear of it, she was teleported inside a castle's portal room. Royal symbols were inscribed in the floor here too in purples and golds. She readied her staff and hurried out of the room.

Gallant ran toward her. "There ye are, woman. Blast it! The portal moved and I couldn't escape it."

Her heart pounded as the adrenaline sparked her rage. She'd fallen into Rosenthal's trap, and Gallant was right...blast it!

She grabbed Gallant's wrist as he held his war hammer ready to do battle. Though she attempted the teleportation spell, neither went anywhere. "It is like Derek's castle. Rosenthal has taken my powers away from me."

"This is not good then." Gallant pointed to the room. "I looked for a button or something on the walls. Nothing revealed the way out of here."

"Perhaps Rosenthal has Grimoria's spell book. If we could at least get it, and..."

An owl hooted, and they turned with a start to see it fly toward them. He flew over their heads. Mexia ran after him, the blood coursing through her body with heightened anticipation. "If nothing more, I'm going to end his ability to watch me through his familiar."

"Aye," Gallant said, tromping after her.

The bird led them down one corridor, then another, each covered in colorful papers, one green, another blue, one purple, and then the next orange. When they reached a yellow corridor, the owl flew into a large open room, the ceilings vaulted into a point some sixty feet high. The owl perched on a brass stand nearby.

Sunlight streamed in through stained glass windows,

drenching the room in a rainbow of colors. The lights shimmered off a bookshelf covered in white leather-bound books. A man stood with his back to them, his white hair reaching the backs of his knees.

"Rosenthal?" she said, incredulous.

The man turned, his teeth as white as his beard as he smiled at her, his blue eyes, warm and friendly. "What took you so long?"

"Rosenthal?" she repeated, her head tilted to the side in her confusion.

"Why would Rosenthal come here to see me?"

"Who are you?"

"The one whom you have traveled a great distance to see."

Mexia quickly curtsied. "Master Parenkin?"

He nodded. "Why did your other companions not come with you? I have a feast spread for all of you."

"Good," Gallant grouched. "Finally, someone is talking some sense."

"The portal was a way to your castle?"

"You had struggled long enough and earned my praise. No sense in making you walk all that way."

"I must return to get my friends. Princess Talamaya had grown too cold—"

Parenkin nodded again. "It is done."

"The owl, he wasn't Rosenthal's familiar?"

"No, mine."

The owl suddenly flew out of the room.

Parenkin replaced a book on the shelf, then faced her. "Harolstin will bring your friends to my dining hall."

"Has Prince Derek ever visited you here?"

"Of course."

Mexia's face heated with anger. He could have brought them to Parenkin's castle then after all.

"But no one can penetrate my castle, unless otherwise asked to come here. You see, you'd have never made it up the trail."

"There were no beasts to fight us on the way."

He smiled. "Yes, well I believe Derek had something to do with that."

"He left his graduation to help me?"

"He has displeased the headmaster of the school much since your arrival."

"The headmaster won't disallow his graduation, will he?"

Parenkin shrugged a shoulder, then motioned to the hallway. When they walked side by side, Gallant fell in behind them.

"So if there were no beasts on the trail, how would we have failed to make it here?"

"The air grows too thin. No one could survive. You'd have had to use my portal eventually. Inside the castle, the air is as you are usually accustomed, is it not?"

She took a deep breath. The fragrance of roses scented the air. "Yes, I can breathe comfortably again." She turned to him. "I wish to ask—"

"After the meal, Lady Mexia."

Mexia couldn't settle the disquiet she felt. She had to know, after all their troubles, would he give her the letter of recommendation or not?

He led them into a banquet hall where a single table was clothed in purple. He motioned to several seats, then sat at the head of the table on a golden throne.

They turned as the princess and Kersta burst into the room. "Mexia, Gallant."

Mexia gave them both hugs, noting that the princess's clothes were damp. Undoubtedly, her slip was wet underneath her gown from when she took a quick dip in the hot springs.

The ladies eyed the wizard with concern.

"Master Parenkin," Mexia said, "these are my companions,

Princess Talamaya and Lady Kersta of Damar, and beg my forgiveness for not introducing him sooner, Gallant of Kern. And this is the High Wizard Parenkin."

The ladies curtsied. He bowed his head in greeting, then motioned to the table. "The food will grow cold. Sit and eat."

None of the ladies moved to their chairs, though Gallant had already grabbed one and sat down, his eyes level with the table.

"Has he agreed to give you a recommendation?" Kersta asked.

"Ye don't happen to have a taller chair, do ye?" Gallant asked Parenkin.

The wizard stared at the chair. The legs grew until Gallant nodded his head. "Aye, that will do."

Turning his attention back to the ladies, Parenkin raised his brows. "Won't you share a meal with me?"

Kersta folded her arms.

Mexia said, "We have traveled a long distance, Master Parenkin. We wish to know if we have done so in vain."

He smiled and picked up a lobster's tail. "You have helped many, so Harolstin has told me. I would think for all you have aided the question is mute. For their benefit have you assisted them for no good purpose?"

Mexia's cheeks burned in embarrassment. "Why no."

"Then sit and eat."

She sat beside him as the ladies sat next to her.

He smiled. "You wish to have a recommendation to go to a school where no sorceress has ever gone. And I know your reasoning also…a good cause if ever I heard one."

Mexia sipped from her flask. "Then you will give me the recommendation."

He shook his head slowly from side to side. "No. I will not waste the school's time—"

Mexia's blood heated. She quickly stood, as did her lady companions.

"You are impatient to go somewhere?"

"Is this what Derek meant? That my coming here had no purpose because you would never give me a recommendation? He knew it?"

"I don't know what my nephew has said to you about what I would or wouldn't do. But you know that patience is important in the mastering of magic."

"You're his uncle?" Her words were spoken in disbelief, and her brow wrinkled with confusion.

He smiled. "Yes, but if he does anything wrong, I disclaim him."

Mexia's brow furrowed deeper. "I've tried to be patient."

"Then sit and enjoy the meal."

She paced across the floor. "I am not hungry."

He chuckled under his breath. "You did not allow me to finish what I had to say."

She paused and stared at the white-haired man. He was wise beyond his years. Shouldn't she at least hear him out?

"I will not waste the school's time trying to teach you when you already know as much as Derek does upon his graduation."

Tears filled Mexia's eyes as her heartbeat quickened, instantly crushed to think he wouldn't give her the recommendation after all. "But I don't want to be just a country wizard. I want to…to have some kind of a level that I have completed. Dragonmage asked me, 'What level are you? Neophyte?' I want to say I'm a graduate of the school. The first one of my kind in Damar. I want someday to be a High Wizard like you. How can I ever be this if I haven't graduated from the school?"

"You helped to defeat Grimoria and his school of rogue mage apprentices, did you not?"

"Well, yes, of course, but—"

"You have already done more than any graduate of the school has done. Those who leave the school will have to face many obstacles in their lifetime, when *you* have accomplished more than they will probably ever have to face, and all of this without having a formal education. There are many ways to learn our skills. Derek has learned in one way, you and your family in another."

He motioned to the table. "Please, eat."

When she and her companions resumed their seats, he leaned forward, his mouth turning up as his eyes twinkled in amusement. "Would you like to know a secret?"

She waited, barely taking a breath.

"I was a country wizard."

"But…but you were the headmaster of the school."

"Yes, I was. For many years. I got tired of seeing all of the boneheaded students we were getting at the school. You do not need to waste your time there. However, I see you and Derek running the school someday in the future."

"But I can never be a High Wizard."

"You will earn the status one day for the accumulated deeds you have done."

"Then I will wed Derek—"

"When you are able."

"Meaning?"

"You are needed at the school in a little while. The graduation ceremony will be interrupted. Rosenthal felt it fitting as he never graduated from there. But he also intends to make you his own. He will be a powerful adversary. Grimoria's spell book must be destroyed and so must he."

"Can you not help us?"

"I'm not as agile as I used to be, Mexia. You will have the advantage over me."

"But when I get upset, I get flustered. I…I sometimes forget my spells."

He smiled. "I forget mine, too, from time to time, but my

forgetfulness is for a different reason. Believe in yourself. Trust your friends, and do what is right."

She rose from her chair. "I'm ready."

He laughed. "You haven't eaten anything. Nor have your lady companions."

"Gallant has eaten enough for the rest of us."

"All right." Parenkin rose from his chair and before Gallant could object, the wizard motioned with his fingers and sent them into the great hall at Langdon Castle.

Mexia took a deep breath trying to settle the butterflies fluttering in her stomach. The room was filled with mages and their families, the distinguishing feature, the coned graduation caps, different colors for the different years. Mexia had no idea which was which until she saw Ros wearing a gold hat, then she knew that was the senior cap that Derek would wear, too.

Suddenly Alinas squealed out, "Mexia, oh my! Talamaya, Kersta! However did you get here?"

Mexia and the ladies hurried to push through the crowd to get to her. "Parenkin sent us."

"Oh. Did he give you a letter of recommendation?" She pointed to the letter Mexia had sticking out of her cloak pocket.

Mexia pulled the parchment out and read the contents.

I, High Wizard Parenkin, do bestow the honor of Level 5 mage on Lady Mexia, House of Sal, Damar, Inherian, for the feats she's performed on both the continents of Inherian and Albion. Under my watchful eye, I have tutored her during several quests, guiding her through the soothsayer, Marinda, the centaur, Chernon, and the boy, Davin.

"Davin?"

"What does it say, Mexia?" the princess asked, as she and Kersta tried to read it, too.

She has excelled at all of the tests, the hardest, maintaining her distance from my nephew, Derek. Having served the mage

*cause so honorably, I hereby affix my seal of office. Signed, High
Wizard Parenkin*

"I'm a graduate of the school." She looked up at her friends.
"I'm a graduate!" She bounced on the tips of her toes with excitement. "I'm a graduate!"

"You've done it!" Kersta hugged her hard. "But then I knew
you would."

The princess embraced Mexia warmly. "You were bound to,
with your determination and hard work, Mexia."

"Two graduates of the school in one family," Alinas said, then
squeezed Mexia. "I'm so proud of you. But we must find Derek
and tell him the news."

"What news is that?" Derek asked, moving in between Alinas
and Mexia, but focusing on Mexia's eyes as if he were attempting
to seduce her.

"I'm a graduate, Derek. High Wizard Parenkin graduated me
from the school."

Derek smiled. "I wish to congratulate you, but somewhere
else. Alone. I need to know exactly what he said about us. And
about Rosenthal."

"I must be chaperoned."

"My sister can go with us."

"No, Princess Talamaya," Mexia said. She squeezed Alinas's
hand. "No offense, but I have to speak about something,
concerning the kingdom of Damar." In truth, Princess Talamaya
was even better skilled with the staff than she was, and if Rosenthal impersonated Derek as Mexia assumed, she'd need the
princess's help. Kersta and Gallant's would have been welcome,
too, but then the man would have grown suspicious.

"Certainly. I will keep Lady Kersta entertained in the
meantime."

They looked around for Gallant. He bit into a chunk of cheese
at a table set up for refreshments nearby.

Derek took Mexia's wrist, but before she could get hold of the princess's, he transported her from the room.

She stared at their dimly lit surroundings. "Where are we?"

"The cellar. They store many of the ingredients for potions down here until they're needed."

"That makes it no fun. Half the trial is in gathering the ingredients for the potions."

"A country mage's wisdom."

"Yes." She eyed his cloak and smiled. Not one golden leaf embraced the velvet material. As soon as he'd greeted her, she knew he wasn't Derek. The response would have been overwhelming, she was certain. What was she doing there? Was she all right? What had happened?

And then his little maneuver to ensure they left her chaperone behind...

"So I take it you wanted to be alone with me for our little discussion."

This was Rosenthal all right.

"You thought right."

She tapped her staff on the floor.

"It won't work in the school. No magically enhanced weapons will work."

"I've never learned this ability you have to make yourself appear to be someone else, even a goat."

The corners of his mouth turned up.

"Grimoria's spell book?"

He didn't utter a word, just continued to smile like a griffin that had cornered its prey.

She nodded, then looked around the room, sighing deeply. Keep a cool head. But would her spells work here? Sure. He'd taken her to the cellar using the transportation spell. She could fight him with her magic.

Stepping away from him, she attempted to put distance

between them. And yet the notion of killing Rosenthal in Derek's image terrified her as her blood chilled...what if it really was Derek?

"So what are we supposed to do now, Derek?" She purposefully called him by Derek's name, hoping to unhinge him if it were Rosenthal. She folded her arms.

He frowned and turned into his own form, evidently bothered she would mistakenly call him by his enemy's name. His long black hair was tied back in a tail with strips of blue suede, while his thick curly beard was neatly combed. Blue eyes stared back at her darkening with what? Anger? Or was it desire that turned them nearly black?

"I like that you can always tell who I am. It means you are drawn to me, no matter what form I use."

Mexia took another step back.

He walked toward her to close the gap. "What are you contemplating, Mexia? You say Parenkin gave you the papers stating you're a graduate of the school. But what does that mean, really?"

"Nothing, as he has said. You see, it is the training we do beyond the school that is important."

"You think you can best me?"

She swung her staff at him. He knocked it from her grasp and smiled. "Here, I have my full powers unlike at Derek's castle. There, I couldn't fight your fury. Where did you ever learn to fight with a staff like that? You are very good at it."

"Thank you. If the idiot guards at Derek's castles hadn't stopped me, I would have killed you."

"Not once we were beyond the castle gates. Then I would have taken you home with me, like I'll do here."

"Why the delay?"

He looked up at the ceiling. "I wish to watch the fireworks upstairs first."

Mexia transported herself upstairs in the main great hall, leaving Rosenthal behind. He quickly rejoined her, lucky guess she figured, and tried to grab her arm. She dodged his grasp.

She saw no sign of her companions nor of Derek or his family. Resorting to unladylike behavior, and not at all sorceress-like, she kicked him in the shins when he tried to get hold of her again.

He cried out, catching Ros's attention.

"Rosenthal!" the mage shouted.

Suddenly, non-mages and junior mages fled the room.

Rosenthal swore. "All right, I will not get my fireworks here today." He pulled Mexia in front of him in the event anyone tried to cast an offensive spell at him.

She attempted to use a command spell on him. He whispered in her ear, "It won't work on me, dear lady. I have the ability to resist mind spells. Did you not learn this?"

The notion horrified her. She hadn't learned how to do this. So if he wished her to do as he commanded, then what? He could have her do anything. Anything at all. She shuddered. "Too bad. But I also have the ability to resist mind spells as well." Not really, but she had to use any resources available to get her out of a bad situation. A country mage's resourcefulness…fibbing.

"I would have figured as much. And that's truly unfortunate. Imagine the things I could have had you do," he whispered to her, his hot breath making her skin crawl.

Once alerted, the headmaster and Derek ran into the room. Rosenthal backed away with her. Derek's blue eyes grew stormy with hatred as he took a step toward Mexia. The headmaster grabbed Derek's arm and shook his head.

Rosenthal smiled. "This is what I've been waiting for." He spoke loud and clear. "Lady Mexia is a graduate of the school, by order of High Wizard Parenkin. And now she is all mine."

Mexia struggled to get free, but she realized she needed to go with Rosenthal. It was the only way she'd get close to Grimoria's spell book. She glanced over at Kersta and Alinas. *Tell Derek I must go with Rosenthal to destroy his spell book. It is the only way.*

Both Kersta and Alinas shook their heads. But Mexia could see no other way.

"I will return!" Rosenthal shouted, then teleported Mexia to his castle.

CHAPTER 21

When Mexia and Rosenthal arrived in his castle, they were in a portal room, but he hurried her to the main dining area. "Your stomach has been grumbling, my dear lady. Are you hungry?"

"No."

He smiled as they walked into the expansive room. "Well I am." He pulled her to a seat next to his throne and made her sit. With a click of his fingers, a woman hurried into the room.

"The meal."

"We hadn't expected you so soon, my lord."

He snapped his fingers twice. "Be quick about it. The lady and I are hungry."

When the servant left the room, Rosenthal ran his hand down Mexia's back, making her shudder as if hundreds of spiders just crawled down her gown. The devil himself had touched her, and she couldn't shake the eeriness. "You are not afraid of me, are you?"

"You cannot take me against my will, Rosenthal." She turned to face him, his eyes and mouth smiling, as if her comment had totally amused him.

"What makes you think you'll not succumb to my desires, willingly?"

She took a deep breath, attempting to keep her wits about her. Where would he keep Grimoria's spell book? In his bedchambers, no doubt. And yet she didn't wish to go anywhere near his bed that was bound to give him other ideas.

"We have time, my dear, if you need it." He leaned over and kissed her cheek, sending a chill down her spine. Then he walked over to the throne at the head of the table and sat.

Mexia played with the ties to her belt, then suddenly had an idea. She hadn't swapped Kersta's cloak back with her. All she had to do was use it when Rosenthal was least expecting it.

Still, she couldn't transport herself to his bedchambers unless she'd been there before. In fact, she couldn't transport herself anywhere but the portal room.

Immediately, she used the transportation spell to take her there. She assumed he'd have the portal locked against her escape, but from there, she could explore the castle and be able to transport to new locations as soon as she'd been in them. Once she arrived at the portal room, she clasped the invisibility cloak together and flattened herself against one of the walls.

As soon as she did, Rosenthal arrived. "I know you can't have gotten far, as this or the hall we passed through were the only places you've been." He smiled. "However, playing griffin hunts the fox should be a pleasurable game to keep us entertained this afternoon. Give the cooks some more time to prepare our meal."

He walked out of the portal room and strode down the hall.

Mexia stepped out of the room and walked in the opposite direction worried either her fragrance or light footstep might give her away if she headed his way.

She explored a library, three sitting rooms, a wing of bedchambers, three more portal rooms and the kitchen. There seemed to be no windows on this floor, making her feel hemmed in all at once as she stood in the kitchen, moving occasionally to keep out of the four cooks' way.

Beef roasted on a spit over an open fire, and the smoke drew into a chimney. Kettles bubbled nearby making the room warmer and more humid than any other. A trickle of perspiration dribbled between her breasts.

"Mexia, Mexia. You are very good at this game," Rosenthal said as he walked into the kitchen where the smell of broth bubbling in one of the pots filled the room with beefy aroma. "Hmm, smells good."

"Have you not found the lady yet, my lord?" one of the ladies asked.

"No, Marn. But I will." He sliced off a piece of bread fresh out of the oven. "She has no way to leave here on her own. And soon she will grow hungry and tired. Then I will find her."

"Several say you shouldn't allow her to use her spells in the castle. That Derek wouldn't permit her to."

"Yes, well, I am not a tyrant like Derek was. She can use her spells. She is not as powerful as some would say. After all, I stole Grimoria's book right out from under her at his castle. She couldn't stop me then, she'll not stop me from having my way with her now."

He headed out of the kitchen, and Mexia followed him, keeping her distance. What she needed was to go through a portal that would take her to another level. Then she gave up on the idea. He'd have to take her to a different level, then she could explore in the same manner she did on this floor. Then she wouldn't need a portal, just transport herself between floors on her own.

In the meantime, she transported herself to the dining area, unfastened the cloak and sat visibly in her chair.

When the bell rang for supper jangling her nerves, he walked into the dining hall and smiled to see her sitting there. "I do believe, my dear, you have won that round."

"I intend to win them all."

"I can see that you do. And frankly, I'm pleased. It is not often I am beat in any game."

He leaned over to kiss her cheek in greeting, then took his seat. Golden platters of ribs of beef, beef stew, salad greens were served and goblets were filled with wine.

Mexia grabbed up a beef rib. If nothing else, she had to get her stomach to quit growling. It would surely give her away the next time she used the invisibility cloak otherwise.

"Did you have a nice time exploring my castle?"

"Where will I be sleeping the night?"

He leaned back in his chair. "You are already thinking of tonight's activities. Good."

"Sleep is what I'm thinking of. I have not had enough of it of late."

"You will have the chambers next to mine. A private entrance leads from one to the other. Should you desire to see me in the middle of the night, do not hesitate to drop by."

His blue eyes sparkled with interest as he sipped his wine. When she drank from her flask, his black bushy brows rose in surprise. "You will not drink my wine?"

"I prefer a sweet tea I keep in my flask at all times." She pushed her goblet over to him. "But you may drink mine if you like."

He smiled at her, the look partly evil, partly seductive. Had he thought he could drug her? Then she might have been more compliant. Maybe he thought of a love potion. Nah, that'd been too easy, and not much of a game.

When she had finished her fill and pushed her plate away, he leaned forward. "A game of chess?"

"It is late. I'd prefer to go to sleep now."

The smile returned to his lips. "Do you plan to kill me in my sleep?"

"I'm sure you'll make that impossible to accomplish."

"Then what do you wish to do?"

She tapped her fingers on the table. "Sleep. I'm exhausted. How can I fight you sufficiently if I can barely stay awake?"

"All right. Then sleep it is."

He rose from his seat, then joined her. When she stood, he took her hand and transported her to her chambers. "Yours," he said, motioning to the expansive room, filled with flowers, from live ones sitting in porcelain vases to the spread covered in roses decorating the bed. "And mine." He crossed the floor and opened the door to the next room.

She shivered. No way did she want to enter his bedroom. However, if she did now, she could teleport herself there later while he slept.

Stepping inside the room, she considered the bed trimmed in black and gold, the bedding, the drapes, the wardrobe sitting in the corner. But what caught her eye were the two doors that led out of the room. One undoubtedly led to the hall. But the other, his office? And Grimoria's spell book.

"Would you like to check out the mattresses? Perhaps mine would be more to your liking."

"Mine will be fine. Besides, I do not intend to stay long."

"You're right about that, my dear. Soon, you'll join me in here. For now, I'll let you have your way."

She walked back into the guest chambers as he followed her to her annoyance. She folded her arms. "If you try anything with me in the middle of the night, you'll wish you hadn't."

"I love it when you threaten me." He leaned down to kiss her lips, but she turned her head. Kissing her ear instead, made him laugh. "Anywhere I kiss you, suits me fine."

She tapped her foot on the carpeted floor. "You are leaving?"

"I know Derek and Dragonmage both had a time parting from your company. Now I can see how this could be." He looked down at the floor for a moment, then met her gaze. "I shall see you in the morning, unless you have a change of heart and wish to join me later."

He walked into his room and closed the door behind him.

She tried the door handle to the hall and found it locked. Her head pounded with frustration. Intending to leave the room and explore the whole floor, he'd thwarted her. What if he watched her through the wall adjoining their chambers somehow? Then if she used the invisibility cloak, he'd know that's how she'd done it. He'd surely take it away from her. He'd transported her directly into her chambers, knowing full well that she couldn't transport now to anywhere but the other floor. And he probably assumed if she entered his room, he'd be waiting for her appearance.

She pulled off her boots and cloak on the other side of the bed away from his chambers. Of course, she considered he could be watching from the room on the other side of her, too. The notion made chill bumps trail down her arms.

After stuffing her cloak onto the bed, she walked over to a brass mirror and unclipped the braids from her head. Slowly, she unwound each fat braid from its silk bindings. Once she was done, she brushed out the waves, wondering if Rosenthal was getting his fill, or if she was being totally paranoid.

Now she'd have to remove her skirt and blouse, but she couldn't do it. She wanted to pretend she was going to sleep, but if he watched her now, she couldn't disrobe, no matter how much she wanted to play the game. Maybe he'd think she worried he'd visit her in the night. Yes, that's the way she'd play it.

She climbed into bed and pulled the curtains shut. Then she slipped the cloak over her shoulders, pulled the hood up, and fastened the clasp. Without further hesitation, she teleported herself into his room near the wardrobe, hoping she had remembered the lay out well enough not to bump into anything.

Standing next to his wall, Rosenthal peered through the black and gold paper lining it. She took a deep breath, trying to calm her nerves, realizing he watched her actions. Then he opened her door to her room and stepped inside.

Now what? Was he checking to see if she was still there?

She had a choice. Return to the bed and pretend to be sleeping or allow him to see she wasn't there. Since he couldn't see her in his room due to the invisibility cloak, he'd have undoubtedly thought she was exploring on the other floor again. Would he search for her down there? Or would he wait for her in her bedchambers?

If he went down to the other floor, she could check out his office. She crossed his bedchambers and peered into hers. He pulled the curtains aside. She smiled as he turned his head. His jaw had dropped, his eyes were wide, but then grew dark. He vanished.

She waited in case he came to his bedchambers and there was a second time-lapse. When he didn't appear, she hurried to the door. The first one was unlocked and opened into the hallway as she suspected. She stepped into it, in case she had to transport there later. Then she closed the door and crossed the floor to the next door. This one was locked. Her heart sank. Then she remembered the key Rosenthal had made for Boras that supposedly unlocked anything. Would it work on Rosenthal's door?

She shoved the key into the slot and turned it. The lock clicked open. She entered the room, then locked the door behind her.

The room was cloaked in darkness, except for a soft green light glowing in one corner. She edged her way over to the scant illumination, tripping over something large and furry in the process. Her breath caught in her throat as she backed away from it.

Whatever it was, did it guard Grimoria's book?

It emitted a low, deep growl. Could it smell her? Very probably. Still, if the creature protected the book, she had to destroy it now, and then the book, too.

She attempted her fireball spell, aimed at whatever made clicking sounds as it neared her in the dark. Nothing happened. Had Rosenthal done something to make her offensive spells not work in the castle? She cast the protection spell over herself, then transported nearer the light.

The creature sniffed at the air. She tried to ignore the feeling millions of insects were crawling over her body, and she neared the light. It was a spell book, but Grimoria's?

She grabbed up the book. Immediately, the room turned white with light. The creature, black, shaggy, bigger than any wolf she'd ever seen, its jagged yellow teeth dripping with saliva, lunged at her.

She teleported to the kitchen. Torn between reading the spell book and learning how to do some of the things Rosenthal could do, and destroying the book before she got caught, she chose the latter.

One of the cooks still worked on cleaning the pots in a cauldron where the fire burned beneath it to heat the cleaning liquid.

A man shouted in the hallway outside the kitchen, "Grimoria's book has been stolen from your library, my lord."

Rosenthal's voice boomed in the hallway in response, "Find her. Let loose the hell hounds."

She shoved the book into the flames, making the cook scream out in surprise.

Immediately, Rosenthal and several of his men rushed into the kitchen. They'd save the book. They'd pull it from the fire.

The hell hounds sounded like horses galloping in a race as seven barged into the room.

"A book just appeared in the fire," a woman screamed out. "It just came out of nowhere. There."

Mexia couldn't use her offensive spells in the castle, but she bet she could will the animals to turn on their masters. Immediately, she worked on her ability to harness them.

Instead of searching for her fragrance, they turned on the men who screamed out in surprise. With breaths of fire shooting from the hell hounds' mouths, three of the men quickly turned to ashes.

Rosenthal hollered, "She's here, she's in the room. Get the book!"

But even he couldn't get close to the book as it burned in the fire while he had to kill one of his hounds that turned on him. "Very clever, dear lady. I can see now why Parenkin graduated you from the school. You will best many. But never me."

Mexia stayed near the fire, intent on making sure the book burned all the way through. The cook attempted to drag it out with a long handled stoker, but Mexia grabbed it from her hands and hid it beneath her cloak.

"She took it!" the woman screamed. "She took the poker from me."

Rosenthal turned to the fire as another hound kept him preoccupied. "She's using an invisibility spell from Derek's book, no doubt." The hound breathed fire on him, but the protection spell he used, stopped it from reaching him.

He raised his fingers to cast a spell on her. She teleported to the other side of the room. "I have just cast a spell of immobility on her. Just grab her and bring her to me."

He turned his attention to the hound and killed him. One of them turned on the cook as the rest of his men fled. The dogs' barking could be heard down the hallway. Mexia assumed they'd meet the same fate as the others piled in gray ashes on the kitchen floor.

The cook dissolved with the hound's fiery breath, then Rosenthal killed the hound with a fireball spell. Once the beast was dead, the mage headed for the book.

Mexia had to stop him. The book was already burned halfway through, but she couldn't allow him to save any part of it.

She attempted a stone spell on him. His protection spell wouldn't allow it to work.

If she used the time stopper spell, it might not have worked, and the fire would have stopped burning the book. Going back in time wouldn't have either. Instead, she dove for him, grabbed his arm and teleported him to his office.

Now that he'd had contact with her, he grabbed her shoulders and slammed her against the wall. Her spine hurt with the jolt, but his hard body leaned up against her, making it impossible for her to knee him in the privates.

"You are undoing my kingdom, Mexia. But you shall not win. Make yourself visible so that I may see you."

He leaned forward to kiss her, but she quickly used her ability to control the beast in the room. As soon as he growled, Rosenthal turned, his rage appearing instantly. "Lie down and be quiet! The lady is privileged to be here."

The animal continued to snarl, then lunged at Rosenthal, surprise evident on his face as his mouth dropped wide open. He'd apparently thought the animal had growled at her, not him. She realized then, he didn't understand she'd had the ability to control the animals...not through a spell, but through an inborn talent.

She turned away, not wanting to see how savagely the beast tore into the mage, but still remaining in the room to ensure he was dead before she returned to the kitchen.

When the beast tore the mage's head from his body, Mexia

shuddered and transported herself to the kitchen. The book was nearly devoured by the flames, making her take a deep breath of satisfaction. She poked at it to hurry the process with the poker and when it was nothing more than ashes, she returned to the bedchambers where her boots were still located.

After slipping them on, she headed out of the room, searching for a portal room, and a way out. In one of the rooms, a young man hid partially behind a bookshelf. Mexia said, "Tell me how to leave here."

He cried out in surprise.

She smiled, forgetting that she was still invisible.

"Tell me, and I'll let you live."

"Where do you...you want to go?"

"Back to Langdon Castle."

He inched his way out from behind the bookshelf. "The hell hounds have gone mad. They're killing everyone."

"I'll protect you if you help me, but we must hurry."

"Yes, yes, I'll help you." Then he paused in his footsteps. Whispering, he said, "But Rosenthal?"

"His creature guarding Grimoria's book made a meal of him."

The man shuddered. "Follow me." He hurried out of the room, and she followed close behind them. When the sound of a hell hound's barking grew near, she cast the protection spell over the servant.

He stopped and looked nervously around him.

"I've cast a protection spell on you. Keep moving."

"Yes, yes." He strode to a portal room, then entered it. "Are you inside?"

"Yes. Proceed."

He pressed a button in the wall. "If you don't mind, I'm going with you."

When they arrived at the great hall, Mexia smiled. The graduation had proceeded, and the graduates lined up to receive their diplomas. All but Derek. Where in the world was he?

"Here's where I bow out," the servant said, then quickly exited the great hall.

Mexia saw her companions sitting with Alinas and her mother. She quickly made her way to their seats. Leaning over a man and a woman who sat next to the aisle and beside Kersta, Mexia said in a hushed voice so as not to disturb the exercise, "Kersta! Where is Derek?"

"Oh!" the woman screamed out as the man beside her jumped from his seat. The graduation proceedings stopped at once.

Immediately, guards ran into the room and surrounded the couple who disturbed the ceremony.

"What's the problem?" one of the men asked.

Mexia's companions hurried out of their seats.

Kersta said, "Mexia's returned." She waved her hand at the aisle. "Mexia, where are you?"

Mexia unfastened Kersta's borrowed cloak and became visible. "He is dead. Rosenthal is dead." Her voice cracked with distress, the whole frantic episode finally settling into her bones.

Kersta and the princess hugged her soundly.

"Where is Derek?" Mexia asked, her heart racing with anxiety to see him gone.

The princess sighed deeply. "He left to find you. He went straight to see Parenkin."

Alinas joined them. "The headmaster will have him returned to the school at once."

One of the men was already speaking to the headmaster, and Mexia turned her attention to the man. Was it awe that she saw in his dark eyes? Or distrust?

The High Wizard Harazod raised his hands in the air, then clapped twice. Immediately, Derek stood before him, the only graduate not wearing a coned hat. The headmaster spoke to him briefly. Derek turned to see Mexia standing in the midst of her companions, knights, and his family. He took a step in her direction, but the headmaster grabbed his arm and shook his head.

After speaking a few words to him, Harazod handed Derek his graduation papers, then shook his hand. Everyone in the audience clapped. Derek bowed to the headmaster, then hurried to join Mexia afterward.

He grabbed Mexia's hand and without a word, teleported her to his school quarters. Before she could speak, his mouth covered hers, commanding, pressuring, his fingers at the same time combing through her hair. She kissed him back with the same kind of longing, her hands wrapped around his waist pulling him against her tightly. Her whole body warmed with his touch.

Then suddenly he pulled his mouth away from hers and stared at her, his eyes clouded with desire. He hugged her tightly against his chest. "I feared I'd lost you."

"What? You thought I couldn't handle a little problem with a mage?"

He chuckled under his breath. "You never cease to amaze me. Parenkin said you'd handle him if you used the knowledge you've learned wisely."

"He had more faith in me, than you."

Derek shook his head. "My feelings for you got in the way."

She smiled and kissed his cheek. Her companions were right. She was stronger than him. But she loved how much he loved her back. Touching his cloak, she was amazed to see more leaves. "A dozen leaves."

"We wed tonight." He nuzzled his face against hers, then kissed her cheek.

Looking up at him, she shook her head. "No. I must see my father and obtain permission. He will require that we do not see each other for at least two weeks, to ensure my betrothed did not cast a spell over me."

He smiled at her. "You cannot be serious."

"I am. After the two weeks, you may come for a visit and meet with my father. If he approves, we will wed."

Derek ran his hands up and down her arms. "You will convince him I am the right one for you?"

She smiled and leaned her head against his chest. Listening to his heart beating made a curl of warmth settle in her stomach. "I believe there will be no other who would play wizardry games with me who I could beat so easily."

He chuckled, wrapping his arms around her, and held her tightly. "I don't want you to leave, ever."

In her heart, she didn't either, but she knew she had to appease her father. "Duty calls, Derek, my love. Once we have had our period of separation, we will undoubtedly wed."

"I can see I have no other choice."

She shook her head, then tilted her chin up. "Give me a reason to remember you."

His teeth shown as dimples dented his cheeks. "As you wish, my love."

~

*T*he next morning, the ladies and Gallant said their final farewells to Derek and his family. When Mexia and her companions boarded the ship, Princess Talamaya had every intention of seeing her betrothed, King Lazarion, first thing once they returned to Inherian. Lady Mexia knew in a little over two weeks' time, she would be returning to Albion to marry Derek.

With the wind in their faces as they looked toward home, Gallant sidled up to Kersta. "Guess that means just ye and me are unattached."

She laughed. "Yes, well, there are three knights waiting for my return to Damar as we speak. And soon my father will insist I choose one of them for my betrothed."

Turning, she caught sight of a man wearing a cloak, hooded, his face hidden from view...the very same man who had bought them drinks in the Dragon's Keep tavern in Langdon. The stranger was a passenger on the same ship as they were? She took a deep breath of the salty air and looked out to sea again.

Little did the companions know, their journey to Inherian would take a deadly detour to the mysterious Emerald Isle of Mists.

ABOUT THE AUTHOR

Bestselling and award-winning author Terry Spear has written over fifty paranormal romance novels and four medieval Highland historical romances. Her first werewolf romance, Heart of the Wolf, was named a 2008 Publishers Weekly's Best Book of the Year, and her subsequent titles have garnered high praise and hit the USA Today bestseller list. A retired officer of the U.S. Army Reserves, Terry lives in Crawford, Texas, where she is working on her next werewolf romance and continuing her new series about shapeshifting jaguars and also writes new YA books. For more information, please visit www.terryspear.com, or follow her on Twitter, @TerrySpear. She is also on Facebook at http://www.facebook.com/terry.spear. And on Wordpress at:

Terry Spear's Shifters
http://terryspear.wordpress.com/